A NOVEL

ANGIE RUBLE

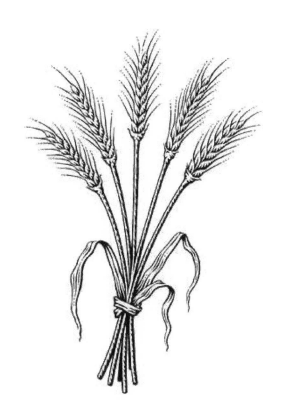

Free

A YEAR AT HALFWAY HOMESTEAD

Free: A Year at Halfway Homestead
By Angie Ruble

Scripture taken from the Holy Bible, New International Version®. NIV®. Copyright © 1973, 1978, 1984 by International Bible Society. Used by permission of Zondervan Publishing House. All rights reserved.

Library of Congress Control Number:2019910249

This book is dedicated to ...

The Keeper of my homestead.
Everything about You is free and sets free.

Contents

I

Winter

New beginnings are often disguised
as painful endings.
Lao Tzu

December

It was a warm rain for December. The windshield wipers
in the squad car kept time. Swish-swash, tick-tock, a
cadence like the march of an inmate on death row to his
final meal before his eyes close in death. Death had been near
lately, marking time; X's marked over dates could have been
X's over her eyes, counting down to its release. Why hadn't
the end of time come? Why was there a click when there
could have been a bullet's final release? Zoe pondered these
things and shuddered at the memory. Instead, time reset,
faster this time. The arrest, the preliminary hearing ... the
rain hammered hard against the car as it roared off to where
her next time would start and the wipers beat faster ... the
plea, the sentence and now twelve more months.

Time.

Her heart pounded in her head.

Time to think.

Time to plan.

Time to waste.

Time.

Slow time.

The rain stopped as they pulled into the drive of an old
mansion. Through the rain-spotted window Zoe stared. The
old place, once grand, was fenced in the front with spans of
arrow-shaped iron spears separated from each other by round
stone turret-looking columns that reminded Zoe of a castle or

a prison. For her a prison. The large iron gates were open next to the fading sign on the fence all but hidden in ivy that announced her address for the next twelve months:

Halfway Homestead
est. 1889
257 River Rd

Why would someone leave the gate to a rehab center open? Zoe wondered. Isn't that like leaving the gate open at a mental hospital? She shook her head befuddled by the irony of the situation.

The car rocked as it continued down the old brick driveway. Leaded windows still held the candles of Christmas which sat glowing in the dusk. This weathered Victorian had seen better days. The cracked paint held together what used to be. Sporting varying shades of graying greens, the wrap-around porch was welcoming even in the wintertime.

The car stopped. The deputy got out and retrieved Zoe's bag and a quilt from the trunk. Zoe sat in the car waiting. For what, she didn't know. She had hoped the events of the past year wouldn't come to this.

New beginnings in a life are seldom marked out in advance, but more often scratched deeply in a soul. A scarring, layered with either regret or rejoicing, not soon forgotten. Today was such a day for Zoe.

"Okay, Ms. Dempsey," the deputy said, opening the back door. "It's time."

Zoe pulled her shirt close around her, threw her purse over her shoulder as she stepped out of the car and took her first breath of new life in and let it out long and heavy.

"Thanks," she said, taking the quilt and bag in her hands.

She tried to blink back tears, but they fell hot on her quilt, leeching the warmth from her body as they splashed and soaked into the fabric. It was a wedding quilt from her grandma, given to her when love still had promise. *Seasons of Love*, her grandma had called it as she passed it to her. It had been so long since Zoe had felt loved. She could scarcely

2

remember what it was like or if she had ever known real love. If she had, what season of love is it when you find yourself at a halfway house? Winter? It must be winter, cold and dead.

"Please find your way to the door. Dispatch called ahead. They are expecting you." His radio squawked as he closed the door. He answered it in low tones and turned to go.

Zoe stood staring at the mansion. The round tower stood in the far corner holding the house firm, reminding her of a simpler time. When she passed this place as a child, she dreamed of being a princess who took her tea on the veranda or a distressed damsel waiting for her prince to rescue her on the balcony. Never did she dream her life's journey would bring her here, imprisoned, with no hope of rescue, marking days on a calendar.

In the distance Zoe thought she heard a violin playing a mournful dirge and a rooster crow. She shook her head to clear it and looked beyond the house at a garden and orchard asleep for the winter. The heads of the trees hung low, looking creepy and dead with no hope of ever blooming again. It was just how she felt.

Behind the main house sat a small cottage painted to match. At one time a servant's quarters she presumed. A dim glow came from one window. Wood smoke rose out of a small brick chimney and hung close to the earth in the dusk, giving the grounds a haunted appearance.

She wrapped herself in grandma's quilt to ward off the chill, but winter had crept into her soul. Her steps were short and unsure as she left the bricks and followed the stone pathway, green with age. As she climbed the steps to the double door entrance, her hand shook while she gave the ancient doorbell a twist, announcing her presence. She couldn't hear any noise coming from inside. She gave a final half twist and fell back into a porch swing to the left of the doors, wrapped up like a papoose.

The chains of the porch swing creaked as it rocked back and forth. The rhythmic swaying soothed Zoe like a child being rocked by its mother. She closed her eyes and buried her face in the quilt breathing in smells of cedar and smoke

3

from the chest which someone had rescued it from. It was one of the few things that had escaped the fire.

The past five years had left its mark. Zoe couldn't remember much of chaos, even though she had lived it out to the last pitiful detail. Why she had made the choices she did, eluded her too. There were plenty of culprits to blame: alcohol, abuse, affair and arson. "And that's just the A's ... " she whispered, licking the tear that rested at the corner of her mouth. Plenty to choose from and the judge had picked freely. She fell from the heights of glory to the depths of hell in a matter of days.

Zoe's insides turned to liquid. Maybe it was time to run. Running from her past was the only thing she knew to do.

When she opened her eyes, there was a huge black man sitting sideways on an old chair by the door. His elbow rested on the back of the chair. A calloused hand held his head. Dark, liquid eyes studied her. Zoe gasped and leaned forward as if to run when she saw him. Her panicked heart raced in her chest, beating loud in her ears. His sweet brown eyes held hers as long as she could bear it. She looked away to the peeling paint on the porch for relief. Hoping to make a good impression, her hand smoothed her hair and her tongue sailed across her teeth. She glanced back at the man who was no longer looking at her. Instead, he had righted himself in the chair with his long khaki covered legs stretched out in front of him. His boots crossed at the ankle. Long arms crossed his chest. His hands tucked in his woolen sweater under his arms.

"I know what y'er thinkin'," he said, rocking back and forth and staring into the evening. "Y'er thinkin' I can out run 'im. He's old and his runnin' days are over." The old man laughed deep and shook his graying head.

"He left the gate open," he said, nodding toward the iron gate. "That's my ticket outta here. Yes, sir. Y'er thinkin' it's not far to a bar and the freedom of a drink. Whatcha order on a night like this? Cold night, you wouldn't be orderin' a nice merlot. No, sir, a person need somethin' stronger— straight bourbon. Yeah, that will do. In fact, make it a double. Settle 'em nerves. Somethin' that would dig and scratch all the way down, remindin' you through y'er numbness you can

4

still feel somethin'. That gift of pain might help rid 'em shakes that are just fixin' to settle into y'er young bones. Then what? After a couple drinks you need a lifeline—so you phone a friend. He come pick you up, you share whatever you gonna share tonight. Then … yeah, you back. Like none of this nightmare ever happened." The old man's eyes filled with sorrow and settled on Zoe's.

Zoe sat in stunned silence, shivering. Her deepest thoughts revealed. A strange way to introduce oneself. She didn't even know his name. The tears had stopped falling and the numbness of self-preservation had set in.

"Or … " The old man turned and stared through the lace curtains into the dining room just beyond the foyer, alive now with the noise of fine china being set, water pouring into glasses and giggles of women. "Or, since you obviously a bright woman, you may be thinkin' I've waited my whole life for this. To come home to a mansion with a room made up just for me. Surrounded by folks drinkin' in the goodness of life, lovin' deep and laughin' hard. Well, Miss Zoe, if that's what you been waitin' for, this is y'er day." His eyes held hers.

"That's more like it. Ain't it, Miss Zoe?" He was still staring at the inviting scene inside the old home.

Zoe's soul was frozen. But her weary spirit jumped within her at the hopeful words, begging her to go.

"Go," its voice long hushed whispered. *Dive headlong into it. Run out of the darkness into the light … "*

His calloused hand now held the ancient door open. Smells of home brought Zoe back to the moment. Her eyes begged the old man for direction.

Stay?

Or go.

"Miss Zoe?" His voice was tender.

She was holding her breath. Hot tears rose again in her eyes as she sat looking through the door at women ready to sit down to a meal of soup and homemade bread. Her breath came out hot and jagged. She breathed deep, smelling the goodness, not wanting to exhale but not knowing what to do next. She held her breath again, tipped her head back and closed her eyes.

5

Light?

Or darkness?

"Miss Zoe, they've set us a place and are waitin'." The old man's head tipped towards the door.

Hope?

Or despair?

"It's y'er choice."

She couldn't move. Her eyes were wild. He walked over and took her arm, tucking it under his, hugging it into his woolen side and tottered toward the door, as if walking with a child. "There now. That's better," he whispered. "That a girl. Yes, sir."

His eyes sparkled. "Just for the record, Miss Zoe, I might be plumb worn out, but I could out run the likes of you any day of the week and twice on Sunday. Yes, sir." His deep chuckle filled the anxious gap.

Zoe recoiled and stuck her quivering chin in the air and said with a defiant, albeit shaky voice, "I—I don't race strangers."

"Well now, I'm Abraham Joseph Johnson," he said, with a bow. "My friends call me Abe. So, you can call me Abe. Now that we friends, we can move forward on settin' a date for that race."

A lady came from the dining room, slipped the quilt from her shoulders, took her bag and handed them to the old man. "I see you've met Abe. I'm Kit." She took Zoe by the arm and led her to the table where a steaming pot of vegetable beef stew was cooling with slices of homemade bread begging for butter, awaiting their plunge into the savory goodness.

Kit squeezed her hand, her piercing blue eyes penetrating Zoe's resistance. With a soft voice she said, "We are so glad you are here." For such a trite statement, Zoe felt welcome given the circumstances.

The old man reappeared, sat at one end of the table and held up his calloused hands to hold as a sign to the others. He glanced at Zoe, winked and bowed his head. She hurried to grab the hands of those on either side of her and half-bowed her head looking around the best she could as his booming voice filled the dining room.

6

"Father, today we celebrate, another child comin' home, a new beginnin'. We thankful for our family gathered here, the food grown on our grounds and the hands that prepared it. Bless it, Father—only through Y'er son. Amen. Yes, sir."

Prayers always made Zoe uncomfortable. They seemed pointless.

"Dear ones, we have a new family member with us tonight. Her name is Zoe. If ya'll would be so kind to introduce y'erself and tell her how long you've been here and what y'er doin' here."

Kit smiled and leaned closer to Zoe. "As I said earlier, I'm Kit," she said, reaching for her bowl, filling it with the stew and placing it by her plate before moving on to the next bowl. "I've been here two years now."

Blonde bangs framed Kit's smiling eyes. Deep crow's feet graced the corners. Round pock marks dotted her face and neck, making Zoe wonder if she might be a recovering meth addict.

"I'm responsible for cooking for everyone and teaching meal planning classes. When I'm not here, I work at the food bank and enjoy the farmers market on Saturdays in the summer." She smiled again while she continued serving.

"I'm Jael." Jael's voice was throaty and dense for a woman. On a brighter day, Zoe would have thought it sultry and interesting matching the mysterious blackness of her hair and the cutting greenness of her eyes. "However, some here call me J." She rolled her eyes as she picked up the bread and passed it to Kit. She was exquisite, but had a toughness that tainted her beauty. "I came here nine months ago. I'm in charge of laundry and maintenance. I ran a crew for Habitat for Humanity that just wrapped up last week. My favorite thing to do is go dumpster diving with Rayden. But my goal for this year is to paint the exterior of the house since it's been at least a hundred years. I'm testing the effects of light. That's why there are paint swatches on the porch."

Zoe hadn't noticed.

The last girl to speak was timid and meek, yet stunning. Her eyes shifted with her slight body and she stared at her plate, occasionally glancing at Abe, who seemed oblivious to the lull. She shifted one more time, stirred her stew, cleared her throat and spoke with the softest voice. "I'm Rayden. I came here six months ago." Her chocolate eyes, pooled with sorrow, peeked out from the veil of hair that hung to her elbows. "I'm in charge of cleaning. When I run out of things to clean, I work at the recycling center downtown. I bring home items and repurpose them into useful pieces. I teach others to do the same," she said, with a shrug and a brief smile. "I also go through the donated items, sort out what we need and sell the rest at our frequent garage sales. My favorite way to pass time is dumpster diving with J."

"Rayden has an immense talent for decorating, repurposing and organizing. She has made this house a home, with the smallest of budgets and the biggest imagination," Kit added.

It was the first time that Zoe had noticed the eclectic mix in the home. The table was an old, worn farmhouse table with mismatched chairs surrounding it and a bench on one side. The conglomeration of china and silver impressed a feeling of home in Zoe.

It was Zoe's turn. Her hand shook. Her eyes burned. She didn't know what to say. Everyone there had a place. She had a past.

"I'm Zoe and I'm an … a … I don't know what I am," she whispered.

"Hi, Zoe," they said, laughing in unison.

" … I … uh quit college." Her eyes were filling up with tears and her voice shook. "I always stayed home, hoping someday I would have a house full of … "

Abe interrupted, "Miss Zoe, here on the Homestead we not focused on what you ain't, but what you gonna be. So, I'll help ya out, just one time," he said, with a wink.

"Ladies, Miss Zoe will be second in command of the garden, livestock and grounds. Past that we don't know yet how she will shine, what she will teach us or how she will serve others with her gifts."

Zoe looked down at her once manicured nails, now cracked and chewed down to nubs. Through tears she glanced toward the door. "I uh … have never done anything like that. I'm more of an inside person."

Abe smiled briefly. "Well now, Miss Zoe, since it's almost January and all, they's not much to do out there in the garden. This is our time to rest. Yes, sir. I call it hibernatin' myself. At some point we'll do a little prunin', some egg gatherin', chat with Bossy some, until stork duties start.

"Let's not worry ourselves about it tonight. We got oatmeal cake and fresh cowboy coffee for dessert. And then we have a special treat for you. Ladies, please do the honors?"

Jael and Rayden cleared the table and Kit skipped off to the kitchen for the dessert and coffee. Zoe started to get up, but Abe rested a hand on hers.

"Sit tight, Miss Zoe. It's our night to serve you.

"Now, if you haven't noticed, we have an empty seat, cause we missin' someone, Miss Ev'lyn. She's been known to run off at the most inopportune times to play bingo and what not. I'm sure she'll be around in the mornin'. An interestin' character, Miss Ev'lyn."

The girls came back giggling. Zoe glanced around to catch the joke but it eluded her. She forgot her worries when she bit into the dessert and took the first sip of coffee. The old-fashioned, caramelized, nutty topping gave way to the homey spice in the cake. Strong coffee was the perfect thing to wash it down. The conversation turned to everyday things.

Zoe turned to her own thoughts. This rehab center or halfway house wasn't what she expected. Where were the stacks of papers to fill out? The doctors. The nurses? The gray walls and institutional lighting?

"Miss Zoe," Abe said. "If y'er all done I'll show you to y'er room."

Everyone was smiling.

"The girls have it all ready for you."

Abe led Zoe upstairs to a room. Not just any room. The room of her childhood dreams, with the rounded, pointed porch. Everything about it was gray: the wall paper, carpet, a queen bed with an aging barn wood headboard, and duvet. *Here's the gray*, she thought. Her bag and quilt sat on the bed.

"This is y'er room, for as long as you need it. Now for y'er surprise." He led her down the hall to a bath room with an old claw-foot tub filled with a bubble bath.

"This is where we'll part for the night. You'll find everythin' you need right here. Soak as long as you like."

Abe looked at the pitiful sight in front of him. Another girl in his care, broken by the world. He hoped she would find healing and restoration here.

He took Zoe's face in his hands and whispered, "You've had a long day. Let's not worry 'bout tomorrow. We've had enough trouble today. Yes, sir. Most things in this life can be fixed by a hot bath and a good night's sleep." He placed his hands on her shoulders. "If you need anythin' you holler and one of 'em girls will come a runnin'. Goodnight, child. See you in the mornin'."

Zoe liked being called child. It gave her a sense of belonging. But she remained perplexed by the reality of her situation versus her expectations.

She closed the door and took her time undressing. She retrieved the soap, shampoo, razor and washcloth from the stand and climbed into the bath. The water was barely cool enough to sit in, but she sank into the bubbles and leaned against the slope of the tub. Haunted by her past, conflicted by the events of the evening and terrified of what the future might bring, her tears fell. She scrubbed until anything angry was washed away. The bath had sapped her of any remaining energy and thoughts of running. Exhausted, she fell into her new bed.

As she drifted off to sleep, she wondered: *When will I see the "in one day and out thirty days and twelve steps later" rehab center?* She hoped she wouldn't, but knew she would.

Tomorrow, she guessed.

Tomorrow she would run.

2

Choices

*You are free to choose, but you are not free from the consequence of
your choice.*
Zig Ziglar

December—The next day

It was still dark when the door to Zoe's room opened. A
gentle hand rested on her arm. A soft voice whispered in
the darkness, "Good morning, Zoe. It's Kit. It's almost
six, time to wake up. The coffee is on and breakfast will be
ready soon. Get dressed, come down to the dining room and
we will help you get started on your new life." Kit got up to
leave.

"Kit?" Zoe said, in a groggy voice. "I don't have many
clothes … "

Kit interrupted, "Rayden left a pair of jeans, boots and
cold weather gear. That should get you through today, until
you can pick out what suits you better." Kit patted her arm
and slipped out.

Thoughts flooded Zoe's mind. If she were to run, today
would be the perfect time, before getting attached to her
"new life" as they called it. But the judge had warned her that
if she ever so much as showed her face in his courtroom
again it would be the jailhouse and not the penthouse. If he
didn't want to see her again, why did he send her to Halfway
Homestead—a joke of a rehab center? Was he trying to set
her up to fail? She cursed under her breath, got dressed, made
her bed and headed downstairs.

The dining room table held an insulated thermos of
coffee, a bowl of oatmeal flanked by a small pitcher of fresh
cream and some honey. A small plate piled high with toast

was covered with a hand embroidered towel. All the girls were seated in their places, except Evelyn.

Abe sat at the head of the table, reading his Bible. He stopped when she sat down, smiled and said, "Good mornin', Miss Zoe, you ready for that race today or you need more time to train?"

Zoe poured herself a cup of coffee and used both hands to steady the cup as she brought it to her lips. "I would like a little more time to train," she said.

He chuckled and looked back at the book that lay open in front of him.

Kit settled in at the table and leaned over to the open book in front of Abe. "What are you reading about this morning, Abe?"

"The promised land," he quipped. "Behold, I lay out before you a blessin' and a curse. Choose a blessin'." He closed the well-worn book. "God may have brought people to a promised land or promised life with everythin' good in it, but now, like then, they's plenty of bad to avoid and people to overcome." He winked at Zoe. "It would have been easier on everyone if He would have just given Eden back. But then I s'pose nobody would have any skin in the game. Can't learn anythin' of substance that way. He left evil right there in amongst the good, so we would have a choice.

"Let's bow. Father, God, we are thankful, Father for new beginnin's—beginnin's with promise. Help us choose a blessin' today. Amen."

Most of the girls echoed his request.

"Yes, sir. Let's eat. Looks like Miss Ev'lyn still ain't with us yet. Bingo must have been a little hard on her last night," Abe said, nodding to the empty chair at the opposite end of the table.

All the girls giggled, except Zoe.

She wondered, *What was funny about that? Why the double standard? How come Miss Evelyn could skip dinner for Bingo then sleep in when others had to work?* It was one of the many things that hacked Zoe about this low rent, joke of a rehab-halfway house. The other thing that bothered Zoe was that the court order didn't give a specific timeline of when she might get to leave. "When offender shows significant improvement regarding destructive behavior ... The judge will review case in six months." Zoe shook her head and took a bite of cold toast.

"Let me tell you how most days go 'round here," Abe began. "We all try an' take breakfast together of a mornin' and supper of an evenin'. For lunch you on y'er own. Miss Kit always has things set aside in the refrigerator, free for the takin'. Throughout the day we all fulfill our duties and some days we have what we call life classes. Those classes will teach you things to help get along in life once you leave here. Like cookin', cleanin', money management, simple mechanics—how to change oil, check your tires and so on. Sometimes our housemates teach, other times we bring in folks from outside. On Wednesday nights, we have a Bible study. Other than that, y'er free to come and go as you wish so long as you are keepin' up with y'er responsibilities. Once a month y'll receive a stipend. It can be spent any way you choose, but you must show a written budget 'fore you do any spendin'."

Zoe wondered again what kind of responsibility Miss Evelyn had.

"Questions?"

The girls got up one by one and took their dishes to the dishwasher and began their day.

Zoe leaned back in her seat with her arms crossed and held nothing back when she spewed, "Yes, I have a question. I have a lot of questions! First off, how do you get off calling this place a rehab center? It's more like Abe's pimp shack! Where you pimp us out to do all the work around here. Where are the doctors and nurses? Where is my carefully crafted care plan that outlines how you plan on healing me while I'm here? Where are the psychologists for group and individual therapy? Where are the freakin' drugs to help me cope? Where are the activities? The computers? TV? You gave a nice speech on being slaves and captives, leaving our old life for the Promised Land and choosing a blessing and not a curse. What do you do when the Promised Land looks like a prison? A prison you say I can run from, but if I do, I

13

get a real prison. What am I supposed to do when what you call a blessing looks like a curse to me?"

Abe got up and put on his coat. "Let's take a walk, Miss Zoe," he said, handing her a coat.

As they walked through the kitchen, Abe picked up a compost bucket with carrot and potato peelings and plate scrapings from the night before. He also grabbed an empty stainless steel bucket and they strode out a side porch to the yard. The air was crisp and cold, with no hope of warming up by the look of the dense gray clouds that had settled in the sky. Abe didn't say a word as they walked across the crunching grass toward the servant's quarters, garden and dry riverbed. Zoe fell in step behind him, glancing back toward the iron gate before walking past a small cabin to the garden. An Australian shepherd dog joined them. Abe stopped to pet him.

"Mornin', Shep," he said. "Miss Zoe, meet Ol' Shep. He Miss Ev'lyn's dog. He just as much a character as she is. He used to be quite a cow dog, but spends most his time with Miss Ev'lyn nowadays."

Zoe petted the dog and they continued walking past an old brick outhouse standing tall in the morning light. Zoe stared wide-eyed as they came to a chicken house, beyond the servant's quarters. Abe dumped the compost bucket over the fence into the chicken run, hung the bucket on the fence, opened the door to the chicken house and held the door while Zoe stepped inside. The chicken house was warm from the heat of the chickens and smelled like feathers and manure. It repulsed Zoe. The chickens hummed and clucked. Abe bent over and talked nonsense to the chickens, like a daddy talking to an infant. Abe took an old metal egg basket off a nail and handed it to Zoe.

"The first order of b'ness every mornin' is to gather eggs," Abe said. His coal eyes shone as he reached into a nesting box, pulled out a brown egg and placed it into the basket. "After we've gathered the eggs, we'll feed and water the ladies and gentlemen and move on with our tour. Now, let's see you have a go," he said, as he nodded toward the boxes.

14

Zoe's hand shook as she reached for an egg. This time the egg was blue. Zoe's eyes met Abe's, but she didn't speak.

"Yes, sir, chicken eggs are the same color as they ears. Did you know chickens have ears?" Not waiting for an answer Abe unhooked a metal bucket with a lid and spilled feed into two feeders that hung from the ceiling and hovered a few inches from the floor.

"Miss Zoe, I heard what you said. I'm not 'noring y'er questions. We just burnin' daylight and need to get a good start on our day. I figured we could talk and work."

Zoe looked at Abe. He had some big ornery looking ears, but they were the same color as the rest of him. She smiled for the first time that day.

Zoe looked at the chickens, studying their heads looking for the place where an ear might be on a chicken. Satisfied that chickens might have ears, she continued gathering eggs.

Abe took the basket and counted the eggs. "How many today, twelve? They slack off in the winter time. Oh, we could turn a light on for 'em since the days are shorter now, to encourage egg production, but the truth is they have a mind of their own. They say 'if you gonna slack in the winter, so are we.' Grab that waterer, Miss Zoe and follow me."

Abe hung the egg basket high on a hook, picked up a larger automatic waterer and walked out the door and over to a hydrant. He dumped the remaining water on the ground and filled it with fresh water stepping back to let Zoe have her turn at the hydrant.

She fumbled with the waterer until she filled it and limped back to the coop with the sloshing water. They set them in place and adjusted the tightness of the lid to let air in so the water could refill itself without overflowing.

Abe pulled up a small chicken door to allow them passage into the run and chuckled as the roosters went first and then the hens. He walked out into the cold air holding the door for Zoe.

"We'll pick up the eggs when we come back this way, Miss Zoe. Let's see 'bout fillin' up that other bucket and feedin' the cattle." They walked to the lean-to of the barn where an old pickup sat. They made their way around the pickup to a small pen where a cow was waiting.

"We late ain't we, Bossy? We late and you hon-gry."

Zoe smiled at the way he said hungry.

Abe eased his way through the small gate holding it open for Zoe and nodded to the right, directing her where to stand. Zoe crept through the gate and stood as far away from the cow as she could. Abe closed the gate behind her, slung what Zoe assumed was a milk bucket on his left arm and dumped a small amount of sweet, smelling grain into a feed pan. As the cow started on the grain, Abe snapped a lead rope already tied to the barn to Bossy's halter and scratched the base of her ears. Bossy didn't seem to notice or care. Abe then plucked a one-legged stool off a hook and sat the stainless steel bucket on the ground under the swollen udders of the cow. He sat down on the stool and looked up at Zoe for the first time letting out a hearty laugh.

"Why, Miss Zoe, you look like you seen a ghost. Don't you know where milk comes from?"

He turned to the task at hand, dusted off the udders while humming to Bossy in his own language and milked the rear udders first. In a few minutes, the bucket was half full and the milk had to cut through a thick layer of foam before mixing in with the existing milk.

"Boss is comin' three this spring. She started as a bucket calf here when she was a baby. Weren't you, girl? Yes, sir. There's no real trick to milkin', Miss Zoe. You start with y'er top finger and thumb and squeeze on down."

Zoe, wide-eyed, moved closer to Abe careful to keep at least part of him between her and Bossy.

"Once you get that, piece o' cake. 'Fore long y'er forearms will be the size of Popeye's and you'll have a crushin' grip. Grip like a vise. Yes, sir."

Zoe stared at him.

"You so young, prolly don't even know who Popeye is."

The milk stopped coming from Boss's rear udders and Abe looked at Zoe with a grin and said, "Y'er turn now, Miss Zoe. You ease down in here and work on the front udders. They the easiest to milk, cause they so close."

Abe got up and stepped behind Zoe in one motion holding the stool up so it wouldn't fall.

"But, Abe, I've never … " Zoe's voice quivered. Hot tears filled her eyes again and spilled down her face. "I'm not cut out for this. Why can't I have a job like Rayden? I have more experience in clothes and decorating, than anything else."

"Miss Zoe, I know y'er scared and unsure of y'erself. You feelin' stretched and wonderin' what in the world does milkin' Bossy have to do with the mess you've found y'erself in. But jobs here pick the people. People don't get to pick the job. They's things in life we do, not 'cause we want to, but 'cause we have to for the sake of others. Right now, you gonna give milkin' a go to ease Miss Bossy before she gets impatient, to feed the girls milk and if we lucky maybe make some homemade ice cream. Most importantly, you gonna finish milkin' to fill the bellies of that family of hon-gry kittens over there lookin' on so they will catch the mice outta the grain. So we don't have to deal with some unnecessary outburst when you come out here alone and run into a country mouse, and give out a city-type scream. Or worse yet a black snake … " His voice trailed off.

Zoe hadn't noticed the family of kittens around an old cast iron skillet, looking on waiting anxiously for their portion of the milk. With shaky hands, Zoe held the udders and let out a gasp when milk came out. After a while, the mama cat came and rubbed back and forth on Zoe's leg encouraging her to finish her job. When no more milk came, Zoe stood, picked the bucket up and walked to the skillet while Bossy chewed her cud and looked on.

"Can I do the honors? I love cats and haven't had a kitten since I was a girl."

"Sure, Miss Zoe, that's fine. Mighty fine."

Abe watched as she poured the milk into the skillet almost to overflowing. This made him smile.

"That was probably too much, but they're so cute, especially this one." She snatched up a calico that had a foam beard and one foot wet from being in the milk. The kitten wriggled around and around in the air until she came to rest

17

on Zoe's bosom mewing to get back to her family and food. Zoe smelled behind her ear before setting her down.

Abe unlatched Bossy and patted her on the hip as she walked out of the barn. He then picked up the milk pail and hung it high on a nail. "It's time to feed the cattle, and give you the rest of the tour, Miss Zoe. You'll have plenty of time to introduce y'erself to the furry mouse traps later."

Abe ambled to the pickup and started it while Zoe settled herself in the passenger seat. He put the truck in reverse and backed out of the lean-to, then drove on toward the pasture ground that lay north of the house and beyond a cattle guard. "I know you've noticed we don't do things here the same way everybody else does, 'cause that don't work. When you look at 'real' rehab centers, as you call them, they an institution, regimented to one-size fits all. Right? Gray walls, florescent lightin', psychoanalyzin', prescribin', counselin', discussin', twelve steppin' nightmare. Where you come through the front door sick and leave by the back door, well, thirty days later. Perfectly—on time just like y'er regimented days. Praise the Lord and pass the ammunition!"

He pulled the truck to a stop at the top of a hill overlooking a valley with a few trees, pointed and said, "Yes, sir. The only thing always on time 'round here is my turkeys, wild turkeys." He was quiet for a time, then continued, "I count them ever' mornin' and it looks like we have 'bout how many? Forty-two head of Thanksgiving feast." He picked up a calendar and pencil lying on the seat and wrote forty-two on that day's date and laid it back down. He watched the turkeys peck and scratch meandering over the pasture ground searching for their food and enjoying the morning.

"Do you happen to know how many head of poultry it takes to fertilize an acre?"

When Zoe didn't answer he went on.

"Only about forty. Pretty cheap, easy way to fertilize y'er ground naturally if you ask me."

He continued to watch his flock of turkeys.

"Tell me, Miss Zoe, in what world does a system that treats everybody the same work?" While he waited for an answer, Zoe looked out her window. When the answer never

18

came, he continued. "That world don't exist. I may not be an institutionally educated man, but even I know that won't work. When you raise kids, you don't treat them all the same. They have different needs, so you give them what they need. Well, grownups are just tall kids. The Lord created everybody different. He created men like stones, with different makeups, shapes and sizes. And man been tryin' to make 'em into bricks ever since." The turkeys were pecking their way into the oak grove. Abe drove on. "We want you to become what y'er created to be.

"So here on the Homestead we look at what everybody else is doin' and do the opposite." He turned the pickup and backed up to a round hay bale, picking it up with the bale mover mounted to the back of the flatbed. "What do you think of that?"

"So, after meeting me last night you know I'm supposed to be a farmer?" she scoffed at the idea, shaking her head. "There aren't even any farmers in my family. I don't want to be a farmer. I don't want to be here. I want to get on back to normal, back to living."

"How old are you Zoe?" he asked, as he drove off toward a herd of cattle.

"Twenty-nine," she said, looking down at her hand-me-down boots.

"And in those twenty-nine years, how many of 'em were good, purpose-lived years?"

"None. Some maybe, when I was growing up. None. I don't know … I'd like to think some … " Her voice trailed off and she looked out the window.

"We leave that iron gate open fer people just like you. Fast livers, hard livers who want to get back to the chaotic normal they call livin'. Who fill their days with gourmet coffee, name brand clothes, pretty cars and the next best phone to keep you connected to all the right people. When in reality real connection with somethin' or someone real, scares you. Don't it, Miss Zoe? Silence and time to think, screams failure and regret. So you tune in and turn up so you don't have to hear truth, cause the truth is too much fer you. People and relationships bring a whole other set of problems. When we

19

done with chores, I'll drive you up to that gate, or anywhere you want to go so you can get on with fast livin'. If you want to go back to life as a brick expecting life as a stone, I'll take you. I'll tell the judge we had nothin' to offer you here. It's y'er choice.

"But, if you want to stay here and learn how to live slowly and live out the most natural of relationships between the Creator and created, and maybe even the created and created, we'd love to have you." Abe pulled up and stopped in the middle of a herd of cows, putting the pickup in neutral.

"They's a word for that, you know. I just discovered it. You know what it is?" Abe nudged Zoe with his knuckle. He didn't wait for an answer before continuing. "Relational permaculture. Here I thought we invented it, yet someone had already come up with a name for it. Do you know what it means?"

Zoe shook her head while watching the cows mill around the truck with curiosity.

"Well relational is easy to figure out—how one or more connect. But permaculture is a fifty-cent word. I prefer the definition as it relates to agriculture: sustainable ecosystems. So it's understandin' how ecosystems or people connect in a sustainable and self-sufficient way. Isn't that somethin', Miss Zoe?"

After seeing Zoe's wide-eyed and confused look on her face, Abe continued on. "You see the problem with America is we more than one generation removed from the farm. Young'ns no longer have a basic understandin' of makin' hay when the sun shines: Plantin' a seed, prayin' for rain, harvestin' the bounty and savin' some of it to plant again and/or sustain you through the winter.

"When a person or society loses sight of how they relate to their surroundin's, they take for granted the price paid for the conveniences they enjoy. In creation there is life and death at every turn and it's important to understand the natural cycle of things to understand the Creator."

Zoe looked scared as Abe rambled on.

"A seed dies to produce more and the plant returns to soil to nourish it. There is give and take around ever' bend. Not just give, not just take—like where most are livin' today. Livin' like that y'er bound to use up a resource and everythin' around becomes unbalanced. When y'er unbalanced in y'er relationships you end up in a place like this. Which is not a rehab clinic, per se. We absolutely into restorin' how we relate to one another and our world around us, but also how we relate to eternity. That's why we call this place Halfway Homestead. If we alive, we halfway home. It's all about getting people home, to their real home. Bases are loaded you might say."

"Huh?" Zoe shook her head perplexed.

"The ball's been hit. The events set in motion. It could be a grand slam. Not everyone on base will make it home, but they do have the option. Part of our job here is to coach you home. Point you in the right direction. Help you decide if you need to be slidin' or not. After all, you halfway home."

Zoe didn't know what she thought of all this. "But why here? Why on a homestead?"

"I can't pretend to know why things work out the way they do. Maybe it's because in pure unadulterated nature you can see the perfect complexity and unity in relationships as they react to one another. It's life by example."

"I can't see that," Zoe admitted looking down at her hands.

"Miss Zoe, I know you have a lot of questions and it's no secret that relationships take trust which you find y'erself lackin'. But give this place a chance—it might grow on you as you find out more and grow y'erself."

Abe dug into his pocket and produced a knife which he opened with one hand and handed to Zoe. "Hop out and cut the twine off that round bale, please, 'fore those cows start relatin' to us in an unbalanced way."

Zoe stared at the knife and then at the cows. "I'll get trampled. I'm not cut out for this." Zoe's eyes were big with fear.

Abe laughed his booming laugh. "Those kittens might charge you, but not them cows. I'm askin' you to trust me on this."

Zoe opened the door slowly and hugged the pickup while walking back to the bale. The cows hummed and smelled around waiting for the stranger to release the hay. Abe chuckled as he watched in the rearview mirror. Zoe cut the strings and wadded them up into a mess around her hands then walked back to the safety of the truck. As Abe pulled forward the hay unrolled until it was all laid out in a perfect line and the cows started to eat and mill over the fresh hay.

"We will start calvin' toward the end of February. That's when our stork duties start. You'll enjoy that. Nothin's more beautiful than when a baby takes its first breath."

Zoe noticed a sadness in Abe's voice, despite his message and wondered what that might mean. She shrugged it off and stared out the window while they drove in silence back toward the barn.

At the barn, Abe took the milk pail from the nail and walked to the sliding door in front of the pickup sliding it until there was just enough room to let Zoe out. Abe latched the door after Zoe and strode off to the chicken house to get the eggs.

Zoe scrambled to keep up. "I have another question. Why is there one man in the house and the rest women? I find that creepy."

"I find that creepy as well. That's why I live out in that little house. There's too much estrogen in the mansion fer me. I've lived happily there fer years. Miss Ev'lyn oversees everythin' in the big house." Abe seemed tired and short.

"You live in the servants' quarters? Doesn't that bother you, being black and all?"

Abe stopped and turned toward Zoe chuckling. "Well now, Miss Zoe, first you call me a pimp and now you insinuatin' that I'm a slave?"

"That's not what I meant. It's just, it looks … "

"Stereotypical?"

"Yeah."

"You'll soon come to know, if you haven't already, we anythin' but stereotypical 'round here." With that he turned, walked to the house and held the door for Zoe.

In the kitchen they placed the milk and eggs on the counter where Kit was waiting for them.

"If you need me, I'll be in my workshop, workin' on a fiddle I promised someone. Miss Zoe, you free until this evening when we milk again and get the grain ready to go again for tomorrow. Enjoy y'er easy days. In February 'er March the dam will break and you won't rest again until after fall harvest. In the meantime, get settled in here, meet the girls and help them as you can."

With a final nod, he left. Zoe watched him go. He looked tired and sad in a way. Like the weight of the morning was too heavy.

"Is he always like that?" Zoe asked.

"Like what? If you mean mysterious and moody, yes. Isn't he wonderful? He is like the father or grandpa many of us never had. Come on. I'll show you what we do with the bounty you gathered this morning." She picked up the egg basket, took it to the old farmhouse sink with drain boards on each side and sat it in the large sink. She turned on the water, scrubbed dirt and manure off of each one and set them on a hand embroidered dish towel to dry. Zoe helped as she continued.

"Eggs have a coating called bloom. They can keep for weeks if you don't wash them, but here in America the idea alone makes us a little squeamish so we wipe and refrigerate." When she finished, she placed the eggs into cartons.

"Know anything about eggs, Zoe?"

"Only that my body doesn't make an abundance of them and in a roundabout way, that is why I'm here."

"I was talking about chicken eggs, but I would love listening to your story over some hot tea and leftover cake later if you will share. We can call it lunch," she said, with a wink. "If the goal is to change every broken paradigm, I vote we start with that one. What say you, Zoe?"

"Sounds like we will live on the edge. I'm in," she said.

Kit smiled and crossed the kitchen to the pantry to retrieve a large hand cranked machine with a large tub on top and two spigots protruding from the side.

"What is that thing?" Zoe asked.

"Well, I'll tell you what it's not, and that is easy to clean. It's a milk separator. If milk sits a while the cream comes to the top and can be skimmed off with a cup or a ladle or whatever. But this will separate it straight from the udder you might say."

After placing a couple of bowls under the spigots to catch the cream, Kit took an old dish towel, laid it over the top of the bowl making a low place in the towel, poured the milk into the large drum and cranked.

"There is an old saying, cream rises to the top. I've found in real life, cream doesn't rise, it makes its way to the top and sometimes the journey makes it sweeter. Ever feel that way, Zoe?"

"Not for a long time, if ever." Zoe let out a deep sigh and asked, "Is this place for real? I mean, is this going to be one more thing I have to survive or is there really hope here? 'Cause I don't know if I can survive much more. You know?" Zoe's eyes filled with tears again and through them she could see the rest of the girls coming into the kitchen. She turned and wiped away her tears noticing that it was almost noon.

Kit quit cranking the separator and turned and looked long at Zoe's back and the other girls.

"Girls, Abe is in his wood shop working on a fiddle today, Evelyn is still MIA, we have a ton of leftover cake, and Jael just washed, which means clean yoga pants. The clouds and drizzle will stay until this evening. What do you think about building a fire with pallets in front of it, have a picnic in the parlor and get to know our new friend?"

The girls squealed and at once there was a flurry of activity. Jael pulled on her boots, grabbed the first coat on the hook and disappeared out the door. She returned with an armful of split wood which she took to the parlor. Zoe followed her to a beautiful old hearth and sat in an old wooden rocker as she watched her work. Jael crumpled up a piece of newspaper and placed it under the iron grate. She then piled wadded newspaper and a pine cone on the grate. After building a teepee of wood shavings around the pile, she took some of the smallest pieces of split wood and made walls and a roof and lit the tinder with a Strike Anywhere match.

Zoe hadn't seen a Strike Anywhere match since she was a child, at her grandma's house perhaps. Watching the fire, she couldn't help but think about her story she would tell in a few moments. Smelling the smoke from the fireplace made her nauseous. More exposure. Why? It seemed her whole life to that point had been all about the exposure of the truth and shortcomings. Feeling vulnerable, out of control and no good, she hugged herself and bent forward rocking back and forth until the flurry of pallet building interrupted her torment.

Rayden came in with an arm load of quilts, blankets and pillows, followed by Kit who had a stack of yoga pants. Rayden kept her head down and worked to turn the cold, stiff parlor into a cozy sanctuary with pillows to hug and blankets to sink into. In the middle, she placed a wooden serving tray with leftover cake, cheeses, spreads, naan, sliced apples, mismatched tea cups with saucers and small dessert plates. It was homey, nourishing and comforting. Everything that Zoe longed for but had always seemed to slip through her fingers. Gone like smoke up the chimney. Zoe wanted this strange place to be real and not a facade. She wanted to submerge herself into the simple but beautiful landscape of perfection. Instead, fear kept her chained to the darkness of her past.

Kit put her hand on Zoe's shoulder. "We've changed into something a little more comfortable. You are more than welcome to join us." She smiled, patted Zoe's shoulder and placed a pair of yoga pants in Zoe's lap. Zoe went to change.

When she returned, the girls had situated themselves around the fire. After she sat down, they joined hands and Kit said a prayer. "Father, we are excited about our new friend. We all remember the wonder and fear of a new beginning and the pain of its vulnerability. We pray this time would be a time of perfect release of the darkness and that Your light of freedom and life would prevail. Amen."

Zoe had never been much on praying, especially in a group. Prayers were always predictably uptight and scripted. But these words were soothing and if Zoe were honest, she would have to admit a life of freedom and not darkness was one of her deepest longings.

Everyone but Zoe and Jael said, "Amen." The others didn't seem to notice. Jael put on a heavy leather glove and retrieved the coffee pot from the fire pouring coffee into the hand-me-down china teacups while Kit passed out plates of cake. Zoe didn't feel like eating, but picked up her cup in hopes the warmth from the coffee would warm her from the inside.

"We all have a story to tell, Zoe. Today is your turn. This is about as close as you will get to the typical group therapy sessions that seem to be so popular in rehab centers. Otherwise, life will happen, things will come up and things will come out and we will work through them. But it's hard to know how we can love you if we don't know who you are."

Zoe's eyes filled with hot tears.

The Fall—years prior

She grew up just a few miles down the road from the Homestead, an only child. Her dad was a real estate broker with his own firm, while her mom stayed home to raise her. He treated her like a princess when she was a little girl. As his business grew, he spent less time at home and more time at the office.

Zoe met Craig, her ex-husband, in high school. It was the stereotypical story of the cheerleader falling for the quarterback. He wanted to be an oil man like his dad, investing in oil wells, wheeling and dealing. She dreamed of being the town's power couple, unstoppable. They talked of the money they would make or inherit and the yard full of kids they would have.

Craig's car was fast and so was he. Zoe was pregnant and scared by eighteen. Deep down she was excited about their dreams coming true even if it was quicker than what they had wanted; besides they would graduate soon.

She told him on a Monday and by Friday it wasn't a problem anymore. A problem is what he called the baby in her womb. She agreed to the abortion to keep him—

26

believing him when he said they were too young. He wanted a perfect life, college, wedding and *then* a baby. A baby in a frat house wasn't his idea of a future.

He broke up with her the following Monday.

Zoe was devastated. Craig had made her promise not to tell anyone—which she hadn't until coming to the Homestead.

After finishing high school, she went to college and dropped out. Seeing him around campus proved to be too much.

She moved home where her dad gave her a job as a secretary. That's when she discovered why her dad had been so busy at work. His former secretary had become his personal assistant—emphasis on personal. When she called him on it, he divorced her mother a few months later.

Her mom turned to the Bible. Zoe turned to the bottle, moved into an apartment and made ends meet by bartending. A handy job, when you are an alcoholic.

Craig graduated from college, moved back home and swept her off her vulnerable feet with promises of prosperity one night while she was working. She believed him.

The wedding was huge. He learned the family business and the money rolled in. They built their dream house, a log cabin, on the hill outside of town and tried right away for a baby, but she couldn't conceive. One of life's cruel tricks. Karma for the life she took, Zoe supposed.

The team of fertility docs tried everything. Nothing worked. Days turned into years and drinks turned into bottles. Craig worked more and volunteered for business trips while Zoe stayed home.

One night she came home early to giggles coming from their bedroom.

They hadn't heard her come in. The blonde screamed when Zoe said, "Someone has been sleeping in my bed, and she's still here."

Zoe ran to the night stand, grabbed the revolver Craig kept by his bed, swung around and pulled the trigger. She never heard the gun go off. The white flash was blinding in the dark room and Zoe fell to the floor.

It was then she realized a gun hadn't made the white flash, a left hook from Craig had. He disarmed her with a backward sweep of his right hand. Then a well-placed hook from his left caused his wedding band to cut her right brow, forcing blood into her eye.

The blonde ran from the room scooping up her clothes as she left. Craig pulled on his jeans and stepped into his boots. The rage for a final reckoning forced Zoe off the floor.

Blondie was getting dressed by the back door when Zoe caught up with her. She screamed and covered her face, but Zoe never connected. The blunt trauma to the back of her head sent Zoe to the floor. Her nose broke her fall.

She never dreamed Craig would leave her. She also never imagined the last picture of him burned in her memory would actually be a reflection. His leaving reflected in the blood pooling from her nose. A mirror image only her left eye could see. Her other eye was swollen shut.

"You're a big man, beating up on a little girl, Craig. Why don't you just shoot me and be done with me for good?" Zoe cursed.

He turned, pointed his Smith and Wesson revolver at her and pulled the trigger.

The hammer fell to an empty chamber with a deafening click.

The gun wasn't loaded.

He threw his head back and laughed his high-pitched hyena laugh and turned and strode to his truck.

"Run you coward," she whispered, as he left. "Run back to your whore."

The heavy effects of booze and trauma took over and darkness fell.

Their dog, Duke, a German shepherd mix, woke her by lapping blood from the floor and licking her nose. She pushed him away and pulled herself off the floor enough to prop her aching body against the kitchen cabinets.

Looking around their once beautiful home through the eye that wasn't swollen shut, she thought about their custom home. It was a wedding gift from Craig years earlier. Twenty acres of prime real estate with a four-bedroom log cabin on a hill overlooking river frontage. Everything she had ever wanted.

"Some freakin' fairy tale," she said out loud. "Now it's just a house made of mud and sticks. Any old pig could build this piece of crap!"

She opened the cabinet under the sink, pulled out a bottle and shook as she bought it to her lips. She gulped the warming liquid hoping to melt the ice encamped in her soul. But the glacier that had overtaken her on the inside was there to stay. It was as deep and cold as Antarctica and as unmovable as Gibraltar.

"That's better," she lied to herself, and let out a long sigh. "Well, the big bad wolf, cometh. He's gonna huff and puff and blow your house down and you won't have anywhere to run."

On cue, the crisp air of fall blew leaves into the house through the door he had left open, promising winter was just around the corner. Little did she know then, winter would come early and camp on the doorstep of her life for more than just a season.

~~~~~~~~~~~~~~~~

The next morning, she had a plan. A plan she had overheard Craig talk about. A slow gas leak from the kitchen stove and a burning phosphorous tipped tracer round through the window would cause an explosion and cover any evidence. And he had everything she needed to do it. Perfect irony.

I'll give them one last night of heat and passion, then watch while our fairy-tale marriage goes up in flames, she thought.

~~~~~~~~~~~~~~~~

The numbing wind felt hot compared to the coldness on her insides. She had heard all of her life of people having a soul or a spirit—the part that goes on living even after death that either burns forever in hell or plucks away on a harp in heaven. But Zoe was done believing in fairy tales.

He would not fool her again. She came in through the woods on their property. The lights were on in the house. She stopped at the edge of the woods behind their home. She wasn't much of a shot, but figured she could hit a big picture window.

Back at the Homestead

"I learned later they weren't home," she said, with no emotion.

"Attempted murder, arson and a handful of other things is what they charged me with. We pled it down to arson. I served just under four and a half years of my five years. I'm on parole now for seven months. So, here I am—halfway home, as you say. Not what you call a fairy-tale ending."

Zoe broke her trance-like stare from the fire and looked around. The girls' eyes were fixed on her. Rayden had been crying. She looked back to the fire.

"I guess what I want to know is, why is it written on a girl's soul to even want the fairy tale? Why do we long for the playful romance and adventure? Why do I have that desire in a world where women are despised, degraded, used up and tossed aside?" Zoe's questions hung in the air begging for someone brave enough to answer it.

"Da whys of dis world are de hardest to answer, yah."

Zoe turned from the fire to match the unfamiliar voice to a face. It surprised her to see a short, dumpy woman in worn clothes. Her pants were too short and her blouse was too long and worn threadbare making obvious the fact she wasn't wearing a bra and by the looks of things, possibly never had. Her greasy, gray hair was mostly in a bun. Close to her right ear lived a large mole whose hair had once been styled into her coif. Deep wrinkles pushed her lips to frame a gray-brown almost toothless smile.

This must be Evelyn, Zoe thought. She looked nothing like she had imagined the famed, wealthy hermit to look. Her shocking appearance held Zoe's gaze as she walked near to the fireplace in her bare, bunion-cursed feet. She filled a cup and shuffled around. Without pause she dumped most of the fresh cream and half the sugar into her cup, stirring it with a slice of apple. The rocking chair near the hearth creaked when she fell into it. She sat looking out the window at the moisture dripping from the eaves, slurping the hot liquid.

The girls sat in silence. Jael poured another round of coffee. Rayden sat hiding behind her hair deep in thought and cloaked with a heavy sadness. Kit sat content in the moment, the perfect picture of a lady.

Zoe thought about the statement that hung in the air. There was truth to her strange statement. The why questions of her life were the ones that kept her in her darkness steeping in the ugliness of the unknown.

More profound was Evelyn insinuating, like Abe earlier, there was more than this world. Preposterous, Zoe thought, but she tucked the idea away, just in case.

Abe had been sitting outside the door listening to part the recap of her life. After Evelyn's statement dissipated, he got up and peeked through the door. It was time for another milking lesson.

3

Pruning

My fake plants died because I did not pretend to water them.
Mitch Hedberg
*Everything has seasons, and we have to be able to recognize when
something's time has passed and be able to move into the next
season. Everything that is alive requires pruning as well, which is a
great metaphor for endings.*
Henry Cloud

January

The sun shone warm for the first time that year. Fifty-two degrees was warm for the middle of January. Wool sweaters were the uniform of the day, along with light gloves and hand-knitted beanies. Since the forecast was sunny and warm, Abe wanted to do some of the winter garden chores and introduce Zoe to the other part of her job—the garden and orchard.

Zoe couldn't believe she had been there almost a month. She was settling into the peculiar life at Halfway Homestead, but still didn't understand why she was there. Weeks there were better than one day in jail. Given the choice, she would gladly stay there.

The garden shed was well kept. Terra cotta pots were stacked from large to small on the floor. Along the wall, oiled garden implements hung ready for use. A work bench housed compost in bins underneath, presumably to start seeds.

"Today, we will clean out the chicken run," Abe explained. "As you know by now, we dump all kitchen scraps, yard waste and wood ash into the chicken run. They pick, dig and scratch their way through it, addin' whatever they add, turnin' it into some of the highest quality compost you've ever seen.

"We'll take these screens," he said, as he picked up two wooden framed screens with half inch openings and put them into one of the wheelbarrows. "Two garden rakes, two shovels and we are ready to head to the chicken run."

When Zoe opened the gate to the chicken run, some of the chickens made a mad dash for the opening. Zoe panicked. Abe assured her the chickens would return before evening. And since Shep was probably inside with Evelyn, they would most likely be fine outside.

They walked into the run. Abe, with little explanation, began by laying the screen across the wheelbarrow and shoveled the black richness on top of the screen where most of the goodness fell through into the cache. Zoe followed suit and was soon enjoying being outside in the sunshine. She would have never guessed a few weeks ago she would have been shoveling manure and liking it. Soon the wheelbarrows where filled and they carted the dressing to the garden.

The garden and orchard weren't what Zoe expected. Wood chips covered the ground in the garden, leaving the area void of plants except in a few places. Gray trees stood, bent with their arms hanging low, as if the orchard was mourning or dead. The haunted appearance was creepy to Zoe.

"This doesn't look like any garden I've ever seen. It looks like hell. Godforsaken. How can anything grow here?"

"Good thing we don't judge a book by its cover 'round here," Abe said, with a low chuckle. Setting the wheelbarrow down he gazed at the garden and orchard that lay before them. "I've been here, workin' this land since before you were born, Miss Zoe. Seen a lot of girls come and go—too many. Although all different, I've noticed some patterns. They all want to know one thing. You know what it is? Do I have what it takes? If you didn't notice, Zoe that's what you asked me about this garden. Does it have what it takes? 'Cause it sure don't look like it.

"You see, those girls were layered, like this garden. When we stopped tillin' years ago I laid down straw followin' the Ruth Stout's 'no work' gardenin' method. It worked okay, but then I heard of this lasagna method where you lay down compost layers, a brown—something dead, then a green—kitchen waste or somethin' recently dead, like leaves or grass clippin's. Then a brown again and so on. You know, layers, like lasagna, but you don't turn or till the soil. The edgy-cates say that won't work. But they don't account for nature, grand design and little critters called worms. As long as the ground is covered, they till the soil.

"Then along came a feller named Paul Gautchi, from Washington, who say all you need is wood chips to cover. So I start goin' to the city recycle center and haulin' wood chips by the pickup load, coverin' the layers and my garden has never been better. Ever' few years I clean out the chicken run and spread it across the wood chips to feed it from the top." He demonstrated by dumping his load and pushing the blackness with his rake tines up. Again, Zoe followed his lead. "But I'm getting' ahead of myself.

"The girls all come through here with layers, complicated—lookin' godforsaken. Just like what you say, like hell has had its way with them—once alive, but now dead. I 'spect you can identify."

Tears filled her eyes. She nodded.

"Come here, child," Abe said, kneeling. "Let me show you somethin'." He removed the top layer of wood chips and dug down. "What do you see?"

"Just dirt."

"Not just dirt. What else?"

"Pieces of different things."

"Like what?"

"I don't know, straw maybe, an egg shell, something unrecognizable … "

"They call that humus. Let's call 'em things that used to be, Miss Zoe. The past. Everythin' good put into you, everythin' bad put into you, layered in. Y'er life.

"Smell it." He bent and stuck his nose in the hole and breathed deeply. "What do you smell?"

Zoe bent low. "It smells good." Breathing in again. "It smells great. Why?"

He got up leaving his rake and headed back to the chicken house with his wheelbarrow. Zoe followed.

"Life," he said.

"Huh?"

"It smell like life."

"I don't get it."

"The question you should be askin' is how? How to get to smellin' like that again?

"You may not know this, Miss Zoe, but you be smellin' like a wasteland. Not good or bad, just like nothin'. You can't grow healthy on nothin'. You girls come here wantin' to forget the past, so you strip it away. Till it in. Hide it. 'Cause the shame of what has been is too much sometime. Understandable, but I think it's the wrong approach for both a garden and a life.

"I wonder what would happen if we didn't hide the hurts? All those imperfections of life. What if we at least took up the weeds of shame, so they not rooted anymore, but left them there on the surface, so everybody could see?"

"Ugh!" Zoe stopped raking. "No thanks."

Abe ignored her comment. "Over time it would decompose. What was once ugly and foul smellin' would morph into somethin' beautiful and rich—feedin' the good things planted."

"Would others be able to see what was?" Zoe asked.

"Oh, maybe if they really lookin'," he said, leaning against his rake. "A piece here and there might speak to what was. But mostly people would see what is—the fruit that comes after shame is laid to rest. Healin' for you. Hope for others. A far cry from the shameful past."

Zoe stopped what she was doing to muse on that thought. "But what if I don't want people to see my scars?"

"You sayin' you'd rather have your past, your top layer stripped away?"

"Yes!"

"Nothin' gonna grow there. Y'er top soil gonna blow away. Nothin' there to hold it. You talk about weeds. When you till in y'er weeds—hide y'er past, y'er troubles gone fo' awhile, but they be back with a vengeance.

"Let's go back to another garden, kinny-garden. What you have to have fo' life, Miss Zoe?"

36

She loved how he said her name. Smiling she said, "Air, water, shelter, food … " Her voice trailed off. "Love, maybe."

"Right. Layers provide shelter like skin. Food is a product of things once alive. Rain comes, to dilute the food and make it usable. If you have all that, worms come makin' air space, turning dead stuff into life-givin' stuff. It isn't complicated."

They worked in silence for a few loads.

"What about love? What represents love?"

"Well now, Miss Zoe. There's the greatest mystery in life. The easiest answer is light—everythin' true. It shows up every day and darkness runs to hide. It's good. Very good.

"Here's the thing, it doesn't matter what you build the layers on. Everybody's layers gonna be a little different. You can use whatever is available. If you have all life-givin' elements, you'll have life. Take one element out and you'll have death. Add somethin' and you'll have death."

"Add something? Like what?" Zoe was perplexed.

"Oh, they's a lot of things a person could add. Right, Zoe?"

Zoe nodded sadly.

"But one word will cover it. Lies."

Zoe leaned against her rake.

"How can a garden lie to itself?"

"You know, Miss Zoe, you a thinker. That's one thing I'm lovin' about you, a grand characteristic. Let's go back to another garden, the first one, Eden. Do you know that story?"

"Of course, I do. I went to Sunday school. I just don't believe it." She raked again.

"I'm not askin' if you believe it. If you believed it you wouldn't be here today. I asked if you know it. So, Adam, Eve and the snake in the garden, where did the snake come from?"

"He's Satan, the head of the fallen angels appearing as a snake."

"Right. Did God make him fall or did he choose to fall?"

"It was his choice." Zoe bowed her head.

"So, was the garden perfect?"

"Yes."

"Really?"

"I don't know."

"If it were perfect what was the snake doing there?" Abe asked.

"I don't know. Maybe the garden was perfect, but the snake wasn't."

"A perfect garden, huh? What about that tree they weren't s'posed to touch, much less eat from?"

"The tree of the knowledge of good and evil?" Zoe asked.

"The tree of the knowledge of good and evil," Abe echoed.

"What about it?"

"I know you say you don't believe in any of this, but let's say you do. Is God capable of evil?" Abe asked.

"I don't know."

"Did you sing in Sunday school?"

"Yes."

"*God Is Love* and so on?"

"Yes."

"Based on those songs, which are quotes outta the Bible—assumin' it's true—is God capable of not lovin' or evil?"

"No. I guess not." Zoe shrugged.

"Why?" Abe inquired.

"I don't know."

"'Cause it's against His nature. Light can't become darkness and darkness can never infringe on light. Do you think it's possible he *didn't* create the tree of the knowledge of good and evil?" Abe's question hung.

"I guess so." Zoe stood staring off in the distance. "If he didn't create it, who did?"

Abe raised his eyebrows and looked at Zoe like she already knew the answer.

"Satan?" Zoe gasped.

"Satan isn't a creator per say. He's a mimicker, a corrupter, a contaminator, but not a creator. When he contaminates something, it's no longer what it was. It's a lie. So, if Satan 'made' or corrupted a tree in the garden, what would God tell His creation to do regardin' that tree?"

"Stay away from it?" Zoe answered.

"Right. Why?"

"To protect them?" Zoe asked.

"Why?"

"Because He loves them?" she guessed.

"Absolutely! From the beginnin' a time." Abe beamed.

"Why the choice?"

"You mean free will?"

"Yes."

"Because everythin' about Him is freein', it either sets free or is free. That's why the religious leaders of Jesus' time were frustratin' to Him. The law was used to control people with no love or grace. Godly relationships have freedom and love. Where within His boundaries everythin' is permissible, but not everythin' is beneficial." He dumped the last load from the chicken run and leaned on his rake.

"If you were to marry again, Miss Zoe, would you choose the institution of marriage or the relationship of marriage? Which offers the most freedom?"

"Relationship."

"Now you seein' the method of our madness around here. We don't wanna brainwash you into a set of rules you must follow at all costs. We couldn't police 'em no-how. Instead we'd like fer you to look at what you added or took away from y'erself to get where you are now.

"We hope you'll seek a relationship with y'er Creator, the only one who can help you change and become who you were meant to be."

"I'm not saying I believe it, but if I did. How would I do that?"

"That's a good question, Zoe. We've spread enough fertilizer this mornin'. Let's go have lunch and we'll talk about it this afternoon over some prunin'.'"

They returned everything to the garden shed and walked to the house.

They found meatloaf in the Crock Pot on the counter with homegrown garlic mashed potatoes and green beans.

Zoe dished the food onto two plates. They sat down and Abe bowed his head. Zoe bowed slightly and closed her eyes only to open them as soon as Abe prayed.

"Father, we all long for a relationship with You the way it was meant to be, with lovin' boundaries yet freedom. I thank you for Zoe, another special creation of y'ers and ask that her life elements be restored to pure. In y'er Son we pray. Amen."

Even if she couldn't bring herself to believe all of it today, the idea sounded good to her. Too good. She silently hoped there was a God that could do such a thing.

Abe cut a piece of meatloaf, ran it through the potatoes and groaned as he took a bite. "Isn't that something? Yes, sir."

~~~~~~~~~~~~~~~

"Okay, Miss Zoe, this afternoon we will need only one wheel borrow, that tarp there," he said, pointing at a folded canvas tarp on a shelf, "two pruners and two hand saws." He turned and picked up the wheel-barrow full of supplies and headed toward the orchard.

He spread the canvas under two drooping apple trees, picked up his pruners and looked at Zoe. "You may wanna watch for a couple trees 'fore you take off on y'er own. Prunin' is easy. I like to think of it as stimulatin' the tree, freein' it to do what it's made to do—grow and produce, while stayin' within the boundaries we set."

He walked to the middle of a tree with his pruners, "The first thing I look for is dead wood and crossovers; branches that have crossed or will cross in the next season if not removed. Take 'em out." On the larger branches, he used the saw and the smaller ones the pruners, dropping the branches onto the canvas. He was careful to cut the branches off almost flush to the parent branches. "The suckers comin' off the branches going straight up won't produce fruit. Take 'em out. Also think about lettin' in light and air, removin' upper branches that will shadow the under branches, kind of openin' up the middle. The Japanese have a sayin', 'a tree

40

must be open enough to throw a cat through it.' I like that. Don't you, Miss Zoe? Why don't you have a go?"

Zoe hesitated, walked to the middle of the tree and pruned. Occasionally she would look up at Abe with a questioning glance and he would nod to cut and somewhat scowl on those he wanted her to leave.

"Not judgin', Miss Zoe," he said, as he snipped here and there on the tree she had just finished. "Just like in life, if you change y'er perspective, it helps you see things you couldn't before." He hummed a tune as he worked soaking up the sunshine until he interrupted her thoughts with a statement.

"The question on the table is how do you pursue a relationship with a god you don't know, and y'er not sure you believe in?"

Zoe didn't remember asking the question like that, but it got to the heart of her deepest query. "Yes. I guess that is the question."

"I think all questions about God can be answered in nature. Like, 'does God exist'?

"The Bible says 'For since the creation of the world God's invisible qualities, His eternal power and divine nature—have been clearly seen, being understood from what has been made, so that people are without excuse.'

"Let me ask you Miss Zoe, were you created or did you come from primordial ooze?"

"I would like to think not from ooze. But I don't know of a good alternative."

"I can't support the minute statistical possibility it would take to get us from nothin' to somethin'. The sheer lack of fossil evidence to support the progression from slime to human tells me there's gotta be another way. '

"The law of biogenesis says life always comes from life. That makes sense to me. They's gotta be some order to it. All the laws of nature adhere to the laws of logic, mathematics, physics, planetary motion and chem-stry. That's a tall order from somethin' that happened randomly. I reason since there's order to nature whether in the heavens or on earth, we must've come from an orderly bein'.

"Whad you think, Miss Zoe?"

Zoe had stopped pruning, dumfounded at Abe's intelligent rebuttal of creation versus big bang. "I don't know. You're talking over my head."

"Let's make it simpler. Did the sun rise on time this morning, so that calendar, seasons and all, wouldn't be thrown off?"

"I don't know."

"I don't know, either. But there's a scientist somewhere who keeps that data and would most certainly panic, with no way to fix it if it didn't. Right?

"It was breathtakin' this mornin'—though, wadn't it?" Abe added.

"Yes, the prettiest I've seen since coming here."

"Are you concerned if the eggs that lay under our broodin' hens will have enough oxygen for the life that grows inside of 'em?"

"Huh?"

"Each egg, Miss Zoe, has enough oxygen in the air sac so the chick can breathe for three days while they peck out of their shelled world. Have you ever worried about the eggs maybe not being randomly made right? Who watches over such things? Surely there's one who keeps the smallest things in nature runnin' smoothly.

"Isn't it beautiful, Miss Zoe, that we have the freedom to enjoy the goodness that surrounds us? Just be, and enjoy nature.

"You see the beauty, Miss Zoe, of havin' the Creator that first made everythin' beautiful, and then wove a mystery into them to be discovered. We don't have to understand the mystery to enjoy the beauty. The mystery enhances the wonder of the beauty.

"You girls that come through here are like nature. Y'er beautiful, mysterious, nourishin', comfortin', inspirin' and capable of givin' life. Y'er presence is sorely needed to balance the world of men. Yet y'er place in creation has been bastardized.

"That's what we tryin' to do here, Miss Zoe. Discover how to relate to our Creator by usin' the principles in nature, on the farm, in the garden, in the orchard and in an old house filled with other creations.

"So, grand design? Or is everythin' in this life by chance? Do you want y'er life to be left to chance or would some Godly guidelines be helpful?"

"Guidelines would be helpful, I guess. I've tried it on my own and the results were less than perfect."

"Guidelines are helpful. Without 'em we worry about things we shouldn't and create 'fixes' when we ain't creators. Guidelines aren't there to discourage us from what could be, but to encourage us in the safety of growth. Guidelines based on truth give us freedom. Life-givin' freedom. Guidelines based on lies can hurt us and hold us captive.

"So today, we here prunin' our trees and our lives. Cuttin' out the dead branches that won't produce again. Removin' the branches that keep us in the shadows and won't let our fruit ripen. Prunin' out everythin' that doesn't let air and light in. And don't forget to cut out the suckers whose only purpose is to suck life from us.

"Some lives have never been pruned. They big and overgrown. Other lives maybe been hit with a mower when they young and cut off from what they coulda been. It's not too late for trees like that; all grown up like a bush instead of a tree. Any tree that still has some life is redeemable, and can be made to produce again."

Zoe felt dormant and overgrown.

After pruning, Abe gathered up the large canvas tarp and handed the bypass pruners and hand saw to Zoe saying, "I'll make a deal with you, Miss. Zoe. If you make sure these get back to the garden shed, after you prune the ivy back from the Homestead sign up on the wall, I'll do the milkin' tonight. The folks who deliver things here are havin' a hard time readin' that sign."

Zoe was giddy at not having to milk. She said, "Deal!" before Abe could even finish his statement and ran to prune the ivy.

Wondering how one might prune ivy, she took one look at the thick covering on the stone and wrought iron and decided a small haircut around the sign wouldn't make any difference.

She proceeded, trying to keep it pretty without cutting too much. At the bottom she could see words covered by ivy. She pulled and snipped until the last line came into view: Isaiah 61:1-3.

The verses were from the Bible, but she did not understand their significance. Something stirred deep within her. Longing to know what it meant, she finished her work. The sun disappeared behind the horizon; another beautiful picture more brilliant than the sunrise that morning.

Her countenance was lighter as she jogged down to the garden shed, put the tools away and turned to leave. Spying a can of WD-40, she thought of her granddad's old, but well-maintained tools. Misting the tools with the oil didn't take long. Satisfied with her efforts she turned and ran to the house more than ready for supper.

Abe watched her from the barn. The way she ran was like a child, carefree and full of joy. "Yes, Sir, Bossy, I believe we makin' some progress."

~~~~~~~~~~~~~~~

Zoe used the homemade sugar scrub that lived on the sink in a jelly jar. Kit entered the kitchen behind her watching her scrub her hands. There was something different about her today.

"Did you enjoy your day in the garden?" she asked.

Zoe stopped scrubbing for a moment and looked up. "It was a great day. There's something about working outside that invigorates me. Makes me feel empowered."

"Fresh air has a medicinal effect. Doesn't it?" Kit replied, as she picked up another dish of food for the table.

Zoe agreed and went back to scrubbing as Abe strode in with the milk. Zoe took it from him and made quick work of the separating, storing and clean up. The dining room was filled with giggles and chatter when she returned. She could see Evelyn was present and made her way to her place by Kit.

They held hands and bowed their heads. Abe began, "Father, we enjoyed spendin' time in Y'er garden today. We thankful for the abundance that will come from the acts of prunin'. Through Christ. Amen."

Zoe didn't say amen but loved how short yet poignant the prayer was. The meal was simple: lasagna, kale salad, homemade bread and apple pie with homemade whipped cream for dessert.

The conversation topic of the night was where you would vacation in the United States if you could pick anywhere. Everyone took turns answering the question. Abe wanted to hike the Appalachian Trail, visit Civil War battlefields and fiddle makers in the mountains of Appalachia. Kit's dream was to ski Vail Colorado by day, dine at the gourmet restaurants by night and finish the evening by relaxing in a hot tub while the snow falls on her head. Rayden longed to drive a box truck from Maine to Florida, buying, selling and trading treasures down the East coast. While journeying, she wanted to experience a clam and lobster bake in the sands of Maine and go deep-sea fishing in Florida. The girls weren't shocked to find J's desire was to hike the deserts of the Southwest stopping to pan for gold, whitewater raft the toughest rivers and experience a cougar hunt in New Mexico. Evelyn wanted to explore the West Coast, feed sea anemones, tour lighthouses, camp in the Redwood Forest and finally take a hot air balloon ride over Napa Valley.

"Miss Ev'lyn is quite a connoisseur of all things wine," Abe said. "She makes some of the finest chokecherry wine you have ever tasted. I see she is indulging in some here tonight."

Wine at a halfway house? Zoe hadn't even noticed until then. It made her wonder why they would allow such a thing. Then again, it wasn't the place she thought it was going to be.

She thought about the verse again, wondering of its significance. The noises Evelyn made while she ate interrupted her thoughts. She was missing quite a few teeth on the bottom, and pushed her food to the top and front of her mouth with her tongue causing it to mash and sometimes overflow back onto her plate. The other girls had made it a practice to ignore her or at least not fixate on the chewing calamity as much as Zoe. She found it especially annoying when she loudly sipped her coffee or in this case wine.

Zoe tried not to stare.

Kit didn't miss Zoe's fixation. She winked at Zoe and smiled. Rising to clear the main dishes and retrieve the dessert from the kitchen she said, "Zoe, would you help me with dessert?"

"Sure. I would love to," she said, with a relieved giggle.

In the kitchen, Zoe couldn't help but bring up the old lady's eating habits. Kit didn't play into the fray. She focused on cutting the pie into six, large, glorious pieces and placed them on the primitive hand-thrown pottery plates. The apple pie was made from the orchard apples and some ground whole wheat flour from their fields of wheat. Bossy supplied the cream for whipped topping. Abe's cowboy coffee washed it down.

Before going back to the dining room, Kit spoke, "One of my favorite things about being here is that we learn to love one another through our flaws. Sometimes that means setting healthy boundaries to protect our freedoms or just loving someone as a child—right where they are." She smiled one last time and pointed over to the coffee and mugs for Zoe to carry. "Would you do the honors?"

Zoe didn't miss the light correction. She smiled back as she thought about her words and let out a short sigh knowing she had a long way to go until she reached that goal. She picked up the platter with the mugs and coffee and followed Kit to the dining room.

As the girls served, Zoe noticed the simple, yet stunning thrown mugs. She had drunk from them before, but hadn't noticed their rustic beauty. Holding one up to the light, she said, "These are beautiful. I've seen some similar in Taos, New Mexico at an art colony, but they were very expensive."

Rayden perked to life, her black eyes flashed with fire and excitement. In her Mideast brogue she explained, "Didn't you know Miss Evelyn is a talented potter? She has a studio in Abe's cabin where she throws her creations."

Evelyn didn't even look up from her pie. Like a pig at the trough, she was enjoying the goodness.

Rayden continued, "She even processes some of her own clay. She will dig and bring it back, running it through a series of screens to remove any rocks and unwanted material. That is what she uses the plethora of claw foot tubs for, that are behind Abe's living quarters by the woodpiles.

Her artwork and willingness to teach others has made her very well known. The reason she isn't often up with the chickens is because she stays up most of the night throwing pottery."

Zoe felt bad for assuming the worst about Evelyn. "Evelyn, you're so talented. I would love to tour your studio sometime."

By this time, Evelyn had plowed her way through the pie leaving pieces around her plate, down her front and around her chair. She had moved on to slurping coffee. Evelyn smiled and nodded at the compliment, continuing to slurp adding fresh whipped cream to her coffee at will.

"What drew you to the medium in the first place?"

"Plenny of time for tink," she responded, staring at the fire in the fireplace, "and pray. Tink and pray. Yah."

Zoe assumed hermits had plenty of time to do both, but what did she know about being a hermit. She didn't spend much time thinking about Evelyn's life. Her mind and body were tired from the long day in the garden. She excused herself as the other girls cleaned up and climbed the stairs.

After her bath, she snuggled into her bed. The room was cold in the winter, but she liked a cooler room when she slept.

Thoughts of the day's events entered her mind: chains versus freedom, the original garden, God, pruning and the verse. What was it? Isaiah 61:1-3. She longed for her Bible downstairs, but she was too tired to get it. Reaching up to turn off the light on her night stand she wondered if there might be a Bible in the night stand. The drawer opened easily. The Gideons would be proud, she thought, picking up the Bible. It took a few minutes to find the passage:

Isaiah 61:1-3

1 The Spirit of the Sovereign Lord is on me, because the Lord has anointed me to preach good news to the poor. He has sent me to bind up

47

*the brokenhearted, to proclaim freedom for the captives and release from
darkness for the prisoners,*

Zoe couldn't believe her eyes. She had to keep reading.

*2 to proclaim the year of the Lord's favor and the day of vengeance of
our God, to comfort all who mourn, 3 and provide for those who grieve
in Zion—to bestow on them a crown of beauty instead of ashes, the oil of
gladness instead of mourning, and a garment of praise instead of a spirit
of despair. They will be called oaks of righteousness, a planting of the
Lord for the display of his splendor.*

"A crown of beauty instead of ashes," she whispered.

She had meant ashes and devastation for Craig. Instead,
she sat like Cinderella in ashes. Now she yearned to be a
princess crowned with beauty. But who could crown her? She
longed to know.

She placed the open Bible on the night stand, shut the
light off, laid her head on her pillow and cried herself to
sleep. Tears of happiness and sadness, joy and sorrow, pain
and hope soaked into her pillow.

Cleansing tears. Pruning tears.

4

Stork Duty

You can't go back and change the beginning but you can start where
you are and change the ending.
C.S. Lewis

February

Although initially hating to milk, Zoe grew to enjoy the
time alone in the barn. The sound of Bossy chewing
her cud and the cats milling around waiting for their
share of milk was soothing. On clear mornings, the sun
would bathe her in light from an east window making the
winter seem further than just outside the sliding doors and
made the winter in her soul long for the possibility of spring,
a new beginning. So far, boards still covered the windows of
her heart and her internal garden was dormant. Waiting.
Waiting for what, who knew?

Zoe fed the cats, unhooked the rope from Bossy's halter
and gave her rump a pat. She meandered out the door to
check out the hay Abe had refreshed in her paddock. Zoe
turned to get the eggs before returning to the house.

The morning was quiet in the mansion. Zoe busied herself
with putting away the barnyard produce. Evelyn was probably
sleeping in. The girls had taken the van to deliver some of the
things they sold. She marveled at the inventive and
industrious ladies she shared a house with and wondered if
that could be her one day, making a profit by doing
something she loved. She longed for a passion and purpose.

Abe came in with what appeared to be a pile of magazines,
two shoe boxes, some graph paper and two pencils. He
grunted as he closed the door with his foot and put his load

down on the table before hanging up his coat and hat. "Good mornin', Miss Zoe. You look chipper this mornin'. I'd say milkin' agrees with you."

"Morning, Abe. What have you got there?" Zoe nodded with her head as she dried her hands.

"The stuff dreams are made of this time of year: seed catalogs. It's not gonna get any warmer out there today. In fact, I think we prolly in for a dreadful chill. Cold brings on stork duty. It seems the colder it is in February, the more those cows wanna calve. What I'm trying to say is our days of hibernatin' are gonna be gone 'fore we know it. Then 'round the clock stork duties for us 'til we get dem heavies delivered. So I believe it's a good day to stay inside and dream 'bout this year's garden. Draw us up a plan and start all the plants indoors we won't sow directly into the ground. That is right after I have me a couple hard boiled eggs, a cinnamon roll or two and some coffee to chase it with. Yes, sir." He rubbed his hands together in anticipation.

Zoe poured two mugs of coffee and placed all the food they would need on the table. She sat down and looked at the notebook of the garden plans from years past. "These are amazing. They're like garden blueprints. I didn't know gardens needed a plan. I thought you planted wherever and it grew."

"Oh now, Zoe, everythin' need a plan. You ever heard, 'you aim at nothin', you'll hit it every time'? I don't care if you talkin' gardens, business or life, everythin' needs a plan." Abe sank into his seat, picked up his coffee and took a long sip. "Mmmm hmmm, it's a great day to be inside. Let's bow.

"Father, God, we thankful for these days of rest and plannin' 'fore the dam breaks. We pray for Y'er guidance on our plan today. Yes, Lord, we askin' You now to whisper to us what might be best and we pray that we'll have ears to hear this mornin'. In Jesus name."

They ate Kit's famous cinnamon rolls. Zoe savored every bite. It was by far her favorite breakfast.

"What's on your mind, Miss Zoe?"

"Do you really believe we can ask God a question and He will answer?"

"Absolutely."

"How? Have you ever heard His voice? Does it sound like Morgan Freeman?"

Abe laughed at this. "Oh, Miss Zoe, you somethin'. I've never heard an audible voice; you know like what you thinkin'. Instead, for me it's more like a random thought, an idea. Usually it's an idea that is counter-cultural and somethin' I would have never come up with on my own. And after I poo poo the idea or thought and maybe even argue some, you know wrestle with the idea, roll it around in my brain for a while tryin' to figure if it's good or not, I figure it's from God."

"That seems convenient. You blame God for all your good ideas?"

"Well, He's the one that's good all the time. He is not capable of anythin' but goodness, love, grace and mercy. So, I figure if the idea produces somethin' good, then He's the one to blame."

"Give me an example."

"Okay. Years ago, when I was gonna plant a garden for the first time I laid out the finest plan I could on paper. I didn't feel like it was exactly right, but it was the best I could come up with at dat time. 'Fore breakin' ground, I realized I hadn't prayed about it. So I did. I asked God, if He was me, where would He plant the new garden?

"A few days later I was out doin' chores, thinkin' 'bout things and I got a random thought: the soil was prolly good in that barn—we were gonna to tear down. A hundred years of manure and composted hay makes for good soil. I argued. I couldn't believe without my eyes, so I went and dug and you know there was almost two feet of some of the prettiest top soil you've ever seen.

"Seein' wasn't enough faith. So I argued mo', 'But, God, it's February and I would have to tear that whole barn down piece by piece, one nail at a time.' And in my spirit I heard, or felt rather, the warm sun on my back. I only had a flannel on that day. Then thought 'bout the forecast and how we were in for at least ten days of some of the mildest weather we had ever had for that time of year. It was like God was saying,

'Yep and I've given you a bunch of nice days in a row to get started on it.'

"So I went to work, straight away every day, one nail dropped in a bucket at a time and one piece of tin at a time and the walls came down until we had nothing but a frame. Course, I didn't know what to do with the frame, until I got another idea. I would need a fence to keep the deer whupped off my lettuce, so I used old wire and some other old fencing supplies we had layin' around and soon I had a garden. The best garden I coulda had on the place."

"What happened to the fence?"

"Well now, Miss Zoe, that was years ago, 'fore we got Shep. Shep keeps the deer away now. We never have to worry."

"I seldom see Shep," Zoe mused.

Abe chuckled. "That may be true. Shep is some-what of a hermit and quite a bit antisocial. He spends most his days inside with Miss Ev'lyn, yet still patrols at night. She has a doggie door for the po' old flea bag until he drags in somethin' he shouldn't. I promise you one thing, Miss Zoe, he can't go too long without causin' Miss Ev'lyn heartburn. The day he decides to be cantankerous you won't too soon forget it." He chuckled again and got up for more coffee.

"Now the seeds we will start indoors will be tomatoes and peppers. We live in zone six," he said, pointing to their place on a zone map in one of the seed catalogs. "The lower the number, the shorter the growing season. Tomatoes and peppers have long growin' seasons. To get a jump start on the season, we will start those indoors. Everything else we will plant in the ground.

"Now I used to think the garden needed to be laid out in rows east to west, spaced out just right. But the mo' women I'm around the mo' crazy I get driven. They can't plant a straight row to save they soul. I'm done arguin' about it. Garden supposed to be fun, a relationship with our Maker, with freedoms at ever' point. So I gave up on the rows and what da books say. I focus instead on what I can learn about the character of God, how can I get in touch with my feminine side and maybe even some, fung shoey."

52

Zoe laughed out loud. "You mean Feng Shui?"

"Whatever, gardenin' all about relationship. If you a row girl, okay. If you into circles, all right then. If you into sowin' y'er seeds like *Jack and the Beanstalk*, that's fine too. Whatever. But we makin' a plan today. Now, here's a list of the early stuff we'll plant in April like potatoes, onions, all the greens, root crops and beans. They all like it cool and early. After they done producin' we will pull 'em, feed 'em to the chickens and start 'em over for fall crops. The later stuff like melons, okra, tomatoes, peppers and corn, you plant 'em once when the ground warms up. You can plant 'em in April. It's better to wait until it's warmer so y'er seeds won't rot."

While Abe rattled on, Zoe was careful to listen and ask questions. She had worked in her grandma's garden as a child and came to realize that Abe was all about breaking as many traditional rules while raising more food than anyone else in the same amount of space. Although his methods were weird, his childlike freedom was exhilarating. In her quest for control over her life and circumstances she had extracted anything that had resembled freedom and loving relationships in her life leaving rules and guidelines in their place. Maybe by making a loose plan and "coloring outside the lines" in the garden Zoe could find a model for living the carefree life she had always dreamed about.

~~~~~~~~~~~~~~~~

After two hours of garden planning, Zoe felt like she was in school again, taking a gardening class followed by a lab. In the garden shed the lab portion began where they filled the flats with compost and brought them inside to seed.

"Now we ain't fancy 'round here, Miss Zoe, we pretty well use what we have to make it work. We will put plastic wrap over these and place 'em in a south window of my cabin where the sun shines in most of the day. When the seedlin's come up, we'll remove the plastic and set 'em out in April."

~~~~~~~~~~~~~~~~

That afternoon, Abe took Zoe out for a tour of the calving barn and to check the cows. The nursery, in the west lean-to of the barn, was a long alley with four stalls barely big enough for a mama and a baby. The stall on the end was the biggest of the four with two panels and a head-catch to hold the cow's head. The side panels would control her body side to side. Zoe thought it looked inhumane, but knew Abe cared about the critters in his care. He was always careful to feed them before he fed himself, something Zoe respected about him.

"This is where the magic happens," he said of the birthing room. "We bring 'em here if they havin' trouble. After the babe is safe on the ground, standin' up and suckin', we put them in a stall overnight or until we think they ready to go. Then we'll turn 'em back in with the other pairs."

"Pairs of what?"

"Pairs are what we call a mama and a babe. They get their own pasture for growin' in. So we have expectin' mothers here," he said, pointing north, "and pairs over here," he said, pointing west. "Bossy gets a pasture to herself on da east there. We can control the traffic flow from these two gates and that way we try to cut down on the chaos of movin' cattle 'round. I'm too old for chaos, Miss Zoe."

Zoe surveyed the layout. Milk cow paddock, heifers and cows and then pair pasture all converge on the barn with all gates easily accessible.

"Now let's go check on the girls."

Zoe smiled and followed Abe to the old farm truck.

He talked as he drove. Zoe opened the gates for him like a seasoned veteran. "We have 177 cows to calve out this year. I culled twenty-three last year and saved back eighteen head o' heifers. A heifer's a female who's never calved before. We down in numbers this year. I suppose there's a reason for that. We've been in a drought for over eighteen months now. Hay's hard to come by. We usually have enough to get us through the winter with extra to sell, but I started hangin' on to it when the rains didn't come. God always takes care of us. We should have just enough hay if we get some rain this spring and early summer.

54

"What we lookin' for is if a critter is off by themselves. If she's away from others: Is her bag full? Is she lyin' down? Does she have anything coming out her hind end? These are all signs she's ready to calve.

"Do you see anything Miss. Zoe?" Abe drove around.

"What about that one?" she asked.

"She isn't thinkin' about a baby today. She's thinkin' about sittin' on that hay and chewin' her cud. That's 'bout all she's gonna accomplish today."

He drove north. In the distance lay a cow on her side. "Here we go. I should have known she would be the first to go. May as well start this calving season with somethin' interestin'." He stopped the truck on top of the hill that looked west into a valley. "Miss Zoe, meet Crazy."

"She a crazy good mama and just plain crazy. She runs me back to the pickup ever' year when I try to tag her baby. I mean fast too." Abe laughed and shook his head. "She never has trouble calvin', so we be spectators on this one."

The cow had turned around a few times this way, then that, showing off a full bag and udders. She finally laid down on her side lifting her head a few times toward her tail as if to check the progress. Abe reached under his seat and produced a well-worn pair of binoculars and handed them to Zoe.

"Here's y'er ticket for a front row seat."

Biology wasn't Zoe's thing, but she realized any being having a baby was a miracle. They watched for a few minutes and soon two feet appeared out of her opening.

"You know what the monkey said when he got his tail caught in the fan?"

Zoe could see the legs attached to the feet and what looked like a pink nose protruded. "No. What?"

"It won't be long now, Miss. Zoe," he chuckled, rubbing his chin. "Yes, sir."

The cow pushed and the head came out. Then a rest and push on the contractions. "How do they know?"

"Know what?"

"What to do and when."

"They just know. Sometimes I think nature and animals are more in tune to their Creator than we are."

They sat in silence for a while watching as the calf came into the world.

"Here we go, Miss. Zoe. Leave it to Crazy to give us a good show."

The cow struggled to get up. She rested somewhat on her belly as if she was mustering up the courage or the energy to stand. The baby came to rest in an awkward looking position.

"Abe, what is she doing? She will hurt her baby."

"It's fine Miss. Zoe."

The cow struggled to her feet. The calf hung upside down like a kid on a monkey bar.

"I think you're right. She is crazy."

"It's called hip lock, Miss Zoe, where the baby's hips get hung up in the birth canal."

"Should we help her?"

Before Abe could answer, the cow spun and the calf's hips came loose. The calf rolled across the frozen ground and stopped in an awkward pile. It lifted his weak head, shaking it and flinging goo. This horrified Zoe.

Abe laughed and slapped his knee. "Yes, sir. That is the best part when they sling they sweet little head as if to clear the cobwebs of birth and open them ears up to a new world. Oh, Miss Zoe, how can we doubt a great Creator at a moment like this? That's grand design."

"What should we do?"

"Nothing. Crazy will lick him off, give him a nudge for his first walkin' lesson, then some dinner. We not needed here. Today, we just spectators on the wonders of creation."

Zoe continued to watch as Crazy did what Abe predicted. Junior got his front feet under him, then his back and fell face first in a pile. Zoe gasped. Abe laughed. Junior did better the second time even taking a few steps. Crazy made her udders accessible and much to the humans' delight, Junior suckled.

Zoe cried.

"See, stork duties ain't so bad, are they Miss Zoe?"

"I guess not," she said, with a smile.

Abe drove on. "After they've had time to bond and Crazy has had time to eat the afterbirth, we will go back and tag the little rascal. I'll see if I still have what it takes, not to get killed by that maniac he calls Mama."

"Ugh." Zoe groaned and felt nauseous. "I thought cattle were herbivores. Why would they eat the afterbirth?"

"Grand design. Their teeth and stomach may be built for processin' grasses, but her instincts are designed for survival. Somethin' Crazy is especially good at. They consume the afterbirth to get rid of the smell and keep predators at bay."

"Predators?"

"Coyotes, wolves, bear, mountain lion whatever you have in the area that would find a calf an easy meal. That's why I keep a rifle with me, Miss Zoe. It's my responsibility to protect my herd. Some people call it killin'. I call it protectin' and preservin'. It's just part of the food chain."

They drove on to the end of the pasture. Seeing no more action they turned back to Crazy. The babe had bedded down and was soaking up the afternoon sun. Crazy was still sniffing around where the afterbirth had been.

"Now if you would take one of those small ear tags and write the number eight on it, so it matches Mama's I'd appreciate it. I'll sneak out of the truck while Crazy is distracted and pierce its ear. The trick here is to keep the baby between you and its mama. It may come close and sniff, but will usually leave you alone. Unless her name is Crazy. You best stay in the truck on this one."

"I'll be here when you get back," Zoe promised.

Abe smiled and eased out of the pickup careful not to make direct eye contact with Crazy. Zoe suspected he meant to leave the door open, but due to the incline it slammed shut. Crazy seemed mostly preoccupied with her motherly duties. Abe got down and quickly tagged the baby's ear. The calf didn't bawl, but hummed a bit and didn't move.

All at once, Crazy was on the move and was on top of the babe faster than Zoe could have imagined. When Crazy made her move, Abe tucked and rolled into a sprinting position. No one had ever left the blocks faster, especially in the senior division. He put one foot on top of the rear tire and vaulted himself into the back of the truck just as Crazy hit the side of the flat bed where Abe had been just a second ago.

Abe hit the top of the cab, barking orders at Zoe to drive. Zoe slid over to the driver's seat and panicked, forgetting the skills she had learned driving a stick shift. She looked at Abe wild-eyed and shrugged her shoulders. Crazy was making laps around the truck with her head high, her eyes wider than Zoe's.

"For cryin' in a bucket, Miss Zoe, make a hole!"

Abe waited until Crazy was on the opposite side of the pickup and jumped down by the driver's side and got in just in time for Crazy to bend the side mirror. She hurried back to her baby for a sniff. She stood over the babe daring anyone to try her waning patience.

Abe looked at Zoe for the first time and burst into laughter. She was shaking from the commotion. "Guess we showed her how the cow ate the cabbage," Abe snorted.

"Or she showed us how the cow ate the pick-up," Zoe muttered. "Is she always like that?"

"Ever' year. Ever' stinkin' year. But I respect her. She a good mama. Crazy, but good. She raises good calves."

Abe looked at Zoe and nudged her arm. "You up for this, Miss Zoe?"

"I think so. I mean that was thrilling and terrifying at the same time … "

"They ain't all like that. She's the only one. Unless one of the heifers came from her, we shouldn't have any more excitement like that." Abe drove toward the barn.

Zoe felt alive. She longed for adventure. Abe was brave and protective. He made her feel safe, but she longed for a soul mate.

"The year Crazy was a heifer, Miss Ev'lyn was checkin' cattle with me. And blame her soul if she didn't lock the doors so I couldn't get in. Crazy ran me this way and that and finally up a tree. Miss Ev'lyn had to pull up underneath to pick me up. I was so mad. But that didn't seem to bother her. She just giggled and snorted and snorted and giggled. I suppose I'll forgive her someday, but not today. No, sir." He laughed in spite of himself.

He pulled the pickup to a stop. "I think we got another customer, Miss Zoe. That's one of the heifers. And things don't appear to be goin' very well."

"How can you tell?"

"See that foot sticking out? It's a back foot, not a front one. That calf is breech. We'll have to pull it. You get out and just walk behind her guidin' her into the barn."

"But."

"But what? You can't drive … "

Zoe didn't have time to argue. She bailed out and walked behind the heifer guiding her into the barn. Abe followed. Abe explained that they needed to get the heifer's head in the head catch by opening the panels wide. The head catch shut automatically when there was pressure applied to it. The heifer let out a tired bawl with a contraction.

Abe had already stripped down to his tee shirt and insulated bib overalls. "Well, Miss Zoe, the only way to learn is by doin'. I hope those ain't y'er good clothes. Take everythin' off on top that you can."

"But it's cold."

"Miss Zoe, this calf may already be dead. If that's the case, we could lose the mama too."

Zoe undressed down to her t-shirt. She panicked, but wanted so to save the baby, so she listened without feeling to what Abe was saying.

"Okay, the first thing we need to do is get that other foot up here. It's okay. She won't kick. She knows we tryin' to help. We ain't going to turn the calf, 'cause time is of the essence. So take that bottle of lube and rub it up and down y'er right arm. Insert y'er arm into the hole where that leg is sticking out and follow the birth canal down to the uterus."

Zoe inserted her hand and stopped. "I don't think I can fit."

"There's fixin' to be a hundred-pound calf come out of that hole, Miss Zoe. I think y'er skinny ol' arm will fit. Wait a second now. We'll have to wait until the contraction is over. Y'er doin' fine. We just got to keep movin' forward. She's about done. Are you ready?"

The cow's mournful beller shook Zoe to the core. She let out a breath and nodded. Her hand shook as she touched the opening for the first time pushing past the existing foot. "Abe, the foot."

"It's fine, Miss Zoe. It won't go far if it goes in.

"You should feel the elbow to that other foot. When you feel the elbow, give it a push, kinda toward the cow's head or body. That should bring the other foot up, so you can get a hold of it."

"Do you feel the elbow?"

"I—I don't know what I feel. I feel the butt. Oh—there I think I feel it now."

"Give it a push towards the head and see what happens."

Zoe's head was uncomfortably close to the hind end of the heifer. She tried to stay focused.

"Okay, I think I got the foot. I hope it's the right one."

"Okay, pull the foot to the openin' as gently as you can. When you get it to the openin' go ahead and pull it out. We need both feet together to attach the puller."

Zoe pulled the two feet out together only to have them pulled back into the heifer's body.

"Ugh. What just happened? I was so close."

"We up against another contraction. You won't be able to over-power that, just wait for a second. You doin' just fine, nurse, now I need you to listen to me. When we get those legs back out here and get the puller attached we will pull as slowly and as gently as we can. With breech births there are no guarantees. There are all sorts of bad things that can go wrong here. But we'll keep moving forward. After the hips and ribcage are out we will hurry the process and get that calf on the ground. Here we go."

It took two hands for Zoe to get both feet out so Abe could attach the puller. He ratcheted the come-along, pulling the baby out little by little. The hips slowed the process and soon the rest of the calf came out and Zoe helped it to the ground.

The calf looked dead. Abe took the pulling contraption off and felt behind the calf's front leg. "You can feel for the heartbeat, here. I think we have one, but it's not breathin'."

60

Abe stretched the calf out on his side, wiped the mucous from the calf's nose. Using a suction tube, he sucked the remaining mucous out of each nostril. He held its mouth shut while holding his fingers over the right nostril. Cupping his other hand around the other nostril he breathed into the calf. Again and again. Finally, the calf breathed on its own.

Zoe started to cry.

"We not out of the woods yet, Miss Zoe. I need you to get a couple towels outta the pile over there and commence to scrubbin' this calf. And I mean scrubbin'. That will be simulatin' to her body."

Zoe interrupted, "It's a girl?" Tears rolled down her checks.

"Yes, Miss Zoe, it's a heifer. Now get her cleaned up. Then we'll try to get her up and suckin'. She's weak. This might not go the way we want it to, but we'll do everythin' we can."

Zoe nodded and scrubbed, marveling at what had just happened. The cow delivered the placenta which lay in the straw. Blood, slime and feces covered Zoe, yet all she could focus on was the survival of the calf.

Abe busied himself milking the cow into a big white bottle. "The first milk, isn't milk at all. It's colostrum full of all sorts of antibodies and nutrition. I'll get as much as she'll let me then we'll see if we can get Little Bit to take a shot or two."

The calf was still breathing but wouldn't lift his head. She was limp as Zoe finished wiping her down.

Abe came over with the bottle to which he added a nipple. "Alright, Little Bit, here we go." He lifted the calf's head and had Zoe hold it up while he inserted the bottle into her mouth and rubbed the underside of the neck to stimulate swallowing. The calf didn't suckle. It was totally uninterested, eyes closed.

"She's very weak, Miss Zoe. We'll tube her, force some of this goodness in her and see what happens." He walked to a cabinet hanging on the wall and retrieved a bucket with a tube coming out the bottom. He put the tube down the calf's throat and said, "Okay, take the lid off the bottle and pour a little in the bucket while holding the bucket over its head. Just a little, now, we gotta see if we are in the esophagus or lungs."

The milk disappeared and the calf didn't respond. "That's a good sign, Zoe, pour the rest in there."

Abe removed the tube and the calf rested its head on the ground.

"What's next?"

"We pray. We've done all we can do. I don't know if she has the will to live. We'll see."

Zoe pulled the baby onto her lap with its head on her arm. "But we can't give up. I can't lose another one. Abe, you've got to do something." Zoe rocked back and forth weeping for the calf and the child she never got to hold.

"Oh, child," Abe settled in behind Zoe and wrapped a long arm around her shoulder. He held her a while before saying, "I didn't know. How you lose a child?"

"Through an abortion, I didn't want, to save a man I couldn't save. Now I can't have babies." The sobs grew louder. "It was a girl too," she whispered. "I just know it." She continued to weep.

"I'm sorry, Miss Zoe. I'm real, sorry."

"It's my fault. I'm the one that agreed to it."

"We all make mistakes. Do things in life we can't get back. If we ever gonna heal, we gotta forgive ourselves, forgive others and move on."

Zoe sobbed.

"There's only one way, Miss Zoe, through God, and the healin' power of Jesus. He came to set the captives free. Y'er being held captive by y'er past. As long as you there, you ain't here. And if you ain't here, you a dead soul walkin' around in a live body. That's not livin' the free life He has for you."

They sat for a long time in silence. Zoe wanted to move on, but didn't know if what Abe said would work.

"What would you have named her?" he asked.

"Grace," she said.

"Grace," he repeated. "Why Grace?"

"I've always liked the name."

Abe smiled.

"I don't think that cow will claim her baby," he said, studying the cow.

"How do you know?"

"I've been at this for a while, Miss Zoe. She not humming to her baby, not concerned about her what-so-ever. She doesn't want her."

"How can she not want her?"

"I can't pretend to know such things, Miss Zoe. If Little Bit survives, you'll have to raise her."

"How?"

"You can take part of the milk from Ol' Boss and give it to Little Bit outta that bottle. Add that to the list of things you do around here. Gardener, stork, midwife and wet nurse."

The thought thrilled Zoe.

Abe got up and picked up Zoe's coat and draped it around her shoulders. "I've gotta go milk. There's nothin' else we can do for that calf. It's not up to us now."

"I'm not ready to leave her."

"That's fine. I'll come check on you when I'm done milkin'." Abe turned to go.

The barn was quiet. Zoe watched the calf breathe breaths so soft they couldn't be felt. Her mama bedded down in another stall and chewed her cud while Zoe sat tending to her baby.

Zoe didn't believe in prayer. At this point, though, she was willing to try anything. She had tried everything but prayer. Nothing filled the void in her soul. It had been so long since she could let out a breath without wondering if she could draw another one. If prayer didn't work, she didn't have a desire to go on. The tears fell hot on the calf's back.

God, I don't want this baby to die. I didn't want my last baby to die either. But she did, and I killed her. I can't go on like this. I can't. The guilt is too much. I want that crown of beauty instead of ashes I read about. Help me please. Help me! Zoe prayed.

The calf lifted its head. Zoe cried and stroked its bottom lip. The calf sucked on her index and middle finger. Zoe continued to rock the calf.

Abe watched from the darkness outside. He hadn't missed this change. Smiling, he glanced up to heaven and said, "Where demons dance and angels sing. Yes, sir. Amen." Abe walked out of the shadows to put some warm life-giving milk into a cold bottle.

5

The Thaw

The path to paradise begins in hell.
Dante Alighieri

March

It takes faith to get to March. When it comes it brings hope to the despair of winter. It's like a cocoon breaking forth to let in the light—a rebirth—an awakening. Although still cool, the weather was different. They had turned the invisible corner and the residents of Halfway Homestead could tell March was a new beginning.

After many false starts, Zoe had learned to drive the pickup. Her new skill took pressure off Abe during calving. They checked the cows every four hours around the clock. Abe took the night shift, claiming he didn't sleep much anymore anyway. Zoe suspected he took night shift because if she worked it, she would have been waking him up to verify a suspicion or for delivery help.

Zoe milked morning and evening to ease Abe's burdens. She enjoyed feeding Little Bit and Dinky the orphan calves. Despite the shared work, their bodies and minds were tired and ready for a change of scenery that wouldn't come until calving was done.

Zoe came to the house with the milk and two dirty bottles around ten. She was happy to see Kit cooking a big brunch.

Rayden and Jael had piled out of bed at three and stripped the back of the van of its seats. Starting in the most affluent part of town, they went curb shopping and dumpster diving for treasures they could recreate. They were giddy about the mother lode they had picked up in the three trips they had made. The whole mismatched family, including Evelyn went out to see the spoils before diving headlong into breakfast.

Their bounty from the predawn escapade littered the driveway: dining chairs, a winged back chair in need of attention, two drop leaf tables, an old mission style recliner, a double bed frame, three mismatched side tables, boxes of clothing, a broken book shelf, a clock, old rusty golf clubs, a sofa from the 1950s and boxes of miscellaneous items that looked like leftovers from an auction.

"Can you believe it?" Jael said. "All of this for free."

"They's a reason for that," Abe said, hugging J from the side. "Where are you goin' to put all this stuff?"

She shrugged him off and stood by Rayden with her arm around her shoulders to present their best case. "Well, we would like to call a family meeting because we have an idea."

Rayden's hair was in a pony tail through a baseball cap, which she made look elegant. Her face was beaming with excitement. "Come, we can talk over breakfast."

Zoe had never seen her so excited and wondered if spring and the Homestead had opened a new world for her too.

They all went inside except Evelyn, who was pilfering through the boxes of auction stuff occasionally stuffing something in her waistband. Jael laughed watching from a window. "Miss Evelyn has to stuff her treasures in her waistband, because she doesn't wear a bra."

Abe looked at her out of the top of his eyes, a quiet reprimand. It didn't faze Jael. "She's liberated!"

They all laughed despite the look and sat down at the table pouring coffee if they wanted it, while they waited for Evelyn. The giggles didn't stop after Evelyn sat down. The atmosphere was fun and festive. Abe cleared his throat and the girls settled and bowed their heads.

"Father God, help me. (giggles) Sometime the estrogen is too much to bear. Lord, we are thankful for Y'er provision, some more than others. (more giggles) I pray for guidance on this family meetin' that's been called. In y'er Son's name. Amen." He breathed deeply taking in the feast with all of his senses.

Kit had made buttermilk biscuits, sausage patties, gravy, scrambled eggs, a cheesy hashbrown casserole and cinnabonbons. Cinnabonbons were a cinnamon roll made from biscuit dough topped with a honey butter or cream and powdered sugar glaze. They dug in.

"I call this meeting to order," Jael said. "Rayden and I have a proposal for your consideration. Since we have had such good luck selling the goods that have been reworked, we would like to buy a computer and get internet here on the ranch, so we can sell our stuff on Craigslist, EBay, Etsy and with classified ads locally."

This caused the eating to stop. The Homestead didn't have TV, cable or a computer much less internet. It had been Evelyn, Abe and the board's long-standing rule that the focus should be on healing, redirecting and growing in relationship with Christ. In fact, those were the words of the mission statement.

Jael, undaunted plowed ahead. "That would give us a bigger market for some of Kit's canned goods, Abe's restored fiddles and some of Evelyn's pottery."

Abe said, "And the money would come from where?"

Jael and Rayden looked at each other, eyes beaming. "Us," Jael said. "We have been saving the money from the projects we've sold since we got here. We have enough for a computer and a few months of internet.

"That is," Rayden interrupted, "if we can't find a donated computer. I'm sure we can."

"What do you think, Miss Evelyn?" Abe asked.

Evelyn shrugged and continued rooting through the plate of food in front of her.

"Miss Evelyn, we would even like to market your pottery. We already have a name for your business. Chamber's Pots." Jael squealed.

The girls laughed. Evelyn's last name was Chambers. It even made Evelyn stop eating for a second, look off into space, smile and continue eating. Even Abe had to laugh at that.

"If that don't beat all. You girls. What am I gonna do with you?" Abe's shoulders were high and his face, low near his plate.

"Love us," Jael said, laying her head on his forearm.

Abe let out a long breath.

"Was that a deep sigh? Or a cleansing breath?" Rayden asked looking back at Abe through the top of her eyes.

Abe returned the stare, putting his forehead on hers, "Deep sigh. You know you'll have to present this to the board at the next board meetin'."

The girls celebrated with a toast of cinnabonbons, "All bon bons to the middle," Jael announced, holding a cinnabonbon like a shot glass. "To liberation!"

"To liberation." The girls followed suit—even Evelyn, everyone but Abe "clanked" bon bons.

"You still haven't told me where you planin' on puttin' all that stuff," Abe said seriously.

Rayden explained they would use the double granary to store the new loot, bringing it into the house to work on a piece at a time. There was one large room upstairs reserved for donations of clothing and furniture. The latest haul would never fit. In fact, the double granary would soon burst at the seams if the girls didn't come up with a better plan.

"That is phase two of our plan," Jael said, with a wink. "We will let you know that part at the board meeting."

"That's fine, then. Miss Zoe and I will be dividin' the perennials today. We don't need any of the divisions. Do you entrepreneurs want to sell them too? I've got plenty of plastic pots and compost if you do."

"Yes!" Jael said. "We'll take them, right after we clear the driveway. You don't mind if we borrow Zoe, do ya?"

"First you take my peace, then you take my help." Abe pretended to huff.

~~~~~~~~~~~~~~~~

All four girls worked on clearing the driveway. They agreed Kit and Rayden would take the smaller stuff inside to be sorted and organized. Zoe and Jael would haul the larger items to the double granary.

Jael and Zoe made quick work of the larger pieces. Jael said there was one more load they could go get if Zoe was up to it. Zoe agreed and soon they were on their way.

Jael's demeanor seemed different from the other girls on the Homestead. The others girls sought a new life. Jael seemed to search for something different.

"How did you get here?" Zoe asked breaking the silence.

"Evelyn brought me." Jael shrugged.

"From where?" Zoe probed.

"Israel. She was on one of her trips. I guess I was a souvenir." Jael stared down the highway.

"I've never heard of a person being a souvenir," Zoe pondered aloud.

Jael's eyes showed pain. "I've never heard of them not being." Her hard exterior softened, exposing her soul for a moment.

The hum of the tires added to the trance-like way Jael continued.

"I was orphaned when I was thirteen, a result of the war in the Gaza Strip. They said I was lucky I even made it into an orphanage. Most kids don't. At eighteen I was conscripted in the IDF—Israel Defense Force, where I served for two years."

"What did you do for them?"

"I was a driver," she said.

"What did you do when you got out?"

"Lived on the streets for a while. Then in another home for women."

"Is that how you met Evelyn?"

"No," She said pointedly. "It wasn't the kind of house you are thinking of. Women weren't valued there. More like a souvenir, like I said. Or a tool—you know, expendable."

The thought of women being used up and tossed aside sickened Zoe. "I'm sorry," she said finally.

Jael shrugged. "It is what, it is, I guess."

"It sounds like you've been through hell."

Jael glared at Zoe like she was dense. It frustrated her when people didn't get it. "It's only hell if you know something different—otherwise, it's just life."

They stopped to load the van. On the way home Zoe probed deeper.

"So how did you meet Evelyn?"

"It was a fluke, I suppose," she said, with no further explanation.

"Why did you come to the States with her?"

"She offered me something no one else had."

"What's that?

"Freedom."

Zoe thought about her statement.

"Was it worth it?"

"Freedom cost me everything familiar. But I get to make my own choices now," Jael said.

"Do you think you can ever have too much freedom? I mean, I became a slave to my choices."

Jael paused before answering.

"How free is too free?" She scoffed. "That's kind of like asking 'how hot is hell?'.

"Hell's hot and free is free," she said matter-of-factly. "If you can have too much freedom, I haven't experienced it yet."

They drove on.

"I bet you love it here."

Jael's eyes were serious. "Love?" She spat the words as if they were a bad taste.

"Now there's one thing I am afraid of." Jael's voice was sad.

Zoe was confused about Jael's vague statements. Yet they gave her a better understanding of the young woman. Maybe being a free pilgrim in a foreign land has its limitations. Maybe a covering can imprison as much as it protects.

Zoe thought about love and hell. Were they a place you fell into and out of—or a condition? She wasn't sure.

Junk has a funny way of bringing people together.

~~~~~~~~~~~~~~~

Zoe and Abe got potato forks and wheelbarrows out of the garden shed to divide the perennials.

"This shouldn't take too long, Miss Zoe. We got recruits to help," Abe said, as they walked toward the house.

"Perennials are plants that come back year after year. Every few years you have to divide them to prolong their life and get your perennial beds back into shape.

"It's real easy," Abe said, sticking the potato fork into the dirt beside a mum. "Just stick your fork in, dig up a clump and divide with your hands. If you can't work the roots loose with your hands, stick the two forks into the clump together and pull 'em apart with the forks. Perennials are forgivin'. Got it?"

"Yes. I think I used to do this with my grandma in her strawberry patch. Are strawberries perennials?" Zoe said, digging.

"They are. Some people treat 'em like an annual for better crops or to control disease."

"My grandma would divide them and put them in an X pattern. It took forever."

"I did it that way for years. Then that wood chip man said to throw wood chips over 'em and God will do the dividin'. The strong plants come through and the weak ones get turned to compost. The best part is, my work is done in a few minutes. Yes, sir.

"How you doing, Miss Zoe?" Abe asked the question like a concerned father. "If I didn't know better, I'd say you kinda like stork duty."

Zoe smiled. Her eyes filled with tears. "That first night in the barn, when Little Bit was born, changed my life. I made peace with my Maker."

"Thought you didn't have one," Abe teased, bending backwards to stretch his back.

"I know now, that I do."

"You say you made peace with y'er Maker, or got peace from y'er Maker?"

"Both."

"Yes, sir." Abe smiled to himself.

71

They dug on in silence.

"That was my lowest night."

"Lowest night here?" asked Abe.

"Yeah, here. Up to that point I had seen little hope here."

"You know what I call that point?"

"Nope."

"Where demons dance and angels sing," Abe said, starting into the distance.

"Why? Seems like a paradox."

"It is. It's the point you let go of the darkest part of y'erself and you start relyin' on the light of God. A point of great despair and of great hope. A beautiful place to be."

"It's a good thing it's spring, Miss Zoe." Abe picked up the full wheelbarrow.

"Why is that?" she asked.

"'Cause the Son's fixin' to burst forth on you and you gonna grow like a bad weed."

They walked toward the garden shed.

Shep came running around the chicken house with a rooster in his mouth which was flogging his face and screaming. Behind him was Evelyn, giving chase in five-buckle overboots, red polyester britches, a flannel shirt (with all the flannel worn off and thread bare where her liberated nipples had lived for years). Her gray hair flew as she swung an old husk broom and hollered obscenities in Bohemian.

"Devil Darebak ... "

Shep slowed and dodged when the girls came out of the garden shed to watch the commotion. The detour gave Miss Evelyn just the chance she needed to connect full force to Shep's side.

Thowonk.

Shep dropped the injured bird and kept running. Evelyn threw the broom at him connecting again. Without taking her eyes off the dog she put one foot on the rooster's neck and pulled the legs up quickly, removing its head.

Shaking a knobby finger at Shep, she walked to the clothesline. The dog scooted a safe distance away from the old woman to a sunny part of the yard. She hung the poor bird upside down, pinning it with clothes pins and walked to the house. She muttered something about the devil, her dog and chicken and noodles.

It was quiet for a few seconds after the door slammed. Jael said, "Liberation."

The girls all howled.

Liberation, indeed.

"What should we do with that?" Kit asked, looking at Abe, but pointing at the bird.

"Not one blamed thing. But you might hold off on whatever you were gonna have for supper tonight. Miss Ev'lyn gonna school you on how to make some of the best chicken and noodles of y'er life."

Soon Evelyn was back, dressed in a black trash bag. Shep stopped licking the dripping blood from the grass and quietly slunk under the porch to watch from safety. She retrieved the bird from the line and went behind Abe's house to pluck and disembowel the bird.

She returned about the time the girls were finishing potting the plants. Shep was happily rolling in the delicious scent of his fresh kill when she disappeared inside.

Abe nudged Zoe on the arm, "You best not miss this. I'll check the cows. It will be highly entertainin' if nothin' else." He winked and nodded again.

The girls hurried to put everything away and get washed up for an afternoon in the kitchen with Evelyn.

Evelyn was busy rinsing the bird in the sink and singing to the sounds of Frank Sinatra coming from an ancient record player that must have come from her room. The girls were generally good about pitching in and helping. Today they gave Evelyn plenty of room to do her own strange thing. After rinsing the bird, she took it to the gas stove to singe the hairs from the birds back and bum. The smell of burnt feathers permeated the kitchen.

Satisfied with the results, she dropped the whole bird into a large pressure cooker without pomp or circumstance. She picked up a metal pitcher and danced her way to the sink to fill it with water to pour over the bird. She stopped in mid-twirl, bowed to the gawking girls and gave them their orders.

"Go down to the cellar for some garlics, onions, carrots, celery and potatoes, yah." The dance continued.

All four girls went to the cave. Kit was the only one who had ever been down there, so she gave the girls a quick tour. She had brought two enamel bowls to carry the produce back to the kitchen and gave one to Rayden and one to Zoe.

"We over-winter the carrots in these bins filled with sawdust. Someone root around until they find four. The potatoes are in those burlap sacks on the far side there," she said, nodding with her head. "We will need to get an onion and garlic bulb from overhead." She pointed at the onions and garlic braids hanging from the ceiling. "The celery is in the blue bins buried in sand. We will need one of those."

Rayden was amazed by the amount of fresh food stored in the cave, not to mention the canned goods. "How can you keep food like this?"

"Well, before refrigerators and grocery stores, this is how people would store their food for the winter," Kit said.

"Yes, but we have refrigerators and grocery stores now," Rayden said, somewhat puzzled.

Kit laughed, "I know Abe and Evelyn's ways are ancient. They don't trust their survival or the survival of others to the food grid. Their motto is waste not, want not. If we can produce it ourselves, it's silly in their eyes to spend money to buy it. Our food bill is low for the amount of people we feed. Our food is simple. We eat close to the ground, but the flavor is top notch."

Back in the kitchen, Evelyn was waiting by the sink sipping wine out of a hairspray lid and staring out the window. She looked over the vegetables and nodded her approval. "You scrub, yah and drop into the pot," she said, to Jael. "Rayten (she forever mispronounced her name) you and Zoe peel the potatoes. Kit, your rolls."

The girls nodded and got right to work on their assigned duties as Evelyn danced over to the skipping record player to turn the record over.

Evelyn returned to set the lid on the pressure cooker after the carrots, celery, onion and garlic were added.

Rayden started asking questions again. "So, how does it work? The cellar, I mean. Why doesn't that stuff rot?"

"I have no idea," Kit said.

Everyone looked at Zoe. "Don't look at me. I just got here."

Evelyn found a deck of cards and her place at the table to relax while they waited on the chicken. "Cool and moist," she said, as she dealt herself a solitaire game. "Ninety to ninety-five percent humidity. Cure your onions and garlics, don't wash the others. Store what you use. Use what you store. This is the best way, yah. Got provides goot food."

When Evelyn tired of the game, she jumped up and took three eggs from the refrigerator. She dropped a palm full of salt directly into the flour bin and cracked the eggs on top of the salt and beat the eggs in the bin. The girls watched in silence. Frank sang on. Milk was added to the mixture in the flour bin. Soon a ball of yellow dough formed.

Zoe guessed if the health department had been there, they wouldn't have approved of the old woman's methods. She also guessed Evelyn didn't care what the health department thought of her old ways. This made her smile.

 Evelyn picked up the ball, along with a handful of flour to sprinkle on the countertop. She hummed while she rolled the dough out with a well-aged rolling pin. "The dough must be stiff, yah. That's what makes it goot." She continued humming.

Soon the dough was as thin as it could be. She took another handful of flour to coat it well and loosely rolled the dough. Slipping a cutting board under the dough roll, she doubled it into a U shape and cut into strips. She picked up the pieces and dropped them repeatedly, like a child playing with the noodles.

She turned and looked the girls each in the eye. "Girls, make noodles the way you live life, with feeling. Salt for flavor, some eggs to bind (the more people you have around, the more you need to bind), add milk and flour, just enough. Like the Lort, just enough. Pressed together, pressure to stretch fuller than you thought possible, yah. Then more flour, just enough to keep you from going back to the way you were before you were stretched. Cut by the Maker into something new and covert with more blessing. Just enough. And dropped into the heat, holding form, making someting new, someting goot. Someting worthy, yah."

Evelyn wiped her gray hair from her eyes leaving a dusting of flour on her cheek and her mole. She smiled her strange smile while Sinatra belted out, "I did it my way." It was a time of paradox. The strange old woman looked beautiful, full of life and wisdom. Full of love and transparency, yet mysterious.

She patted Zoe's arm leaving a dusting of flour, knocked foreheads with Kit, smiled at Jael and stopped to tuck Rayden's hair behind her ear on one side, cupping her wrinkled hand around her sweet face. Rayden smiled, her eyes filled with tears and she looked down at the floor. "Goot girls," she said, patting her face.

"Time to take the weight off the pressure canner to release the steam," Evelyn said, farting as she walked to the stove. The girls giggled. Evelyn had a way of making the heaviest days a little lighter.

Evelyn backed away from the stove, pointing and nodding at the pot. Kit, always on task, picked up the pot and took it to the sink where she had readied a colander in an enamel Dutch oven and poured out the contents of the cooker through a sieve and into a holding bowl. "When the chicken cools, we will debone it, yah. Now we cook the noodles. Now is a goot time to boil the potatoes and bake dah rolls."

Zoe sank into bed that night with her belly full of the best chicken and noodles she had ever tasted. Feeling loved by a grandmother, safe in a father's home with a complete family of assorted sisters.

The tundra of her soul was beginning to thaw. "Three months," she said, breathing out a long breath.

"It takes faith to make it to March," she whispered, quoting Abe.

She looked over at her Bible still open to Isaiah. If the goal of this confinement was freedom, she was on her way. A single happy tear fell to her pillow and she patted her Bible.

"Liberation," she whispered to herself.

6

Burying the Dead

When you sow, you don't plant the body that will be, but just a seed.
1 Corinthians 15:37

April

April always brings dark days and rain, but gives way to buds, blooms and plenty of sunshine. The Homestead was being washed clean of the coldness of winter and made new by the change that only a season of growth can bring. Seasons in life and seasons in nature aren't forever. For the resident guests of the Halfway Homestead this was good news. Calving was nearly over. That season coming to an end was reason enough to celebrate.

Zoe had overslept and rushed into the kitchen to get the milk bucket only to find Abe just coming in the back door with it full. Zoe hurried to get it from his hand so he could remove his wet boots.

"Well good mornin', Glory. You done hibernatin'?" he said with a low chuckle.

"I'm sorry, Abe. I guess I'm just catching up on the sleep calving took from me." She poured them both a cup of coffee setting his on the table beside the coffee cake Kit had left for them before she went to the food bank to teach menu planning classes. "I'm surprised you're not hibernating too." She smiled and looked at him quizzingly.

"Those blamed girls and their schemes," he huffed, as he reached for a piece of cake.

"Who?" Zoe settled in her chair.

"Oh, the dark-headed hoodlums we call Rayden and Jael."
He shook his head and continued. "They put on quite a show
at the board meetin' last night."

"Oh yeah. How did that go?" She bit into a piece of cake.

"They missed their callin'. They should 'a been lawy'ers,
the bof' of 'em. Or at least had their names changed to
Bushwhacked and Sabotage. They gonna be entrepreneurs if
they keep messin' around." He shook his head.

"I don't know whether to praise 'em or pity 'em, Miss
Zoe. They had flow charts addressin' their finances, short-
term and long-term goals and their business plan.
Unbeknownst to me they'd gone to P-Dub and begged him
for the church's old lap tops. AND ... AND the use of his
'store front' as they called it. In actuality, it's a church. And
the devil said yes." Abe took a long drink of coffee.

"Who's P-Dub?" Zoe asked.

"Oh, I'm sorry, Miss Zoe. Pastor Wyatt, I call 'm P-Dub,"
he said, softening a little when he spoke of his pastor. "I used
t' call 'em friend, but now I don't know." He chuckled while
staring at the wall.

"He an interestin' feller, P-Dub—prolly one of my best
friends if I had t' pick one." His voice trailed off before
picking up again where he left off.

"Course they promised him they would do some paintin',
curtain sewin', website buildin' and Facebook help in trade fo'
the use o' the buildin'. All these things they claim would bring
awareness to our church. Help the down 'n out by givin'
them a purpose in helpin' run the store and reclaim all these
treasures. Leavin' nothin' to chance, they produced before
and after pictures of things they have remade and sold. Glory
be. It was impressive." He bit into a second piece of cake,
then got up and filled their cups with more coffee.

"If that weren't enough, they went on and on about how
they could also have quilters into the shop (not church, mind
you—shop!) to use the scraps of material that can no longer
be used for clothes. Then of course, Miss Ev'lyn's pottery got
brought up again. Chamber's Pots as it's affectionately called
now, would have a corner in the shop—givin' Miss Ev'lyn a
place to teach and sell her goods.

"The board called it inventive, forward thinkin' and the like."

The sun broke through the clouds for the first time in days and filled the house with its warm glow. He paused and looked out the windows on the sun porch.

"So? Did they vote to let us have internet service here?" Zoe asked.

"They did, six to one."

"Let me guess. You're the one?"

"Yep. They agreed to time restrictions and some website blockin', however. Whatever that means ... "

They sat in silence.

"Miss Zoe, it has always been Miss Ev'lyn's and my vision for the Homestead to be a place to give girls a place o' belongin'—like a forever home. Teach 'em skills that have been lost in a society that doesn't value these girls, but by design needs them desperately. Teach 'em the beauty of being a nurturin' woman, the way God intended."

"What did Miss Evelyn have to say about this change?"

"'Freedom to the captives,' she said." He nudged Zoe's arm with the back of his hand. "She sees you girls as slaves that need to be set free. Savvy?" he said, with a questioning nod.

"Slaves?"

"Yes, slaves. Slaves to beauty, the latest fashions, cell phone, cars, home and what have ya. You mentioned bein' a slave to expectations I believe.

"Basically, Ev'lyn *is* liberated. Not in the sense ya'll make her out to be, but truly free. She lives, loves, creates, nourishes and basks in the goodness of bein' the woman she called to be."

"You mean God calls people to life as a hermit?" Zoe asked.

"Wait a minute now, Miss Zoe. Miss Ev'lyn ain't no hermit. Eccentric maybe, but no hermit. And no, I don't believe God calls anyone to be a hermit. Again, it ain't about rules or rituals but relationships. When you in a relationship, there will be community."

"Community as in church?"

79

"A church can be a community, but so can a prison." Abe looked off into the distance. "To commune with someone is to share with someone; or to relate to 'em on a spiritual level—or soul level. I can do that with God right here. My favorite place to do it is in my garden or horseback—in nature. That's where I feel closest to Him. I can see His character in nature. Today I can't see His face, only His works. Someday, when my faith be sight, I'll see bof. Yes, sir!"

"So, it's only about community with God?"

"Yes and no, Miss Zoe. What I'm talkin' 'bout is takin' that relationship and copyin' it into the others in y'er life through natural livin'; sharin' time, sharin' space, sharin' life. It's the hardest of relationships 'cause you dealin' with imperfect beings. Community, like love is messy, time consumin', heart breakin' and confusin' sometimes. It is also the only thing we can 'do' on earth that can go with us into eternity. In that light, nothin' else matters."

"So why does church matter?"

"Let me ask you this. Are you talkin' about the buildin' of church, the rituals of church or the imperfect bein's seekin' out relationship called the church?"

"We have to define it?"

"Of course, we should define everythin' with Truth, the person of Jesus. Not the relative truth that changes depending upon the perspective of the mortal person.

"What's church to you, Miss Zoe?"

"Ugh. A beautiful building with stained glass, that smells like Pond's night cream and baby powder, sounds like an organ, feels like the cold, hard pews, acts like courtesy smiles, forced giving, recited prayers, a hellfire-and-brimstone preacher and an unseen scorekeeper. As far as I'm concerned, the only things churches do well are potluck dinners and the much-too-sweet Kool-Aid and cookies during vacation Bible school."

"Hmmm," Abe rubbed his chin and studied Zoe.

"That's why I don't go. If there is a God and He loves us like you say He does, then why would He make that His house?"

80

Abe continued to study Zoe, leaving her question hanging. She shrugged and looked away. "What's church to you?"

"A buildin', or not, that may smell like a back alley, urine and vomit or my garden after it rains. It sounds like a heart breakin', a child's laughter or a fine fiddle on a good day. You may find eyes red with tears of joy and pain, or a pastor or a former prostitute who speaks the Truth with love. And I'm with you on the potluck dinners, variety as diverse as the people. Food's always better consumed together."

Zoe stared at Abe. "What are you trying to say? What you described is—is … "

"Life?" he asked.

"Ugly … " she shrugged and stared at her cup, "and beautiful."

"Yeah, that's life; life in a community without boundaries of space or time. Life in a relationship with the highest of highs and the lowest of lows; with the common goal of focusin' on a great God and becomin' more like Him."

"If there's a church like that, I've never seen it."

"Never?"

"Never." Zoe crossed her arms and stretched out her legs. "And I rather doubt it exists."

Abe got up and bent backwards, popping his back. He took their plates to the sink. "You know what today is Miss Zoe?"

"April fifteenth? Tax day?"

"Yes, but no. Today is the day we bury the dead."

Zoe was perplexed. "Who died?"

"Come on out to my cabin. I'll show you what I mean."

Zoe had wanted to see inside his cabin since she got there but never had the opportunity. She jumped up and slipped into muck boots and a light jacket.

Smoke rolled from the chimney of the tiny cabin. The warmth of the fire met them as he opened the well-worn tongue and groove door. The door reminded Zoe of a Hobbit door with the curved top. Inside, the cabin walls were lined with knotty pine that had yellowed with age. The main room housed a small kitchen with a few open shelves and a wood cooking stove with a rocking chair on one side and a baby's cradle next to it on the other. The cradle had a tiny cream, colored sweater draped over the side, as if waiting for the small owner to come fill it once again. There was a twin sized cot along one side with an ancient gypsy quilt with strips of mismatched fabric sewn together and overlaid with beautiful squares of every variety. Beside the bed was a small table with a lamp, an old Bible with spectacles on top, a hand-crank alarm clock and a black and white picture of the most beautiful black woman Zoe had ever seen. There was a small table with two chairs next to the south facing window. The table was covered with the plants they had started near the end of February. The place was as neat as a pin and smelled as unique as its owner, a mixture of faint cherry pipe tobacco, fresh wood shavings and the simple clean scent of lye soap.

Zoe walked around taking it all in. Abe poured coffee into two tin cups from the white enamel coffee pot that sat on the stove. "Thank you, Abe," she said, taking the mug. "I love your cowboy coffee." She took a sip.

Beyond the main room was a tiny bathroom flanked by two doors.

"You have two bedrooms?"

"Not anymore. The one on the lef' is my workshop where I work on my fiddles and the one on the right is Ev'lyn's workshop where she throws her clay creations. Years ago, I added an outside door, so she could come and go as she pleased."

Zoe lifted an eyebrow as if asking to see. Abe nodded and held out his hand as an invitation. Zoe opened the door to the art studio first. It was a total mess. The shelves that lined the room were piled full of projects in varying forms of completion. Old tin and enamel buckets full of dried pieces of clay littered the floor. In the midst of the chaos was a pottery wheel stained with clay and a small stool. A clay baking oven stood in the far corner.

"A mad scientist's lair," Zoe said.

"Def'nly," Abe said, closing the door. He then opened the door to his luthier shop.

It smelled of wood, hide glue and a hint of pipe tobacco. Fiddles lined the walls. The workbench was clean except for a fiddle that had been glued, clamped and left to dry. Old hand tools were organized on a peg board. A worn apron made of soft, pliable leather hung waiting to be filled.

"The master's den," Zoe said, with a wink.

Abe smiled, shrugged and said, "Maybe."

He closed the door and walked over to the stove to check on the fire. He opened the door, stirred the coals and closed the door again without adding any wood to the fire. "It's time to bury the dead, Miss Zoe," he said, walking over to get a box labeled: seeds.

"April fifteenth is supposed to be the last frost date for this area, so it is a good day to sow." He produced the garden plan they had made together in February and handed it to Zoe along with the seeds. Then he gathered up as many plants as he could carry and started for the door.

Outside the sun was warm but the breeze was cool. A perfect day for working outside. They walked to the garden, set down the seeds and plants and went to get the rakes.

"Ever' since I put woodchips on the garden it has made it more enjoyable. I'm glad this no-till, no-work method came in my old age. I can enjoy the journey of producin' my food without the work. Age may bring wisdom, but it takes with it a once vital body."

"You're in good shape for someone your age."

"Well now, Miss Zoe, don't think for a second you would win if we raced. I can beat you on a bad day."

Zoe thought for a while and smiled. "Someday we may have to see."

"Yes, sir." Abe stopped and surveyed the garden. He looked at the plan laid out on paper. Zoe was a row person. "Plantin's real simple. You take y'er rake and make a trench down to the soil, plant the seeds and cover with soil. When the plants come up we will bring the woodchips back close to the plants as a mulch or coverin'. They will monitor the moisture and we won't have to water. Questions?" Abe had already planted a row of carrots in the time he took to explain the process.

"Aren't you going to use a string?"

"This supposed to be fun, Miss Zoe. Gardening is like life, it ain't about rules, it's about relationship. Besides you can get more in a crooked row than you can in a straight row. It'll all work out." He stopped and studied Zoe for a few seconds and then continued. "You try." He handed her an envelope with radishes in it.

Zoe looked like a child who was trying hard to mimic her parent. "How deep do you plant them?"

"I do every seed at a quarter inch, just cause the experts say it can't be done. God doesn't plant things deep—so I don't either. I'm just tryin' to mimic nature." Abe picked up another packet of seeds. This time it was cabbage.

"We only plant non-GMO, nonhybrid, heirloom seeds. You know what that means?"

"No."

"GMO is a genetically modified organism, where they actually change the DNA of the seed in a laboratory. Some people call them Frankenseeds. You can't save and replant the seeds from a GMO. They won't produce.

"A hybrid is a plant that has been crossed with another to breed character traits in or out of them. If you save a seed from a hybrid it may or may not produce fruit. If it does, you bound to get a plant that will revert back to one of the parents it came from.

"We plant heirloom seeds or open pollinated seeds here. You can save their seeds and replant them ever' year. It seems heirloom seeds make the most sense in God's economy. One plant can produce many seeds. It's a system that is always giving. Just like our Creator. Abundance is how He rolls."

They planted, following the plan with few modifications.

"It's a miracle, really," he continued. "It takes faith to plant. You put a seed in the ground, it grows into somethin' that looks nothin' like the seeds and produces life-givin' fruit." He stopped and looked at Zoe. "They's a lot of things buried in my garden, secrets, pasts, old selves, bad memories, lies, shells of people who once was. Seeds or people done with their old lives and ready to sprout into what they were meant to be.

"Miss Zoe, I think it's time you bury whatever keeps you from bloomin' into the creation you meant to be. Let it decompose and be the fertilizer for y'er new life. If you agree, then plant y'er seed today. Pray over it and see what sprouts. I think you ready. Will you do that?"

Zoe's eyes filled with tears. She bit her lip and nodded.

"That a girl. One other thing. It's Easter Sunday this Sunday. Will you come to church with me? Not for ritual sake, not for religion sake, not to give church a chance, just for me; because you want to commune with me. This Sunday you bound to hear how Jesus was buried, like we be buryin' these seeds today, and how He bloomed into His eternal life." He paused and looked at Zoe. "It's okay if you say no. This 'bout relationship, not rules. It's y'er choice."

Zoe nodded again, giggled and said, "I'm not wearing a dress."

"I never asked you to." Abe went back to planting.

Abe's Church

Zoe didn't have much to choose from in the way of clothes. Hoping khakis would be dressy enough for church, she hurried downstairs to find everyone in the van waiting for her.

Abe put the van into gear and started down the street. The van was quiet except for Evelyn humming a tune. It didn't take long to get to the downtown area where businesses once thrived but empty shells remained with a few stores still open. This area stood for the past and not the future.

Evelyn looked as nice as Zoe had ever seen her. She had on a polyester pant suit with simple leather shoes. Predictably, she wasn't wearing a bra, but it wasn't as noticeable as usual. Her hair was clean and twisted into a bun. The hair from her mole was combed upward like the rest of her hair. Smelling of baby powder, she sat in the front seat clutching an old, black hand bag, humming and rocking without a seat belt. Zoe admired the rebellious freedoms she seemed to enjoy.

Abe pulled the van into an alley and parked near an open door with five questionable looking tattoo-covered guys standing near it, two of them smoking cigarettes. He nodded to them as he pulled up. One with blonde dreadlocks made his way over and shook his hand while giving him a quick hug, then opened Evelyn's door while Abe helped the girls out.

"Miss Zoe, I think you the only one who ain't met Pastor Wyatt or P-Dub as I call him."

Zoe was a little perplexed and bothered by his appearance but tried not to stare too long. "Hey, nice to meet you, Pastor." She shook his calloused hand. Apparently, he didn't put food on his table by pastoring.

The pastor didn't spend much time shaking hands. Instead, he helped Evelyn out of the van, offering his arm to hold while she walked. Inside Pastor Wyatt sat Evelyn at a small table and served her coffee and a donut.

He turned and gave Kit a hug, asking about things on the Homestead. She filled him in on the latest happenings and asked about his family.

Jael punched him on the arm, jockeying for his attention.

"There they are. The Homestead tycoons." He smiled at Jael while hugging Rayden. "Exciting times for you girls, huh? Come see me sometime. You can pick up the computers and let me know what else you need."

The two girls agreed and turned to explore the space and people.

"It's Zoe, right?" His eyes sparkled when they met hers.

His penetrating stare made her breath catch. Despite her first impression, Wyatt was quite handsome and endearing. "That's right," she said, not much above a whisper.

"Abe tells me you're taking to country life fairly well. I think a lot of what they are doing over there. They grow good things on that farm."

Zoe blushed at the compliment. "Most days I feel like a fish out of water. But I think I'm starting to find my feet."

"Or fins." Wyatt laughed at his own joke.

Zoe noticed his perfect teeth. He wasn't like any pastor she had ever met. His easy demeanor calmed her nerves.

"I'm glad you're there. And I'm glad you are here, today," he said, shaking her hand again. "If you can't tell, we are a little laid back here. Make yourself at home." His head pointed to the retired biker behind the bar serving coffee. He turned to go.

Kit and Zoe sat down with some coffee to take in the strange scene.

The old building once housed a hardware store. It still had its original bank of wooden bins complete with a sliding ladder to access the higher bins and a wood and glass counter. An old hand-powered elevator was still intact and hung suspended in the corner waiting for someone to dream up a modern use for the quaint item of yesteryear. Tin squares covered the ceiling. Their peeling paint exposed the layers of dreams they had seen over the years. Brick walls once held painted advertisements. Now they held a second floor, where Pastor Wyatt was rumored to live.

"Isn't it perfect?" Rayden gushed, joining them for coffee. "I mean seriously, look at this place. When we get done with it, downtown real estate is going to go through the roof."

There was a loud squeal from the sound system while the band warmed up. The music wasn't mournful like Zoe had expected, but was closer to heavy metal. Conflicted, Zoe longed for a familiar organ music she once hated. But the lament never came. Instead the music was intense and edgy.

Abe found the girls and offered Evelyn his arm. The group settled near the front.

The people filled the seats, wearing anything from suits to cut offs, wing tips to flip flops. This amazed Zoe. She was surprised at the number of people who called this place their church home.

A guy leaning against the brick wall caught her eye. The man was a skinny, sore-covered meth user in dirty clothes and greasy hair. Unable to hold still, he paced back and forth, sitting down and standing up repeatedly.

Pastor Wyatt made his way to the front shaking hands with him on the way. He welcomed everyone to church and without waiting for the fray to quiet he stood in the front row and nodded at the band.

The band played "House of the Risin' Sun". The crowd went crazy with whistles and shouts of yeses and amens. An atmosphere of a heavy metal concert had overtaken the building.

After a long intro, the lead singer started to sing, "A-mazing grace ... "

The familiar lyrics were being sung to the tune of "House of the Risin' Sun". Zoe had never heard it that way before.

Some people in the congregation sang the original words and others sang "Amazing Grace" lyrics. Regardless, the vibe was one of old versus new, saints and sinners, haunted and blessed. It moved Zoe greatly.

Pastor Wyatt stood with his hands held high singing. Zoe stared trying to read his lips, but couldn't make out which words he was singing. The song ended, the band took their seats and Pastor Wyatt began.

"I love that song. Don't you? I love it how we sing it here. It reminds me of the depths that God is willing to go to save us and the heights we are one day promised to ascend to. Our rebirth from sin, to love, submerged or baptized in His grace ... "

Zoe thought about the word, grace—then the name, Grace.

"Blood shed on a cross, for forgiveness of our sins—freedom from sin's grip. That's grace—undeserved merit."

The meth head, now sitting with his elbows on his knees, hands hanging limp between his legs, looking at the floor, shaking his head, "Praaaise Je-sus" was all he managed to drawl. His head shook with a praiseful tic.

Zoe looked at the pitiful soul and wondered why he was here in such a state. Was this the only place that had ever shown him grace despite himself?

Pastor spoke about how Jesus didn't come to judge, but set the captives free. How His gruesome, life-giving death on the cross was the ultimate sacrifice. For freedom, you only had to ask and receive.

He continued, giving the history of the first Passover. Jesus had celebrated it the night before He died with the breaking of bread and drinking of wine ...

"Praaaise Je-sus," again from the boy-man.

Many people were crying, tears of joy and deep sadness. Abe's church seemed raw. Raw with emotion and tragedies of life, whether self-infected or world-inflected.

Normally this would have made Zoe uncomfortable, but today she felt at home. She could be real about her situation, here. These people weren't here to judge choices made or the battles fought. They were here to heal and help—repent and be restored.

This church was about freedom. Here, revealed secrets, equaled freed captives.

"The truth of light, holds the keys to the death of darkness." Pastor emphasized her thoughts.

Some men were passing out donuts, Doritos and grape juice.

Pastor Wyatt laughed as he took a Dorito and a thimble full of juice.

"We were supposed to have unleavened bread today, like Jesus did. I won't name any names … " He looked at the bass player who just shrugged and smiled. "Instead we will make do with what we have and that is stale donuts and Doritos (probably stale too) out of Jessie's pickup." The drummer shrugged.

On que, the troubled man said, "Praaaise Je-sus."

"It doesn't matter. Unleavened or not. Stale or not. It represents a broken body, His blood poured out for our sin to pay our ransom. He rose on the third day, that's today. To overcome the darkness of sin and set the captives free. That's you and me … "

"The body." He raised his Dorito and ate.

"And the blood." He raised his thimble and drank.

The congregation followed suit while the band played.

The ride home was quiet. Everyone lost in their own thoughts about the morning.

It wasn't what Zoe had expected, but neither was the Homestead. She decided it was more of a blessing than a curse. Besides, if you could get past the dreadlocks and the tattoos, Pastor Wyatt was easy on the eyes. He alone was enough to make a girl want to go back for seconds.

Easter Dinner

Kit made a nice Easter dinner: Shepherd's Pie, grilled asparagus with reduced balsamic vinegar on spring greens, homemade rolls and rhubarb pie for dessert. Abe excused himself before dessert and went outside toward his cabin.

The girls ate in silence until Rayden broke the silence. "What is wrong with Abe?"

Jael shrugged and kept eating. Zoe just shook her head and looked at Kit. Kit looked at Evelyn but said nothing.

Evelyn went on eating her dinner until she was through and pushed her plate away. "He is 'memberin' dah dead, yah."

"Who died? You mean Jesus?" Zoe said.

Evelyn ambled to the back porch and stared out the door to the North. "Nah. His wife and daughter. Dey died years ago—yah." She stood staring off into the distance chewing her tongue and shaking her head. "Today is his day to 'member." She nodded with her head to the small grave up on the hill behind the barn.

The girls moved in behind Evelyn peering over her shoulder at the broken man on the hill.

Rayden's eyes were huge. "Should we go sit with him?" she whispered.

Kit answered, "He wants to be alone. I think it best we leave him to his … memories."

Rayden placed a small hand on Evelyn's shoulder and leaned close to Evelyn's ear. "What happened so long ago?"

"Come. Sit. I will tell you, yah." She pointed at the pie and coffee and grunted as she shuffled past. Evelyn wasn't one to skip dessert.

After settling in with the pie and coffee, they waited for Evelyn to speak. She was grunting and smacking her way through her pastry. Enduring Evelyn's eating exhibitions wasn't easy, more an act of grace. When she finished she sat back staring at the wall, stirring her coffee while she licked the pie crumbs from her mustache.

"It was 1959, dah Vietnam War was four years old, yah. Mudder and Fodder had just gone to be wit dah Lort.

Sometimes I tink dey knew dey were leaving because dey had hired Abe, home from dah war, to help me care for dah farm. It's too much for one person—always too much for one, yah.

"He had married Adriel when he came home from dah war. Never a more beautiful woman, was dere than Adriel. During the day she would care for dah garten and sing, willing dah plants to grow. In dah evening, dey would sit outside and Abe would play his fiddle and Adriel would sing and knit or sew. Dey were deeply in love and soon her belly grew, a baby, yah." She smiled thoughtfully at the memory.

"My parents died in a car accident late dat spring, yah. Dey had gone away and I was sad. Very sad. The thought of a babe here on dah farm made me happy. I would sit outside and listen in dah evenin' to her songs—and dah music would hold my tears for a moment, yah." Evelyn drank her coffee down and blinked as tears made their way down the creases in her checks. She poured another cup and added sugar and cream.

"Precious Lort," she nodded looking around the table. "Precious Lort," she repeated, "it was my favorite she'd sing. 'Precious Loooort, take my hand … '" Her voice wavered as she sang. One hand stirred coffee. The other wiped her tears and nose on her sleeve, leaving a streak on her jacket.

"Goot times we had dat year. Playing cards, making ice cream, canning, sewing for dah babe. Dis house was filled wit laughter and family again, yah. I wanted a big family to live here wit me and it was happening. I watched it sprout and grow. Very blessed. Got is goot.

"The following spring, Adriel was heavy wit child. Abe finished the handmade cradle just in time. Mrs. had knit a white sweater suit for dah babe with matching blanket and was ready for dah coming day. It was almost Easter of '60 when her labor started—easy at first and den hard. Abe rushed her to dah hospital. She gave birth to a perfect girl who lay still as a whisper. Adriel hemorrhaged and was soon still too. Miss Adriel and baby Hannah have laid on dah hill by my parents over sixty Easters now."

Evelyn drank her coffee down again. The girls sniffed and held napkins to their eyes.

"Got's plans are a funny ting. Mostly tings I don't understand, yah. When I prayed for a family to fill dis house, I hoped my parents would have more. But no, just me. When I prayed for Abe and Adriel to fill dis house wit their children—no. I quit praying for my house to be filled. One day Got filled it anyway—wit orphans, strangers from other countries, felons, addicts, dah poor and brokenhearted—His family. When a room is empty, He fills it. Today dis house is full."

Evelyn's body popped and creaked as she got up. She looked aged as she shuffled to her room and closed the door.

They put away the dishes in somber silence. It was a day of reflection.

~~~~~~~~~~~~~~~~

As Zoe milked, she watched the sun-bathed hillside where Abe sat weeping in the warm light. Her heart broke for him. Sometimes understanding comes a little piece at a time.

Bossy stepped out of the barn and stopped to watch Evelyn amble to Abe. She had a bucket in one hand and bag in the other.

Miss Evelyn laid a towel on the ground and removed Abe's shoes. She dipped water out and washed his feet with great love, drying them with the corners of the towel. With much effort she waddled to Abe's side, sat down heavily and poured two tin cups of wine.

She never spoke. There are no words for some losses. She patted his hand and stared at the setting sun as she took a drink.

Zoe looked at the calves they had saved together through calving season, bucking in the last light. The kittens nearly grown, took a bath in the same light. She picked up the bucket of milk and walked to the house with Evelyn's first words to her ringing in her ears. Sometimes the why's of this world remain unanswered. If answered, sometimes the reasoning eludes us.

~~~~~~~~~~~~~~~~

The paper that held Abe's place in his Bible at Genesis 17, was yellowed and brittle with age. It held a few words, a prayer. *Let this not be for naught. April 17, 1960* scratched out by a hand palsied by the shock of the death of someone or someones dear.

7

Sorting

You can't reach for anything new with your hands full of yesterday's stuff.
Louise Smith

May

April was supposed to bring showers and give way to May flowers, but this year May held her cards close. Instead of rushing into blooms, the blossoms tarried, protecting the budding hopes of Zoe and the other newcomers to Halfway Homestead. May is a time of sorting—cattle, found items and the lives that encompass them. There's an excitement that comes with letting go.

Light rain pelted the windows for the fourth day in a row. The girls sat in the parlor where Zoe shared her story months ago. Besides Bible studies on Wednesday nights, it was the first time they had been back in the room together just to hang out and drink coffee.

Zoe loved fresh cream in her coffee. Her life was transitioning to love the simplest things. She pondered this as she sat in the bay window staring out at the lawn drinking in the moisture. Thinking about her upcoming review, she wondered how it might go. Would she get to stay? Did she want to stay? These questions and others plagued her.

Halfway Homestead was her home now. The thought of having to leave its safe walls scared her. Learning new skills relating to the farm was enjoyable but she knew they weren't very marketable in the real world. She wondered what awaited her beyond the gates of the Homestead. Having made great progress in rediscovering herself in six months, there were plenty of mysteries that remained in her soul.

"What do you say, Zoe?" Rayden interrupted her thoughts with her quiet voice.

"About what?"

"We can't go dumpster diving until the weather clears. And we have limited access to the church until the biker gang finishes their redemption rally. You have mentioned wanting to convert the gloom and doom of your room into something cheerier. We can go look at the possibilities." She smiled her meek smile.

Rayden rarely said much. Jael seemed to be her spokesman. Lately the tides of change were ebbing and flowing in every life here. It seemed she was finding her voice.

"I would love that," Zoe said.

Jael jumped to her feet. "Well, paint won't buy itself. I'm off to the hardware store to get paint for the exterior of the house."

"You're ready for paint already?" Kit inquired.

"Not really, but I get bored quickly. I decided to paint a section at a time. I'm too A.D.D. to strip, prime and paint everything in three stages. I would lose interest before finishing. This way I can mix it up and enjoy the process more. If any of you fools aren't doing anything, you can help me."

The girls agreed to help her when they had time, if she shared the paint colors with them now.

Jael whipped the paint swatches from her pocket and with much drama laid them out on the coffee table along with a picture of a Victorian house with the colors already on it. "Ladies, the transformation of our painted lady … "

The girls gathered, studying intently.

"Painted lady?" Kit asked. "Sounds like she should be on a street corner."

All the girls giggled except Jael.

"Yeah, I guess that's what they called the old Victorian houses. I went with some forms of green again, as a salute to the past. Mossy Crag for the scallops and a lighter Zen Green for the main color paired with a punch of Burnt Burgundy for the door. As a look to the future, Awakened Pea Bisque, a creamy yellow-green for the trim. What do you think?"

"It's fresh and amazing," Rayden said, studying the swatches quickly. Her natural decorating sense didn't need to tarry on paint swatches to make a solid decision.

"It will bring this old heifer into the twenty-first century," Zoe bellowed. Everyone laughed.

Jael swooped up the swatches and walked to the door. Throwing her scarf over her shoulder, she said, with much grandeur, "I'm off."

"Kit, you are welcome to join us, if you aren't busy," Rayden said, while straightening the pillows.

"I've got a full day of cooking ahead of me. Nothing says rainy day like soup and homemade bread. Besides, I want to bake a few things for the freezer."

The girls groaned. Nothing tasted as good as Kit's homemade soups. "What kind?" Zoe asked.

"Cheesy cream of potato with bacon, homemade crusty bread and cherry pie."

With homey smells to look forward to, they tramped off to Zoe's room for some redecorating therapy.

~~~~~~~~~~~~~~~~

The rainy day made the room look even drearier. Rayden walked around the room taking in every detail. Breathing deeply as to ingest the nature of the room, she let the scent speak to what it was to become. She stopped to feel the gauze curtains that hung over the bed from a round hoop mounted to the ceiling and ran a hand over the gray duvet. Her hand felt the gray and white paisley wallpaper.

Zoe watched her friend. "Institutional gray. It's so depressing."

Rayden finished studying the white dresser that stood resolute in the corner between a window and the closet and watched the rain streak down the window while tracing it with her finger. "It's gray all right. I like it. It's timeless and beautiful."

97

"I was thinking of something more vibrant like yellow. You know, something that screams life and not death."

Rayden continued to stare out the window. "Screams life and not death … " She rested her forehead against the pane of cool glass. "That is why we are here, to pursue life instead of death, right?" Her eyes filled with tears. "Most days my ears are full of screams of my former life still not dead. I would love to have a room deadened to the sounds of my past and alive with hope and a future. Instead I live in constant fear of the real demons that still hunt me."

"What kind of demons?"

"My old god is the god of my demons. The words I studied as a child, taught as truth, condemn me now to die. Even my mother and father have vowed to pursue me to death."

"To death?"

"Yes, death," her voice caught in her throat. "For me it's a death of an unbeliever."

"Unbeliever?" The statement confused Zoe. She lay down on her bed, forgetting about the dreariness of her room for the moment.

Rayden lay parallel to Zoe to tell her story.

"I came here from Michigan; the seventh child of seven and the only girl. I was treasured as a child. However, as I grew my parents conditioned me to serve, perpetuate and build-up men. I was strictly veiled when I came of age.

"They promised me to the oldest son of a prominent family. My wedding was beautiful, extravagant and traditional. Everything little girls dream of—except love. It was a marriage of arrangement."

"You were married?" Zoe's eyes were wide. Rayden looked like a high school student.

Rayden held Zoe's eyes with hers and nodded then continued. "Our house was one of stunning glory. My imported clothes, although hidden, were made of the finest silks and materials from the East and Middle East. We even imported our food from the Middle East harvested with the proper protocol. I found out soon enough that no amount of wealth can buy what truly matters. How can it? It can't buy a

98

son to fill a womb, the love of a man or even the freedom to see a breath-taking sunrise without a veil."

The statement hung long in the damp air.

"You are Muslim?"

Rayden shrugged off the question. "It was the renouncing of my religion that brought me here."

"You mean faith, the renouncing of your faith?"

Rayden sat up. "No! Not faith," she said, louder than Zoe expected, then paused taking a deep breath. "Religion." She dried her eyes with resolve. Refreshed by shedding tears, she stared out the window where the sun brightened, a warning to the clouds that light would prevail. "It is written that 'faith is the substance of things hoped for, the evidence of things not seen.'" Her now joyful gaze returned to Zoe. "Do you understand what that means?"

Zoe lay on her back and stared up through the gauze causing her to ponder a veiled world. A world dimmed by cloth and the control of others, fueled by hate. The words that Rayden had quoted were foreign to her. Where had they come from—her current faith or past religion? What was the difference?

"Not really. I mean faith is so abstract it's hard to grasp. It means something different to everyone." Zoe shook her head.

Rayden pivoted, bouncing Zoe on the bed. "No! A frustrating thing about Westerners is they have no resolve. Any wind can blow them. Whether or not we want to admit it, there is only one truth. This relative truth of which everyone speaks isn't truth at all. It enables mankind to worship themselves as truth-telling gods when nothing could be further from *the* Truth."

The outburst and monologue confused Zoe.

Rayden resumed, "I grew up praying five times a day to a manic god, obsessed with salvation by works. Who commands followers to kill anyone who doesn't believe these words set forth by a man—claiming vision. At some point you must ask yourself 'do I believe this? or is there something else?'.

"That is why the teachings of Jesus challenge religion. They are opposite of the bondage of works, where you ask 'how good is good enough?'. They speak of love and freedom, not blood-spilling hate, yet don't tolerate a lukewarm stance. There is no other religion in the world based on a sacrificial love that brings peace.

Rayden was more relaxed. She pulled her hair back, twisting it into a bun securing it with a pencil. "I changed from a radical religion of zealous hate, to one just as radical based on a pursuant, persistent love."

She shooed Zoe off the bed and gathered the gray duvet from it. Zoe crossed her arms and stood looking out the window.

Rayden continued, "I've heard you speak of this place— your room as a dungeon, as a place of captivity. I see it as a place in the trees, oaks no less." She referenced the oaks outside the windows. "I see a nest, open, without doors. Yet the bird in the nest neither flies nor sings. You know nothing of physical captivity as I do. You are a blind, emotional captive, held in the darkness of your past. The difference is I have always been able to see freedom but not achieve it. I had no keys until now. You let choices, long past, imprison you today, even though there's no door to the prison therefore, no keys. You are a captive of the worst kind."

She turned and walked toward the door, with not even a glance over her shoulder and said, "Come. Let me show you what I have in mind for your transformation," she said, as she rounded the corner.

Zoe stood there in shocked silence, not sure if Rayden's statement of transformation was pertaining to her personally or her room physically. For the most part she could not follow the apologetic rant that Rayden had laid out before her.

She didn't miss the glimpse of strength that normally cloaked itself behind the veil of black hair like a prowler waiting on its prey. A passion long-squelched fueled her covert, yet fiercely bright light. Anyone who guessed Rayden to be a meek, ignorant push-over would be mistaken and would miss a beautiful, bold, complicated princess masquerading as a peasant.

Zoe was intrigued. Pulled by the vacuum Rayden left in her wake, she followed her into den of creativity.

~~~~~~~~~~~~~~~~~

The room itself was sixteen-foot square. Stripped of the layers of wallpaper, the plaster walls were washed in color, reminiscent of the plastered walls in Europe.

Along one side of the room, shelving units held fabrics organized according to type and color, sewing notions, craft supplies, old lamps and electrical parts. The other side of the room had two sewing machines pushed up against the wall—one tidy, the other with a quilt top draped across the machine. Two long tables in the middle created a working space. Soft music played in the background and a candle burned on a dresser

Rayden had a swatch of burlap and aqua, white paint, a paint brush and two mid-century lemon-colored lamps on the table for Zoe's consideration. She was pilfering through a box of buttons when Zoe came into the room. She looked up and smiled briefly while Zoe took in the interesting things the girls had acquired while living there. The room made Zoe feel creative and young.

She picked up the gypsy quilt and took it to the window to inspect it in better light.

"This is beautiful. My grandmother used to quilt at the church every Monday and has made many in her life. I have never seen a quilt like this. What is the pattern?" Zoe asked.

Rayden took the quilt from Zoe and spread it out on the large table. "It's called a Gypsy Quilt. I enjoy the whimsy of mismatched blocks and wild colors. Sometimes they are edged with simple squares. They are a perfect way to use up the pieces we have around here. Do you like it?"

"Like it? I love it!"

"My goal is to make everyone who passes through these doors a quilt that has a part of each of us on it to take with them. Like this block with the Middle Eastern Bedouin quilt pattern reminiscent of the fabric of nomadic tribes there would represent me, this tribal pattern might be Abe, this very traditional pattern might represent Kit, Jael, well she's hard to classify, her fabric may be dark and complex." She pointed to another piece and continued, "I took this piece off an old quilt of Evelyn's." Rayden folded the quilt and put it back on the sewing machine.

"It's no secret we are on a budget here, and we are all very busy with our jobs, so your dream of stripping wallpaper and painting will not happen. Besides we must give Evelyn's home respect by not straying too far from the essence of a Victorian. With that in mind, I find the gray paisley wallpaper a nice way to remember this old girl was born around 1890. We will never paint the woodwork and cover up all that workmanship or natural beauty. So that leaves us with my vision. Let's take down the mosquito netting over the bed, but leave the white curtains. Depending on how much fabric I have, the duvet will be white or aqua. Your homemade plank headboard will get a new wash of white. The white bedside tables will remain and we will put these funky yellow midcentury lamps on them."

Zoe squealed when she picked one up. "They are perfect."

"I want to swap out your tall dresser with a lower one with a mirror. I'm thinking distressed white with whimsical black lettering—think vintage French post card. That will give you a place to do your hair and make-up. Some days, one bathroom upstairs for four women, just isn't enough.

"I also have a wingback chair that is almost the same color as the lamps that would make a great study chair by the window where the old dresser used to be. It is a little ratty and smells funny. A few days in the hot sun will fix most of its problems. The worn look may have to stay. I can make a throw and pillows to tie it all together. How does that sound?"

Zoe hugged Rayden. "It sounds perfect. Thank you. What can I do to help?"

"Take your headboard off and bring it in here. You can paint while I get started sewing. And, Zoe, you may have to sleep on the couch for a night or two, so pack your bags because I will not allow you back in your room until the big reveal."

Zoe squealed a second time, picked up the wrench Rayden had laid out for her and headed to her room. A day inside with another woman was a welcome change of pace. She adored Abe and his fatherly perspective but she longed to have relationships with other women that were neither toxic nor laborious. Most of her relationships with women up to that point had been heavy laden with expectations. The thought of doing life with sisters of all ages sounded so refreshing to Zoe.

She returned to the studio with her headboard to find her workspace all ready with a drop cloth in place. Rayden had cut out simple pillows and was measuring the duvet cover.

Zoe picked up the chip brush Rayden had laid out for her and set it back down. Outside the gray room the old barn wood took on a rustic beauty lost on Zoe in her bedroom. She ran her hand over the planks cut off at different lengths. In her former life she would have owned nothing so shabby. But she was learning to look at the world through the eyes of possibility instead of her comfortable yet poisonous world of expectations and competition.

"I don't think I can do it."

"Do what?"

"Paint this. It's beautiful, albeit too gray for that room."

"True. Sometimes we have to remove things in our life and hold them in a different light to see their offerings—raw beauty. Light always gives way to truth." She floated across the room. "Might I suggest dry brushing it? Give it a hint of white—a faint white wash."

Without waiting for an answer Rayden picked up the brush and barely dipped it in the paint, and brushed on a coat that enhanced the texture without covering it up.

"Careful now," she said, handing the brush back to Zoe with a wink. "If you go too far, you must paint it all white. Just take your time and think of it as a piece of art, a creation uniquely incomplete, not a task to be done. You are enhancing what's there, not covering up the greatness."

Zoe wasn't an artist. "Uniquely incomplete," she said, coaching herself under her breath. It felt good to let go of perfectionism in the name of art and freedom. She was determined to learn the technique that came naturally to Rayden in life and in medium.

The room was brimming with creativity, good smells from a candle, music familiar but without words and richness and excitement that comes with learning something new. Zoe felt alive in the moment and rich in every good thing.

"Who held you captive?" Zoe asked

Rayden didn't answer right away. "An ideology."

Rayden seemed to always speak in riddles.

"I guess I don't understand," Zoe confessed.

"My former husband is Muslim and a radical follower of Allah and the Koran—as I once was and my parents still are. This involves many things like Sharia Law, female circumcision and teachings you may not be familiar with." She plugged in an iron to heat. "People whisper and say it doesn't happen in America, but people tend to only see what is comfortable.

"My husband held me captive in my home. He had spies, cameras and ways of knowing what I was up to. When I produced only girls, my husband said Allah was angry with me. He beat me and left me for dead. This was of no matter to him. I'm sure he has moved one of his wives from another country to the U.S. by now."

"Other wives?"

"Yes, he had wives in other countries."

"Wives who gave him sons?"

"Most assuredly. I can relate to the story of Leah in the Bible. I know what it is to be rejected, not the favored wife."

Zoe couldn't see Rayden through the tears. "What happened to your girls?"

"I don't know. My prayers are for their safety and peace." Her voice weakened but her fierce resolve didn't.

"How did you get here?"

"By the grace of God. I was in the hospital for many months. They did extensive reconstruction to repair the damage done to my face. My case worker had been a former

104

resident here and convinced them that this would be the safest place for me, miles from Michigan with a new face and a new name."

"Did you get to choose your name?"

"I did."

"Why did you choose Rayden?"

"Because it means … light. Have you ever seen the sign out front? Isaiah 61," she said.

Zoe bowed her head as the tears fell in her lap.

" … release the prisoners from darkness … now I choose light. Before I had no choice."

This hit Zoe hard. She had been born in the light but retreated to the darkness by choice. A flippant disregard of the preciousness of the gift.

The things she once thought of as precious had grown dull in the light of the Homestead. A new day was coming. Dawn hadn't broken forth yet. Its colored light was sending a warning to the darkness. Darkness had only one choice and that was to flee.

Zoe's Review

The hand-me-down couch was an interesting piece, but wasn't a great bed. Zoe would be glad when the upstairs room was hers again. The day was supposed to start early anyway.

Her six-month review was today. The thought of this day turned her insides to liquid. They would review every aspect of her life at Halfway Homestead, but the benchmarks of recovery weren't clear to her. Every time she asked Abe about it, she got a vague answer. Would they let her stay? If not, where would she go? These questions weighed on her mind.

She peeled herself from the couch and headed upstairs for a bath. Rayden had given her a few dresses to choose from for the occasion. Zoe chose a gray short-sleeved t-shirt dress, with a white scarf with the lightest yellow flowers and gray foliage, a three-quarter sleeved sweater in a matching gray and white flip flops. It was conservative yet pretty and looked stunning on Zoe.

Zoe studied her makeup-free face in the mirror. She had aged. The furrows in her brow were deeper and the lines around her eyes more defined. There were other more obtuse changes. Her face had the underpinnings of peace. For the first time in her life she had a radiance that came from a healed spirit and not out of a bottle of makeup, hair dye or alcohol. She wondered if that counted as "an amazing transformation" she could share with her parole officer.

She learned there aren't enough products or whiskey to fill the wrinkles of life. Being real held the most redemption. Regardless, she felt she could embellish her new aura with some foundation, a little bronzer for her eyes and cheeks, light mascara and some lip gloss.

Pleased with her final appraisal, she was ready for whatever the day would bring.

~~~~~~~~~~~~~~~~

Zoe was shocked to find Abe, Pastor Wyatt and Charlene, her parole officer, sitting at the dining room table waiting on her. By the empty coffee cups and saucers, it looked like they had been there awhile. They stopped talking when she came into view.

"Mornin', Miss Zoe." Abe said. He and Wyatt got up when she came into the room. "Why, you look like you just stepped out of a band box," Abe said.

Wyatt retrieved a cup of coffee and a cinnamon roll for Zoe while she exchanged pleasantries with Charlene and Abe.

"I thought we were meeting at the courthouse this morning," Zoe said perplexed.

"Normally that would be the case, Ms. Dempsey," Charlene said. "But I always enjoy the opportunity to come to The Homestead." She smiled at Abe. "Abe and Pastor Wyatt have filled me in on your progress, however, I need to hear your side. Please sit down and tell me how it's going here."

Zoe nodded. "I must admit the court's reasoning to send me to this place was a mystery to me. I expected the gray walls of an institution, but Halfway Homestead is anything but impersonal and bureaucratic. Abe tasked me with the job of tending to the livestock, garden and orchards even though I had no experience and little desire to do that sort of thing. Since then, I've learned how to milk cows, calve cattle and am learning how to garden. At first, I did it because I didn't want to go back to prison. I do it now, because I want to do it. I don't know how all this translates to the real world, however."

Charlene nodded and asked, "Ms. Dempsey, has this experience changed you for the better? You have touched on the vocational aspect, but we are also interested in the mental and social aspects of your treatment. Are you rehabilitated?"

Zoe continued, "As far as socially, honestly I'm struggling there. It was a long way to fall from my former life to where I am now. My parents still won't talk to me. I don't get out much except to go to church or to the barnyard, so my exposure to the public is limited." She glanced at Abe. He smiled and winked. "Living here challenges the paradigms within me and if it has taught me anything, it is you can't put people in a box—they don't fit.

"Mentally, I'm sorry for my choices. I regret the things I've done, but can't change them. I've been sober for years now. Is that because I've changed or is that due to geography? I don't know. Truth is, somedays I am still held captive by my paradigms, alcohol being one of those— captors. And like a victim of Stockholm syndrome, I've developed positive feelings toward my captors." She smiled through her tears. "But that is changing daily."

She knew the message in her heart wasn't being conveyed as accurately as she wanted it to be, but she pressed on quieter now. "Frankly I wonder what would happen if I were free to go. What would I choose? I don't know. I wish I could say with certainty I would always choose wisely, but I don't know. Abe taught me on the first morning I was here that there are blessings and curses and we are free to choose. One leads to redemption and the other to destruction. I desperately want redemption, but I don't know if that's what I would choose."

Her parole officer stopped making notes and took off her glasses.

Zoe studied her parole officer. Charlene had heard it all, so there was no use trying to skirt the truth. She sipped her coffee before continuing.

"I hope you're not looking for a canned answer or a sterile response. Reality is I can't do that. Instead, I'll tell you I've spent the last six months or so learning that my expectations and fears have always guided my decision making. Am I rehabilitated? No. And I don't want to be." Tears lined her face. "I looked it up. It means to be restored to a normal life through training and therapy after imprisonment or addiction. I don't want to go back to my normal."

Charlene leaned back in her seat, crossing her arms over her chest. "Ms. Dempsey, if you don't want rehabilitation, what is it that you want?"

Zoe looked at Wyatt. His lips rested on his hands. He nodded slightly.

"Redemption," she answered. "I looked that up too. The action of saving or being saved from sin, error or evil." Her voice cracked and fell silent.

Charlene looked over her notes. "By all reports, Ms. Dempsey, you have settled into life here easily. You are a hard worker, doing what is asked of you and more. According to Abe and Wyatt, you have shown no inkling or signs of returning to your old patterns of poor decision making. I wish all my parolees were as easy to check up on as you. Furthermore, you seem to have the unique ability to self-evaluate rather honestly, sometimes to a fault."

She gathered her files. "As far as canned answers, Ms. Dempsey, I've heard enough of those to fill an ocean. The goal of living redeemed sounds like one of the best plans I've ever heard. I'm going to report that you have met your parole requirements, but suggest you continue with six months of probation as you finish up here."

Zoe nodded and whispered, "Thank you."

"Pastor Wyatt, Abe ... " She shook their hands. "It's always a pleasure. I'll show myself out."

"That was just right, Miss Zoe. Yes, sir." Abe hugged Zoe.

Zoe was touched by Abe's response. "That didn't go like I had planned."

Wyatt held his left hand out to bring her into his side. "The funny thing about truth is, it always sets you free. That doesn't make speaking it any easier, does it? Well done, Zoe."

The girls appeared from the kitchen. They were giddy having overheard the news. They hugged Zoe.

"This calls for a celebration," Rayden said. "I have a surprise for you."

They blindfolded Zoe. The girls led her upstairs to unveil her room.

It was exactly how Rayden said it would be with two special additions. On her bed was a burlap pillow on which Rayden had painted a branch with a bird sitting on it. The symbolism wasn't lost on Zoe. She remembered their conversation well. When she turned to say something to Rayden, she saw her hand was resting on a wire bird cage and the door was wide open.

They met in the middle of the room and hugged.

"It's perfect. Thank you."

Rayden whispered back, "It's your time to fly and sing."

Zoe hoped so, more than anything.

~~~~~~~~~~~~~~~~

Zoe sank into her bed early, the day's events racing through her mind. It was good to be back in her room.

She had turned a corner today. The goals of the Homestead were clearer to her now and could be reduced to two words: relationships and redemption. She still had miles to go, but there was something about putting a name to the goals that helped her.

Cattle Branding

There is something unnerving about an alarm sounding at four in the morning. It was branding time and that meant all-hands-on-deck. Call in the neighbors and any unpaid favors from passersby. It was time to brand the calves and turn the cow-calf pairs out to pasture for the summer or as long as the grass lasted. Zoe knew Abe would be froggy this morning. It seemed anything that had to do with the cattle got his spirit zooming.

Branding is a long-standing tradition in the history of the United States. It started when open range or free grazing, was popular as a way to identify your cattle permanently in order to protect your cattle from cattle thieves. Although free grazing was a thing of the past, Abe insisted on branding the old-fashioned way, "ropin' the calves and 'draggin' 'em to the fire", as he said it. A day where neighbor helped neighbor. The reward, a big meal under a fine shade tree and help when you needed it.

Zoe drug herself out of bed and pulled on her ball cap, jeans and boots. Kit had a grab-and-go breakfast of burritos, coffee and cinnamon rolls. The kitchen was full of cowboys, cowgirls and a surprising number of bikers from the church spilled out onto the lawn. Conversations were lively for being hours before sunrise.

Zoe poured herself a cup of coffee and was reaching for a burrito when she felt hot breath on her neck. She turned with a start, brushing her lips on Pastor Wyatt's arm while her burrito bounced off his leg and onto the floor.

"Whoa there, Zoe! Sorry 'bout that, didn't see you there. I was on my way to get Miss Evelyn another roll and wasn't paying much attention." He picked up the now contaminated pile of egg, tortilla, cheese and green chilies.

He looked more handsome than she had remembered; at home in his faded Levis, simple white t-shirt, an open flannel and dingo boots.

"Whelp! Shep has to eat too, I reckon," he said, as he stood and lifted Zoe's hand with one of his. He placed the burrito on her hand goo side down.

It had been a while since she was that close to a man. His scent was clean and unassuming like Ivory soap.

"Good morning, by the way. It's nice to see you again, even if I have to clean up after you." He squeezed her hand into her food and winked playfully as her thumb went into

110

the egg mixture. He took two cinnamon rolls back to Miss Evelyn, who was up uncharacteristically early.

Zoe's heart beat in her ears. She watched him settle into a conversation with the old eccentric as if it were nothing. She put what was left of the burrito into the chicken scrap bucket, wiped her hand on her jeans and got another burrito.

Kit came to restock the burrito pile bumping her hip, then shoulder into Zoe's and said, "Not a horrible sight to see first thing in the morning, huh?" She glanced toward Wyatt and back to Zoe.

Zoe smiled while taking a bite of the burrito.

"Are you ready to see if you are fit to be a cowgirl or not?"

"No. In fact I'm somewhat worried," Zoe said, taking a bite from the burrito. "I never dreamed in a million years, I would be a cowgirl-in-training at some halfway house in the middle of nowhere."

Kit laid her head on Zoe's shoulder, "It feels like home though, doesn't it?"

Home. The word sat light on Zoe's ears—like a butterfly alighting on a flower. Home should be something familiar and easy to describe. To her it was something distant and smelled like a fire freshly stomped out. "I hope to define it one day," she said, to herself, or maybe to God.

~~~~~~~~~~~~~~~~

The sun hid its face a while longer while the cowboys were bringing the cows and calves into the pen where they would brand with lots of noise and commotion.

Zoe watched as they cut the mothers away from their calves. It was quite a sight to see the horses work, zigging and zagging as cowboy and horse willed the separation in this strange barnyard dance. The mamas would escape the corral, humming or bawling for their babies to follow. If a calf made it past the sorters, a mounted cowboy would return it to the branding pen.

Abe rested his elbows against the pipe fence, his hands together out in front. "Diddy always said if y'er gonna move cattle, get up 'fore they do and make lots a noise."

111

Abe always called his father, Diddy. It touched Zoe when he said it.

"Why?" she asked.

"It works better that way," he said, with a shrug.

The barnyard was alive with energy and people moving and doing. A large propane stove and branding pot to heat the irons was set just inside the paneled alley. Two people would rope and drag the calves, and two teams of two would wrestle the calves and holding them while they are branded and castrated if needed. The Homestead's brand was a milliron cross, centered on the right hip.

Since the Homestead sold their beef as grass fed, organic they wouldn't administer any shots today.

"Why do we still do this?" Zoe wondered aloud, already half-knowing the answer.

"Well now, Miss Zoe, just like everythin' here on the Homestead, we believe in tradition and relationship. Everybody knows there are calf cradles now—chutes to run them through taking half the time and a fraction of the people. But where's the relationship in that? Like most things automated now days, they're efficient but lack human connection. Today is all about relatin' to people—in remembrance of how things used to be. You can't find relationship in a blamed cell phone or on the internet, but you can find it here today." Abe threw his leg over the fence, ready to start the day's events.

Zoe hollered after him. "What do you want me to do?"

Abe stopped and turned around. "Miss Zoe, just be."

Zoe held out her hands, palms up, and shook her head with her mouth open.

Abe said, "Like teachin' a toddler to walk ... If that means you find yourself wrestlin' a calf with someone, then wrestle. If that means fillin' up the tea or water jugs to keep folks hydrated, then fill 'em. If the ice cream freezer needs to be cranked later, then crank on it. Just be. There's no expectation here today or any day. Just be."

Zoe was relieved and confused. She didn't want to do barn work today, but she didn't know what else to do.

The dining room was void of people but there were a few reclaimed boxes of goodies that hadn't made it upstairs to Rayden's roost. Zoe looked through them. One was filled with items that a person might keep in a study: a stapler, a ten-key calculator, a fine pen set, an old magnifying glass, a carved pipe set and a mini martini bar. Another had a red plaid woolen throw, a leather bag and an ancient typewriter. Zoe wondered if an old globetrotting journalist had died and these were among his possessions.

The hard leather russet colored bag worn with miles and stories, piqued her interest. Buckles joined the cracked leather strap that kept its contents safe. Zoe couldn't help but open it. A leather journal was tucked in the front pouch. Hand scrawled notes littered the pages. *Alexandria Egypt, 17 March* was written on the first page. *Fort Qaitbey, Roman Theatre, Lighthouse at Al-Muntazh* … she turned the page.

Amman, Jordan, 30 March. Petra, Temple of Hercules, King Abdullah Mosque, camels … Zoe was mesmerized by the pages and flipped through to find the year the previous owner had made their voyage to other parts of the world unknown to her. Istanbul, Turkey, Tripoli … ink sketches of camels, landscape and veiled women, but no year to claim the dates. She set down the journal and looked into the main compartment expecting to find a Pentax K-1000 or something older, instead it held an aging Cannon digital camera.

Zoe looked into the bag again finding inner pouches with batteries and a charger. She plugged it in to see if it would hold a charge and left her bounty to go upstairs.

She knocked on Rayden's door, Rayden came out of the room, the door closing behind her. "Yes?" she said.

"Rayden, I was hoping you were up here. I was just going through the boxes downstairs. Do you know where they came from?"

"No. I haven't looked through them yet. Why?"

"Oh, it's just I found a camera in there, a digital one. And I was wondering if you would mind if I used it today."

Rayden shrugged, "That's fine with me. Help yourself."

"Okay. Thanks, Rayden."

"Sure."

Rayden smiled and slipped away. Zoe went back downstairs to see what Jael was doing on the porch where she was when Zoe had discovered the boxes of treasure.

The porch was abuzz with conversation. It seemed Jael had manipulated Pastor Wyatt into helping paint. Jael had already made terrific strides in painting the old house. Zoe listened near the window.

"Really, it would be so much faster if we announced a work day to finish this beast," Pastor Wyatt argued. "I bet we could come up with at least one sprayer, a couple of lifts and paint it in a day or two max."

"Finish? I'm just getting started. Who would show up to help slap paint on this old beast anyway? Besides, this is me. It's what I do." Jael would rather die that admit she needed help.

"After all you and Rayden have done down at the church, I'm sure I could rally the troops. Besides, the food alone will draw most of the guys. Some of the guys may need public service hours anyway," Wyatt contended. "I'll announce it tomorrow at church and we'll see where it goes … "

Zoe smiled at the possibility of seeing Wyatt around more but couldn't help but feel a tinge of jealousy that Jael was the point of his attention.

The camera battery had charged quickly. She turned the camera on and wondered if taking pictures of relationships happening would count as relating—or "just being" as Abe had called it earlier. She hoped so.

~~~~~~~~~~~~~~~~

The smell of smoke hung heavy in the yard. She watched the cowboys rope the calves and drag them to the fire. Upon arriving, one wrestler would take the rope and the other the tail and throw the calf down. They would hold it there until branded, cut and then release it to its mother.

An odd tradition, but beautiful in a lot of ways. A dance with no music and Zoe wanted to capture every aspect. From

114

the people dirty with manure and dust, to the dogs sneaking snacks from the bucket, it was like nothing she had ever seen.

The work was hard. Abe was the castrator. A job saved for seasoned cowboys. Even at his age he moved like a cat. He looked younger today, happily singing his nonsense songs and dancing jigs with the ladies.

Zoe had to get closer. She climbed the fence and clicked her first picture of many. If nothing else a few framed pictures would be a wonderful gift for Abe's birthday coming up later that summer.

~~~~~~~~~~~~~~~~

Midafternoon found her filling the water jugs as Abe had predicted.

"Hey there, Miss Kitty," Pastor Wyatt said, while reaching around her to get a cup to fill with water. "Wanna wrestle a calf with me later?"

Zoe turned into his chest and stepped away quickly.

"Looks like you've already been trying your hand at wrestling," he said, brushing off the dust on her cheek.

"I've been taking a few pictures," she said, wiping her reddened face with the inside of her shirt. "But, yeah. I'm game. I've been trying my hand at being a cowgirl the last few months and don't feel like I have made much progress. Maybe a tattoo covered, dreadlock wearing Pastor will turn it around for me." Her eyebrows lifted as her head tilted and she returned his playful smile.

"Well, all right then, Miss Zoe. Let's go leave our mark on these cattle." He turned, adjusted his make-believe cowboy hat and sauntered off toward the corrals, his hands resting on a pretend belt buckle.

Zoe felt dizzy and a little exhilarated as she followed Wyatt.

After a brief lesson in calf wrestling, Zoe and Wyatt took to the corral to wait on the next calf. Soon a cowboy drug a calf over to them. Wyatt grabbed the rope in front of the head and Zoe caught the tail, both pulling in opposite directions, throwing the calf to the ground. Zoe pulled at the hocks, while placing her boot near the hind end. She lost her grip on the top leg. The calf kicked, violently connecting with her top lip. Blood spilled down her chin. She got control of the hock, leaning back and pulling hard until they had finished branding and cutting. Zoe got up and headed to the hydrant to clean herself up and assess the damage.

Wyatt steadied her with one hand holding the hand closest to him and his opposite thumb looped through her furthest belt loop. "I think we'll make a good team, Zoe."

Zoe looked through him trying not to pass out. The sight of her own blood always made her feel woozy. His face faded quickly …

She woke up under a tree near the water station with her feet on a cooler and her head near Wyatt's lap. He was cleaning the blood from her lip when she came to.

"Hey there, Sleepin' Beauty," he said, with a smile. "Wakey. Wakey."

Zoe tried to sit up, embarrassed by the circumstances.

"Shhh. After going a few rounds with a young bull I think you need to take it easy for a little while, cowgirl." Wyatt's voice was soothing while he pressed her shoulders down into the cool grass.

He was right. The world didn't make a whole lot of sense at that point and Zoe didn't quite know if the butterflies she felt were from her whole ordeal or from being close to Wyatt. After a few minutes, Wyatt helped her sit up and take a few sips of water.

"Thank you." Her words came out with a lisp due to her swollen lip.

"Yeth. You're welcome," he teased, tucking her hair behind her ear on one side to keep it away from her lip.

"Well that wath embarathing," she said, overemphasizing her lisp.

Wyatt looked down trying to contain his laughter. "Really? I thought it was rather heroic." He tugged her a little closer.

Zoe felt loopy. She stared at Wyatt without thinking.

"Listen," he said. "I'm sure the meat in the smoker is in its happy place by now. How about you and me head up to the house? So I can keep my eyes on you while I cut up the

116

meat." He didn't wait for an answer as he helped her to her feet.

"Do you phink I'll need shtitches?" Her lisp continued.

Wyatt cupped her face in his hands and turned her face to the sun pulling his head in for a closer look, "No, your lip will be fine. It's pulling together nicely. Your ego, has taken a beatin', though. Might outta have someone look at that."

They walked together toward the house. Abe stopped and watched from the barnyard after dropping another mountain oyster into the bucket. "Yes, sir," he said.

~~~~~~~~~~~~~~~~~

The work was done: calves branded, meat smoked, food placed, ice cream cranked, folks gathered, hands washed, hair slicked down, prayers and amens said. It was time—time to partake in relationship. All the pomp and circumstance of the day had brought them here, under a large oak in a circle holding hands—Zoe beside Wyatt, Abe beside Evelyn, and so on. A mismatched family of uniqueness.

It felt right to Zoe. She wondered how the patchwork of society—these misfit, broken humans could come together and prosper in harmony.

Evelyn hung on Wyatt's arm while nodding and grunting at the food she wanted. Wyatt chatted while dishing the food and helping the old gal to her place at the head of the table. It was a beautiful show of selfless love. He came back to Zoe at the end of the line. He talked easily with the people around him, at home with himself and in relationships.

If there was one desire in Zoe's heart it was to become who she was created to be. She pondered what that might be like. Had she ever been close to her calling or purpose?

Zoe watched as Wyatt held a small girl and spun her in circles. The girl giggled, head back and mouth open to catch as much of the blessed time as she could. She envied the girl. Living authentically without a predetermined outcome wasn't Zoe's strong suit. How do people find their way—their plans for the future? She knew whoever held that answer was her way forward.

117

The line had moved but Zoe hadn't. Wyatt placed a hand on her back, guiding her to the line, "Hey there. You okay?"

"I'm better," she said, a nod to the future.

His blue eyes sparkled, softened and became serious, looking directly into her soul and said, "I can see that."

~~~~~~~~~~~~~~~~

The concrete slab, once home to a building was decorated simply with square bales and Edison-style light bulbs on strings, strung back and forth on temporary poles to give light to the pickers and the dancers. Next to the slab was a stone encircled bonfire that would help to light the area after the sun set. The sounds of instruments being tuned, people talking and kids giving chase filled the evening.

The circle of music kicked off with a song now familiar to Zoe "Cluck ole' Hen". It was the first song she had ever heard Abe sing in the chicken house what now seemed like years prior. The players took turns picking out the melody around the circle. When Abe's turn came again for a solo, he sang.

On cue, Evelyn danced. Not used to this much excitement, she had to force her old body into a performance. Everyone hollered and clapped, encouraging the eccentric to continue. Wyatt joined Evelyn in dance. Zoe had a hard time keeping up with the photo opportunities, prevalent during this kickoff event. Soon Rayden and Jael joined in. Rayden's dance was reserved and Jael's outlandish and boisterous. Kids followed suit, one trying to outdo the other with their gyrations.

Abe stood. The instruments quieted and kept time while Abe bent and ripped into a solo on his beloved fiddle. After his solo, he danced a jig. He finished the song with a final phrase on his fiddle and everyone erupted with shouts, whistles and clapping. Wyatt dipped Evelyn slightly and kissed her on the forehead as he brought her back up.

Sharing whatever talent or instrument available, the musicians started another song, playing anything from bluegrass to blues, rock and roll to gospel. Two hours later, most of the players took a break for cowboy coffee, pie, ice cream and s'mores. Many went home after dessert. It had been a long day.

Zoe was changing out a trash bag when Wyatt found her.

"Is your dance card full or do you still have a place for me?" He took the bag from her hand and set it down while filling the void in her hand with his.

Zoe giggled. "I don't dance, Pastor."

"Oh, it's Pastor, now. Earlier when you were loopy you were calling me Wyatt and Cowboy. Come on. This is a waltz, all you have to do is follow my lead." He pulled her to the dance floor.

There were only a handful of people on the dance floor. Pastor Wyatt was careful to keep his body the obligatory distance that one might expect from a pastor, but seemed to dance closer to her than he had with others he had danced with that night. At least part of her hoped that was true.

Abe's fiddle moaned out the melody while a twin fiddle, the harmony. The song seemed like a song she should know.

"What's the name of this song?"

"This would be the "Kentucky Waltz"," he said.

In the background, an old, strong voice began to sing ...

Zoe was quiet, thoughtfully looking into the distance trying to place the song.

"A penny for your thoughts?"

"How do you do it, Wyatt?"

"Do what?"

"Do this," she glanced around, shrugged and shook her head. "Life ... without ... I don't know ... walls ... without ... expectations ... "

"Without captivity?" he asked.

"No. Not really. Yes. I don't know what I mean," she babbled.

"Stated positively you might say I live in freedom?" He raised an eyebrow, twirled Zoe around and brought her back to him.

"I guess ... I guess that's what it is. If I knew what it was and how to do it, I wouldn't be asking about it now. Would I?"

119

They swayed to the music.

"You're just ... you're just comfortable in your own tattooed skin and dreaded hair." She touched the back of his head beneath where his hair piled in a loose pony tail and squeezed. "You cherish old women, play like a child, and love people where they are—even if it's an ugly place."

He closed his eyes as if to soak up her touch, then looked down at her. "You don't like my hair or my tats?"

"I don't mean it that way ... "

"I know," he interrupted.

He was quiet for a while before saying, "I can teach you."

"Teach me what?"

"How I do this." He twirled her again, brought her back and dipped her down as the band wrapped up the song. He clapped for the band, whistled through his teeth and held his hand out to guide Zoe off the dance floor.

Near the fire, he found two dirty tin cups, dumped whatever remained in the bottom on the ground and filled them full of coffee. He handed one to Zoe who was sitting on a hay bale. He settled on the ground next to her, half turned with his elbow resting near her leg on the hay.

"It hasn't always been this way," he started. "I wasn't always a preacher man. After high school a few of my buddies started a band, a metal band called Unzipped. We were a pretty good, regional band with hopes of record deals and going large. We would open for national bands when they came to town, were the house band at a huge club and even went on tour once. All that comes with what one might expect: alcohol, women, drugs, porn ... you know. Tattoos, dreads ... " He winked at Zoe and tapped her leg with his elbow then took a long drink of coffee.

"We lived fast and played loud, living the dream as they say. It doesn't take long for the things you've longed for to enslave you and hopelessness to set in. Other people's lives aren't always what they seem. Sometimes a man-made dream is just another version of hell.

"The gig was up quickly. With no money coming in, and habits to support, I did some stupid things and wound up, not unlike you, in a court appointed dry-out center somewhere, albeit quite different from this homestead.

"I've been clean for five years now. I'm on the other side now. No longer dependent on this man." He pointed to himself. "But dependent on that Man." He pointed towards the stars of the sky. "I promised Him, before I was convinced He was real, if what they said about Him was true, I would play for Him the rest of my days and would show others how to do life, in freedom and not chains."

A star streaked across the night's sky. They both watched it fall and fade from sight.

"My tattoos and dreads are just scars from the open wounds of my old life. Healed over now they are a reminder that God 'makes the valley of disaster an anchor of hope'. I'm not ashamed of what He has done for me. I'm thankful and I am redeemed."

There was that word again, redeemed. But with it came a glimpse of the source of redemption.

Zoe put her shaky hand on his elbow. "I want that too."

Wyatt stood up and pulled Zoe to her feet and wrapped her up in a bear hug while she cried tears onto his chest. He held her. This wasn't a man holding a woman he desired but a man holding a broken child.

"I just want you to know. The day of your review, I was so proud of you. You said everything right."

"I really didn't," she cried. "I failed. They still have my case open. I had hopes of getting on with my life. I should have told them what they wanted to hear."

"No, you didn't fail. That's a lie. And never tell people what you think they want to hear." He held her at arm's length. "You spoke the truth. Truth always sets us free. Always. Not on the world's time, but God's."

She couldn't see his facial expressions since the fire had burned low, but she guessed his eyes were serious.

"If you're ready to learn, I can teach you."

Butterflies swirled in her stomach. She nodded. She was excited about the possibilities of being with Wyatt, but nervous that maybe it was wrong to have the feelings she had for him. Rehab wasn't the place to fall in love. But she wasn't

121

in rehab. She was in redeem. (Was that even a word?) She didn't know but somehow that made it okay.

They were dancing again. Each lost in the moment and their thoughts.

When the song ended, Wyatt tucked her hair behind her ear on the right side. Holding her face in his hands he leaned in to kiss her on the cheek. Instead, he whispered in her ear, "Class starts tomorrow."

He gave her forehead a light kiss, her hand a squeeze and walked away into the night air.

It was becoming clear that hope changes everything.

8

Trust Empowered

Trust starts with truth and ends with truth.
Santosh Kalwar

June

Summer wasted no time getting to the Shenandoah Valley. With it came hot, muggy days and much work to be done.

True to his word Pastor Wyatt announced at church that Halfway Homestead needed help updating the exterior of the house, to include power washing, priming and painting. He solicited power washers, sprayers, and lifts, promising the Homestead would provide paint and food, if the church provided the brains and brawn. At days end they had everything lined up to get the job done.

They would power wash one weekend, and prime and paint the next. Jael was responsible for finishing the trim work by using a borrowed lift. The projects would take place the second and third weekends in June.

The thought of getting the house done sooner rather than later secretly overjoyed Jael. Helping Rayden transform the church excited her more than painting an old house. Rayden had been working tirelessly, but with just one person, it was slow going and she had more plans than time.

Bossy's milk dried up, ending milking duties until she calved and came fresh with milk the next spring. She and the pairs were enjoying summer pasture, leaving few cattle chores until fall.

The garden would be Zoe's main focus for the summer. She occasionally helped Abe check the cattle, but mainly she would be on mulch and weed duty for the duration of the growing season. As the garden produced, Kit would teach her how to process the food they would eat throughout the year.

Classes with Pastor Wyatt had started late May as he had promised. Zoe secretly called them dates. Today's class was berry picking since the strawberries were in full production. It would be nice having help picking. Kit had offered to teach them how to freeze the bounty and make strawberry jam.

He showed up at sunrise hoping to get the berries picked before the heat of the day set in. Before going to the store, Kit set out two baskets stained with berry juice from the years prior—adding to the magic of the day. Jael and Rayden were busy getting ready for the grand opening of the store. Abe was on horseback checking fences, cattle and water. Wyatt and Zoe were alone with the morning.

Wyatt's hair was piled high on his head to keep his neck cool. He looked ready to garden in a light t-shirt that said "not all who wander are lost", khaki shorts, sunglasses and flip flops.

"I like your t-shirt," Zoe said causally.

Wyatt smiled and popped a couple of berries in his mouth. "Thanks. I like it too. It reminds me of how far I have come." He continued picking the red berries, stopping to eat another now and then.

"How do you mean?"

"Well, you know … I spent the first part of my life wandering around in a parched land. A land of my choosing—music, groupies and booze. I thought it was heaven. It was all I had ever wanted, but it was lonely. How can a life be filled with people, and music and food—every desire fulfilled—yet be as empty as this basket? Just meaningless." He shook his head.

"Time passed. Regrets came. I settled for the life I thought I wanted, even though it was killing me. I was content with the hell I had built for myself. I lived there in the past, not present in the moment and with little thought of the future.

"Know what I mean?"

Zoe nodded. "All too much."

124

Zoe contemplated his words. Wyatt was so real and wore his heart on his sleeve. She hoped that someday she would heal enough to share like he could.

"One day I had a thought. Maybe I was designed to be a part of something bigger, or at least bigger than what I could do on my own. I wanted my life to have purpose—to count for something."

He moved to another spot to pick. "I reasoned if I had a higher calling then there must be a Caller, right? And His way, must be the best way.

"So, I started seeking. I found that left to my own devices, I would wind up in some dark places that just feel yucky."

Zoe giggled at the simple childlike statement, but knew how true the words were.

Wyatt's eyes held hers a while before he turned back to picking berries. "Yucky people with yucky pasts have no promise, little hope and not much of a future. The Caller must have something good for me, but there's no way for me to be as good as He wants me to be."

Zoe stopped for a moment. "See that is what I don't understand."

"What?"

"How good, is good enough?"

"Perfect is good enough," he said.

"Exactly. That is why there is no hope for me."

"That's where you are wrong, Zoe. We don't have to be perfect, because the Caller, in His wisdom, has three parts: Grand Designer or Artist, Redeemer and Counselor. The Artist, God, designed us for a purpose. The Redeemer, Jesus, lived perfectly and died horribly so we can live redeemed. The Counselor is my favorite, the Spirit that dwells in us, guiding us."

"So, say we accept that as truth. What would keep us from living in our past?" Zoe asked.

"Nothing!"

Zoe's shoulders slumped.

"There are people that believe, but live in the same hell they have always lived in …

"That's where the wander part comes in. It's a choice—our choice. We can become a new creation, and stay in the wonder of being a new creation and thrive. Or we can wander back to the familiar ways of our past and thrash."

"Blessings and cursings ... " Zoe said, under her breath, remembering her first day at the ranch.

Wyatt smiled at Zoe. "Yeah. Blessings and cursings. Wander in his promises, with hope and future or wonder how you can get yourself out of the self-centered and self-contained hell you've created.

"I choose to wander in relationships and in His provision. It's freedom at its best. I make plans, but hold loosely to them."

"But that means you have to trust," Zoe said, with a defeated look still on her face.

"Yes, it does." Wyatt's eyes were sparkling. "And unlike any human, I've found Him trustworthy."

"Why is that so hard?" Zoe asked.

"Because we have to give up thinking we know what's best for us."

"How do you do that?"

"Honestly, there isn't much *you* can do except surrender."

"Doesn't that require me to trust what I'm surrendering to?"

Wyatt giggled at the statement. Zoe threw a mushy berry at him. He caught it in his mouth and promptly spit it out, causing them both to laugh out loud.

"I'm serious, Wyatt."

His smiled faded a little, but the ornery look remained. He continued picking like there had been no reprimand. "I know you are and I am too. It's just, people seem to only vet God before being willing to trust Him. Everything else like music, sex, booze, food, material possessions, other humans ... whatever, get total blind faith and complete adoration, without vetting. What gives?"

"Ugh! I don't know. That's what I'm trying to understand. Some days I feel more lost than when I came here."

Wyatt ignored her outburst and answered his own question. "For me, it's because I can see and feel tangible things. It's easy to trust in those things—especially if they make you feel good. But I can't always see God, at first anyway. So it was hard to trust what I couldn't see."

"So, what caused you to trust in someone you can't see or even explain?"

"At the risk of putting it all out there, it took me a long time. I would only trust Him with the parts of me I either had no control over or that didn't matter to me at the time.

"For example, when they threw me in jail, I had all my freedoms taken away, because I was hurting myself or potentially others by my actions. When you're not free, you have no choice. That's true, whether you are behind bars or not. You're imprisoned or set free by your choices—location on earth is just geographical."

Zoe thought about the statement and how it pertained to her and then each person on the Homestead. Some were imprisoned by their own hand, others imprisoned by people and Jael, both.

Wyatt continued. "In jail, I had hit rock bottom. They saved me from myself. As my release grew closer I prayed, *God if you are real, provide.* The halfway house where I landed wasn't what I had in mind, but it was provision. I got a job as a construction worker to begin the process of getting back on my feet. I asked Him again, *God, provide a place to live.* That old hardware store sold for taxes owed, exactly the small amount of money I had saved while at the halfway house. My boss provided the tools I needed during the day and at night I scrounged through the piles of leftover materials to build my apartment upstairs. Was it my dream home? No, but maybe I wasn't grown up enough for my dream home. God was just being a good dad and giving me only what I could handle.

"He proved Himself able to provide. Not always what I thought I wanted, but what I needed at that time in my life."

"What did you trust him with next?" Zoe asked.

"Friends. My boss contracted installation of a new roof on that old house and that's how I met Abe and Evelyn. Abe invited me to his church and over the years I became an ordained minister. His old church wanted to open a church downtown and thought the old hardwood store would be as good a place as any."

"So, you've known them for a while now?"

"Yep, five years. I know we look like unlikely friends, but I love them and I cherish the time I've spent playing bingo with Evelyn and music with Abe. They changed my life. Everything they have brought into my life has been good." He looked thoughtfully at Zoe.

She blushed and looked back down at the strawberries.

"They grow good things here. If it wasn't a halfway house for women, I would love to live and grow here too. But for now, anyway, I have to be content with where I am."

"What will you trust Him with next?"

Wyatt lay in the woodchips that covered the ground staring at the cloud formations being baked away by the heat of the sun and let out a sigh. "You," he said, and continued to look up into the sky.

Zoe didn't know what to say. She felt giddy and scared of the thought, but dating Wyatt had crossed her mind more than once.

"I don't say that to scare you. I've been so focused on my growth, I haven't thought about dating until I met you. Abe keeps me posted on your progress and we've been praying for you and your journey since you got here. I'm interested in at least continuing our study together of how I try to do life trusting instead of testing God."

"I would like that," Zoe said softly.

He got up and extended a hand to help her up. They had picked the ripest strawberries, more than enough for strawberry jam and to freeze. It was time for a lesson in jam making and berry freezing. He held her hand longer than he needed to. They carried the baskets to the house.

~~~~~~~~~~~~~~~~

Kit was in the pantry putting away the last of the groceries she had bought at the store when Wyatt and Zoe came in the back door.

"Hey you two, just in time. I stocked up on sugar for the jam. I'm thinking we can make strawberry jam and scones, then have a spot of tea later when we taste to see how we did."

She picked up the jelly jars, four in each hand and headed for the kitchen while Zoe and Wyatt took off their shoes.

The intensity of the sun made the kitchen glow even more than usual. Almost pulsing like a heart—there was life in Kit's kitchen. Although aged and well worn, the 1940s cabinets that stretched from floor to ceiling held to the past. Adorned in aqua and cream they cradled the farmhouse sink and drain boards under the window. Kit's homemade soap lay in the corroding silver dish. Years prior, Abe had suspended a weathered ladder from the ceiling over the sink to dry herbs throughout the winter for seasonings, teas and tonics. The 1940s white enamel gas stove held two ovens and warming areas. The flecked linoleum floor showed little wear from all who had passed over it for years. The kitchen was like coming home. It made people feel welcome and wanted.

Zoe and Wyatt scrubbed their hands. After removing the green tops from the strawberries, Kit tossed the topped berries into a large colander.

"You kids work on this and I'll gather what we need to make jam and scones. We will freeze what we don't use."

Wyatt and Zoe nodded in agreement.

Soon all implements of canning, freezing and baking were organized in work stations. It was time to chop and crush the berries.

"Zoe, you're in charge of the scones. I've been around Wyatt enough to know he is great at smoking meat and he has wonderful youthful enthusiasm, but his baking skills are lacking. The scones need one to two cups of strawberries diced small, sprinkled with sugar and placed in the freezer for now."

"Wyatt, you're in charge of the jam. You will need to measure two quarts or eight cups of strawberries into the Dutch oven and crush them with the metal potato masher on the stove. I'm sanitizing the jars in the oven at two hundred twenty-five degrees for twenty minutes. You may also boil them for ten minutes. I find the oven is the simplest way with this many people. Notice the pan of water with rings and seals and tops simmering on the back burner there. You may shut that off until we use them."

Comfortable in the kitchen teaching and directing, Kit had taught cooking classes every week at the food pantry and farmers market. She was called to cook and she embraced her calling.

"Which is it? One or two cups of strawberries," Zoe asked.

Kit hugged her and said, "Oh. You're one of them."

"One of who?"

"A specific kind of person, one who wants to know exact-ly how much of what goes into whatever."

Zoe shrugged. "Aren't you?"

"No. I'm a recovering idealist. Before I came here, I drove myself and everyone around me crazy trying to be a perfectionist. That's part of the reason meth had such a hold on me. It exacerbated the problem. I became more O.C.D. than before.

"Now I like to live in the freedom of ... "

"Chaos," Zoe interrupted.

Wyatt and Kit laughed.

"No, not chaos, more like controlled chaos or artistic freedom. I enjoy the freedom of grace. If it's not quite right, that's ok."

"How do you do that?"

Wyatt looked at Zoe and then Kit and then went back to focusing on mashing the strawberries.

"I feel it," Kit said.

"Wyatt?" Kit asked.

"Yes, Ma'am." He continued mashing the berries.

"Do you read music?"

"No, Ma'am."

"How do you know what to play?" Kit asked.

"I feel it," Wyatt shrugged.

"Exactly," Kit said.

"Yeah, but how?" Zoe insisted.

Wyatt quit what he was doing and turned around. "You know that inner voice we all have? Not the one the screams at you to have a second bowl of ice cream or take a drink or whatever. The other one, the quiet and peaceful one. You know that voice?"

Zoe shrugged and nodded.

"You listen to that voice."

Zoe was perplexed. "How can a voice show you?"

"It's like a guide, an idea, a way. *The* way. It will teach you. But there's a catch. You have to get out of the way—release what you think is right and let *it* lead," Wyatt said.

"Yes. Exactly," Kit whispered. "It's not like following your heart or your feelings. It's more like tuning out your way and long, established paradigms and tuning into His voice and trusting that."

There was that word again. Trust. Zoe proceeded cautiously. "So, it's a quiet voice?"

"So quiet it can't be heard, only felt. It sounds like the greatest truth you have ever known," Kit said.

Zoe, intrigued by the dialog, but confused about cooking, asked, "So how many strawberries?"

Everyone laughed.

Kit opened a cabinet door wide for everyone to see. On the inside of the door were recipes. The old scribe, beautifully handwritten in pencil had faded with time. Kit studied carefully, closed that door, and opened another. "Here it is. Ida Mae's scone recipe."

Everyone gathered around.

"Who's Ida Mae?" Zoe asked.

"My modder, yah." Evelyn, still in her pajamas, had snuck into the kitchen.

She shuffled over to the cabinet door grabbing a handful of berries on her way. She looked up at the scrawl while gumming the strawberries. "My modder taught me how to cook and I teach my girls. Yah." She patted Kit on the face and tottered off to find coffee to slurp.

"This is the only record of Ida Mae's cooking we have except what Evelyn remembers. Aren't they precious? I've written down all these recipes and everything that Evelyn has

131

taught me to preserve them. That is one place in my life I am still O.C.D. I hope to put together a cookbook to honor her memory and call it *Ida Red's Pantry*."

"Why Ida Red? Why not Ida Mae?" Zoe asked.

"My fodder called her Ida Red, because of her hair." Evelyn was looking out the window miles, maybe years away in thought.

"So … how many strawberries do I need? You still haven't answered the question." Zoe sighed.

"A cup and a half, yah, these aren't terribly juicy." Evelyn flopped down at the table with her coffee to work a crossword puzzle.

The matriarch had spoken. Satisfied, she measured, sugared and froze the strawberries. Zoe knew the scones would turn out perfectly. For now, she didn't have to channel her inner voice.

"Ok, Wyatt, add about six cups of sugar according to how sweet you prefer it. Bring that to a boil and cook it for about forty minutes. Stir it often to keep it from scorching."

"How will I know when it's done?" he asked.

"When the jam breaks from the spoon in a sheet all at once, it's ready— that is called jelly stage. If it falls in 'drips' it needs to boil longer."

"What if it doesn't set up?" he asked.

Kit smiled and shrugged her shoulders. "Then we'll put it on our pancakes and ice cream like syrup. No worries."

Kit handed Zoe a recipe card with the scone recipe on it. Zoe got right to work on putting the scones together.

"So, what's for lunch?" Wyatt asked.

The girls laughed.

Kit brightened, "Since we have an English theme going, it would be fun to have a ploughman's lunch."

"What's that?" Wyatt asked, raising an eyebrow.

"It's a cold lunch of meat, cheese, bread, onion, apples, pickles and hardboiled eggs. We could shop in the cellar and garden for everything we have grown and canned here in the last year: smoked sausage, cheese, dilly beans, sweet pickles, fresh green onions and apple chutney. Its traditionally served

132

with ale, but we could have hot tea or cider—and scones for dessert."

"Right-o!" he said, in his best English accent.

Soon the smell of baking scones wafted through the house. The jelly jars were ready to fill. Kit took the jars from the oven and showed Wyatt and Zoe how to use the jar funnel to fill the jars, leaving at least a quarter of an inch of head space. Then setting the lids and rings on the clean rim, she screwed the lid tight and set it on a towel to cool.

"Some people would water bath the jars for ten minutes, but I seldom do that for my jams and jellies. Just 'cause that's how my grandma did it," she said, with a wink. "Let's focus on setting out lunch and enjoying an English feast."

Abe came in the back door singing one of his nonsense songs. "Well hello there, P-Dub. What brings you over to these parts?"

"Hey, Abe." He extended his hand to shake and hugged Abe with his other hand. "Good to see you, man," he said, while hugging Abe.

He pulled away to answer. "Kit had promised me a lesson in jam making when we were over painting the house. She and Zoe recruited me to pick strawberries today. What are you up to?"

Abe finished slipping off his boots, "I've enjoyed a quiet ride on horseback this mornin'. Watched the sun come up from the top of Oak Ridge, counted our pairs and spent some time with the Almighty. I believe I'll spend the rest of the day workin' on fiddles. It's too hot to be outside today." He filled the teapot with water and put it on the stove to whistle.

The men settled into talking about people from church and future plans.

The front door opened, Jael exchanged pleasantries with everyone while Rayden retrieved an old hairbrush and brushed Evelyn's hair. She twisted into a bun, securing it with the bobby pins that were never far from Evelyn's head. Jael had settled into helping Evelyn with her crossword puzzle while snacking on the fresh berries.

Zoe surveyed the patchwork of lives represented in the room, people from around the world. These unlikely saints she now called family. The only word that came to mind was respect. The thought of leaving its protective walls set cold in her heart. She was falling in love with her simple life and the relationships that came with communal living. There was no pretense here, just love. She supposed if she was to trust, her future would be as good a place as any.

Kit interrupted her thoughts with a nudge from the basket she had filled earlier. It was time to "shop" for goodies for lunch.

The damp cellar felt good compared to the air outside. The stores held there always impressed Zoe with a feeling of security. From the work of her own hands she was learning to provide for herself and others in the simplest ways. The law of the harvest was evident here. There was a time to plant and a time to harvest. The cellar was always at its lowest in the spring, but their cellar was often an exception. Once in a while, Kit culled out the aged canned goods, and fed them to the chickens to make way for the new. Zoe couldn't help but think of Wyatt's earlier statement of faith. Provision.

Kit didn't say much as they shopped. Zoe had always labeled Kit as astute in knowing when to speak and when to just be. It was time to just be.

The simple lunch took minutes to set out. It wasn't a meal of kings, but a meal of working men. The food grown from the earth where they lived, offered strength to those weak in flesh or spirit. Abe directed his flock to join hands and asked Wyatt to give the blessing.

Wyatt obliged. "Father God, we are impressed with Your creation from Your sunrise viewed from a horse to the wonder of Your provision from this land. We are thankful for it. Help us trust You." He squeezed Zoe's hand. "In Your Son's name. Amen."

~~~~~~~~~~~~~~~~

Rayden came downstairs from her studio carrying a box long forgotten, her face ashen.

134

Abe rushed to her side, catching her as her knees gave out. "Easy now, Miss," he said, as he lowered her to the floor.

Wyatt took the box from her hands and set it on the table. Zoe recognized it as the box from which the camera came on branding day.

"H-h-he has found me," Rayden stammered.

"Who has found you?" Abe asked, has he knelt over her.

"My husband," her voice a whisper.

"Is this his stuff?" Jael's voice was dark and fierce as she looked through the box.

Rayden nodded. "When did this come?"

"On branding day. That would explain the pictures on the card when I uploaded them," Zoe said. "Why would he come all the way here from Michigan to leave a few boxes of stuff?"

"To send a message," Rayden said, her hands shaking.

Wyatt and Abe locked eyes.

"What kind of message?" Wyatt asked.

"Telling me I can't hide from him," Rayden said. "Telling me he is all powerful."

The heaviness of the moment hung in the air. One of their own was in danger. The outside world had come to the Homestead and Zoe felt like there was nowhere on earth they could go to make themselves safe.

Abe got up and called the sheriff, requesting his presence on the farm. Jael took Abe's place by Rayden's side protective and strong. Abe hung up the phone, his shoulders squared and unwavering. He slipped his boots on and went out to his house summoning Wyatt to follow.

The girls remained to help Rayden to a chair and get her a glass of water. The mood was solemn and heavy. Once a spirit is broken and suppressed, it is easy to go back to the familiar. There wasn't a spirit in that room that hadn't found the familiar in being a captive at some point in life, except for Evelyn that is.

Often masquerading as naïve or simple, Evelyn was anything but. Having lived with plenty of troubled women with a plethora of issues over the years, Evelyn was perceptive and shrewd, not easily shaken. She had survived jealous exes, addicts, nonbelievers and the like. This was just another day. Rocking at the table, humming the same song she always hummed, she dipped apples into hot tea with too much cream and sugar. The same way she had the first day Zoe met her in the parlor.

With a sticky hand, she reached over and patted Rayden's hand and said, "The Lort is goot, a refuge in times of trouble. He cares for those who trust in Him," and went back to rocking and humming.

Trust. It seemed to be the word of the day.

~~~~~~~~~~~~~~~~

When the sheriff arrived, Abe and Wyatt met him at the door. After a brief exchange they invited him inside where Kit set hot tea and a scone in front of him. There was only one thing on Abe's mind and that was keeping his tribe safe at any cost and he wasted no time getting to the point.

"What we need to know, Sheriff, is what can we do 'bout this?" Abe leaned across the table to press his question.

"Well now, 'fore we go to jumpin' to conclusions, we need to establish where these boxes came from. When did they show up? Were they delivered by FedEx, UPS or dropped off? Did anyone see who dropped them off?" The sheriff took a careful sip of tea while his eyes traveled from person to person.

Jael spoke first. "Three boxes were placed on the front porch the day of Zoe's review."

The sheriff interrupted, "What day was that?"

Zoe answered, "May twenty-fifth."

The sheriff nodded.

Jael continued, "FedEx or UPS didn't deliver them because they were all open on top with no address. I saw them out there, brought them into the living room that day and took them upstairs days later."

"Why are you calling on this now?" he said, while looking through the boxes.

"People drop things off here all the time. We are getting a reputation for a place to take unwanted items. It's not

136

uncommon for them to just appear on the porch with no explanation. Yet, sometimes we don't go through them for a while. Rayden just went through them today and discovered they came from her husband's house in Dearborn, Michigan."

The sheriff scoffed. "With no witness or concrete evidence, your claim is hard to prove."

Rayden's voice wavered, "These are gifts I have given him, for his den. It's his way of saying. 'I found you and I am watching you.'"

"Has anything been removed from the boxes?"

The collective answer was no.

"Actually," Zoe began, "I did remove something." She looked at Rayden nodding. "Remember when I knocked on the door and asked if I could use the camera out of the box and you said it would be fine?"

Rayden stared at the floor and nodded, "Yes, I remember. But I didn't know what boxes you were talking about."

"A digital camera?" the sheriff asked.

"Yes," Zoe said.

"Did it have a memory card?"

"Yes, a few, but only one with pictures on it. I kept the pictures because they were exotic and beautiful." Zoe left the kitchen to find the camera and cards.

Jael broke the silence, "Can we press charges?"

The sheriff shook his head, "No laws have been broken."

Jael huffed and stabbed the sheriff with her green eyes.

He returned his gaze to Abe and Wyatt, his head shaking. "I understand how this might shake you up, but there's nothin' I can do for y'all. I'm sorry."

"So, you're saying we have to wait for him to come back and kill her for good before you can do anything about this?" Jael fumed.

Abe shot Jael with his look. Zoe had only seen that look on his face a couple times since coming to the Homestead. Everyone knew he had heard enough. It quieted Jael for a moment.

"Here's the camera. I put the SD card in so you can review the pictures that were on it before it came here. There

137

is also a journal of sorts that recorded the dates, times and places the pictures were taken. It might come in handy in the future."

Jael huffed again but didn't speak.

"Dang fine photographer," the sheriff said under his breath. "Wonder where this one was taken." He adjusted his bifocals then turned the camera toward Rayden.

"Alexandria," she said dryly.

He pursed his lips and raised his eyebrows as he nodded. "Don't see any pictures of people in these ..."

"He isn't one to care about people," Rayden said.

"Whelp!" He handed the camera back to Zoe. "We can't build a case on what we think is right. We have to have tangible evidence to support a crime, but no crime has been committed here. I suggest you keep a better eye out. Close that gate and sort folks out there at the road or somethin'. There's nothin' I can do for you today." He finished his tea, nodded his thanks to Kit and started for the door.

Wyatt stepped in front of him to help with the door, but paused before opening. "Is there any way we could get a written report on why you were called out here today? Just to build a case for the future, if needed?" Wyatt smiled an easy smile.

The sheriff's patience was wearing thin as he let out a sigh. "I s'pose I could fill out somethin' for ya. Maybe stop by my office tomorrow and pick it up."

"Will do." Wyatt stuck out his hand and thanked the sheriff for coming out.

The kitchen was a mass of activity and murmurings when Wyatt returned.

Abe stood and announced they would all be learning how to shoot tomorrow. Class would begin at daylight and all were to be present. He finished his announcement by asking Wyatt to accompany him to the gun shop to buy ammo. Wyatt agreed. The men left by the back door.

The girls took the boxes back upstairs leaving Evelyn alone in the kitchen, humming her odd tune. As she filled her mug, her big bunioned toe found the strawberry jam that was on the floor, swirling it round and round. She hummed and swirled the jam and the tea. Hum and swirl. Hum and swirl.

"No reckoning today, yah," she said. "No reckoning today." She swigged her tea and looked out the window at Shep panting in the shade of an oak tree.

Evelyn was right. Reckoning wasn't to come that day. Instead it tarried as it often does, until its appointed time. Today, like most on the Homestead, was a day to tend to what was planted, water and weed. Hold on to the good and let go of the bad. Reaping would come, but not today.

~~~~~~~~~~~~~~~~

Out behind the barn, Abe had a conglomeration of firearms laid out on the make-shift table—a piece of plywood resting on two saw horses—along with enough ammunition to start a small conflict. Eye and ear protection lay in neat piles. Targets stood at twenty yards, fifty yards and one hundred yards. Eight bowling pins were lined up on the twenty-yard line.

None of the girls were excited about learning to shoot except for Jael, who had already handled weapons during her short stint in the Israeli Army. But they showed up on time and would do their best out of respect for their old friend and to calm their nerves shaken by Rayden's discovery the day before.

"Good morning, ladies." Abe chuckled. "Don't y'all look enthused?" His mood turned more serious as he went on.

"I appreciate ya'll humorin' me on this. I believe Americans should have a gun and know how to use it. Today is as good as any to learn.

"Questions 'fore we get started?"

Jael piped up, "Where's Evelyn?"

"Well now, ladies it might surprise you to know, Miss Evelyn was a crack-shot back in the day. A reg-lar Annie Oakley. Yet I highly doubt she'll be makin' an appearance here this mornin'.

"They's four rules when it comes to shootin'. We'll boil 'em down to two: muzzle management," he said, as he pointed a pistol toward the targets, "and trigger finger discipline." He tapped the side of the pistol with his index finger.

"Down range is that way." He pointed toward the targets again. "You will *not* make y'er gun ready until you take the line. Y'er finger should be off the trigger unless you plan to kill whatever it is y'er pointin' the weapon at. Understood?"

His attention turned to the guns. "I have here a few long guns and various hand guns. We will go over each one. Just like y'all, one pair of shoes don't go with every outfit. One gun doesn't always work for every situation."

The girls giggled and Abe continued his monologue on the make, model and attributes of each gun and what you might use it for. Kit and Zoe listened as well as they could to the lecture but it didn't appeal to them. Jael, confident in her gun knowledge, only half listened to Abe. Rayden locked on and absorbed as much of the information as she could.

"Well, it ain't gettin' any cooler. Let's move on. We gonna start out easy with a .22, the smallest caliber I have. I want everyone to don a pair of earplugs and safety glasses 'fore we move on."

The girls complied.

"The pistol is the hardest thing to master 'cause of the short distance between the sights and the fact you usually don't have a rest for y'er weapon. There are five things to think about before pullin' the trigger: stance, grip, sight alignment, sight picture and trigger control."

Abe explained shooting fundamentals until he was ready to demonstrate. "Finally, we ready to pull the trigger—slow and steady to the rear until the gun goes off. We not slappin', jerkin' the trigger or anythin' like that. We gonna let it surprise us."

The gun fired and Abe hit just below the bullseye on a target at twenty yards. The gun shot sent Shep to the safety of the porch and made the girls clap and scream.

"Now, since this is a single-action pistol I must cock the hammer back ever time 'fore pullin' the trigger. To do that, don't break y'er grip, just use y'er support thumb and fire again—slow and steady." Abe shot five more times, emptying the pistol.

"When I'm done, I keep my gun pointin' down range while I unload it and check it for empty. Then and only then can I holster my weapon or head back to the table or whatever. Even if the gun is empty, we don't point it at anyone. Is that clear?"

The girls nodded.

"Any questions?"

Rayden said, "That didn't sound as loud as I thought it would."

"Y'er right, Miss. A .22 ain't as loud as the others and don't kick much at all. Like I said, we startin' you out easy today. They's nothin' here that you won't be able to handle readily by the end of the day.

"Rayden, why don't you get up here and show the others how it's done.

"We gonna go up to the ten-yard line, reload, shoot six, back up to the fifteen-yard line, reload, shoot six and back to the twenty-yard line, reload and shoot the last six. Here we go."

Abe stayed close behind Rayden's left, coaching and reminding as she shot. Her hands shook with anticipation while she fired the first cylinder but became steadier as she went through the drill. Her groups got tighter and closer to the bullseye even though the distance from the target became greater.

Abe gave her a one-arm hug. "That will certainly do, Miss."

The girls clapped and squealed, cheering on their friend. After the pistol was placed back on the table, Jael picked little Rayden up in a bear hug and swung her around. The normal shy and sheepish look on Rayden's face was replaced by a proud and determined one. She pulled her hair back out of her face and twisted it into a perfect knot, securing it with a clip.

"There's one other thing, I forgot to mention when it comes to shootin'. We all right-handed here today, so most likely y'all right eye dominant. When it comes to awareness and shootin' a pistol or shotgun we want to keep our eyes open. When you focus on your front sight, you'll fuzz one eye, y'er weaker eye. No need concentratin' on that. It should happen naturally."

"I'm next," Jael shouted.

"Yes, sir. Miss Rayden set the bar pretty high for ya'll to follow." He motioned for Jael to take her place on the range.

Abe didn't coach Jael much since she overflowed with confidence and knowledge. Conversely, her target told the truth of her skill level. Most of her shots were high with a few to the right of the bullseye. Abe explained if you switch your focus from the front sight to the target (to see where your shots go) it has a tendency to push your palm into the heel of your grip and may cause your bullets to go high.

"It's better if you concentrate on y'er front sight. It should be clear and the target fuzzy when you pull the trigger. Don't worry about where it went. It's already gone." Abe slapped her on the back and told her to get back in line.

They put up fresh targets for Zoe and Kit.

Kit was up next. She said everything out loud as she did it, asking questions as she went on everything Abe covered. This made Zoe smile to herself, it seemed when Kit was out of her comfort-zone she would resort back to her old O.C.D. ways, which made her a decent shooter.

"Okay. Look here, ladies. See how the bullets went left of the bullseye—some are low left?"

They nodded.

"That may mean she is milkin' her grip." Abe stopped and looked at Kit, then at Zoe. "I'd expect Miss Zoe to be milkin' her grip, since she is our milker 'round here."

Everyone laughed.

"To correct milkin' the grip you have to become accustomed to movin' y'er trigger finger independent from the rest of y'er grip. It's a slow and steady squeeze to the rear with y'er index finger only. Not y'er whole hand.

"All in all, Miss Kit, very nice groupin'. We will just work on not milkin' the grip and that should move y'er group to the ten ring or center there. Well done." Abe hugged his old friend.

142

Zoe went last. She had shot before and enjoyed it, but the last couple times she had a gun in her hands it wasn't the best of circumstances. The memory was hard to shake. Not wanting to let Abe down, she tried letting go of the past as she took her place beside Abe.

Her hands shook violently. Abe patiently explained another shooting tip to the group.

"Movement when y'er tryin' to get on target is natural. Some move more than others."

The girls giggled.

"The older you get, the mo' shaky y'er hands may get. Just remember you'll never be able to hold perfectly still, so embrace y'er movement, know it's there and don't snap y'er trigger when it's perfect. Just pull slow and steady to the rear while keepin' on target the best you can. You'll be surprised how well you do.

"Okay, Miss Zoe, you up."

Her shaking calmed a little once she shot.

"Now here's a classic case of jerkin' the trigger. This happens when folks are afraid of the recoil or noise firearms make. They anticipate the gun going off and jerk or slap at the trigger. Bullets will go low and left on a right-handed shooter, low and right on a left-handed shooter. You wanna *let* the gun go off, don't *make* it go off."

She shot again.

"Oooh wee. If a bad guy come 'round here and you jerk like that, you may shoot him in the pinky toe, Miss Zoe. Then you can out run 'im." Abe laughed big and shook his head.

The morning passed. The group shot three different pistols Abe had for them to shoot. Rayden dominated the girls in accuracy and speed. They cleaned up the range and took the guns and ammo to Abe's cabin before heading inside for lunch.

A light lunch was in order with the high heat index. The group munched on chicken salad sandwiches, apples, sun tea and molasses cookies for dessert.

Even though the Homestead was on heightened alert, the conversation was lively, lighter than the day before. They had never seen Rayden so silly and animated.

143

"I'm gonna start callin' you Calamity Ray. Dad gum, child, you a shooter!" Abe said reaching for another cookie.

"What you think 'bout all that, this mornin'?"

Rayden sat with perfect posture. "I feel empowered, Abe. Thank you."

She reached a hand over and squeezed his. Their brown eyes held each other for a moment.

Abe placed his other hand on hers and said with a slight catch in his voice, "Awww you welcome, honey."

He cleared his throat. "But we ain't done yet. Losers still got guns to clean."

Jael laughed and threw another cookie at him, which he caught and ate.

Empowerment, the essence of the Homestead, had found its feet in many forms over the years. Today it came faster than the speed of sound in the hands of a half-pint woman at the behest of an old man.

What you couldn't hear was the sound that fear makes when it's defeated. It's too bad too—a sound like that never gets old.

9

He Speaks

I love to think of nature as an unlimited broadcasting station,
through which God speaks to us every hour, if we will only tune in.
George Washington Carver

July

Summer had set in with a vengeance in June and doubled down in July. Zoe was thankful Abe could take care of the cattle during the summer so she could focus on the garden, canning and helping Rayden and Jael get ready for their grand opening in September.

The sun was relentless on the garden. The heat made the peppers, tomatoes, cucumbers, melons and corn thrive, but pretty well devastated the early cool weather crops like green beans, beets, peas, onions, cabbage and broccoli.

Zoe's main task became weeding and cleaning out the cool weather crop beds, readying them for a late planting and fall harvest. She would work in the cool of the day, from daylight until noon, clearing the area of aged plants or weeds much to the chickens' delight. Since Shep was a great cattle dog but a poor chicken dog, the incarcerated chickens looked forward to the garden goodies in lieu of braving the lunacies of Shep. The fresh greens supplemented by some grain kept the Homestead in eggs and Shep under the porch.

Zoe hadn't been a gardener when she first arrived, but now loved the time she spent there. She had tried to put into practice some of the ideas Pastor Wyatt had been laying out for her on their dates, as far as reading the Bible and praying. Since prayer was such an abstract thing to her, she settled the issue by resorting to just talking to God either out loud or in her head while working in the garden. Mornings in her garden were like a cleansing workout—physically and mentally. The days that her sweat mixed with tears seemed the most beneficial, bringing her peace. Other days brought direction in the oddest of ways.

One day in particular she had been weeding and clearing and came across a squash plant covered in beetles. The plant was all but dead. She said out loud or to whoever was listening, "What in the world are these?"

Abe was wandering by at the time and stopped to talk to her. He explained they were blister beetles and they attacked only stressed plants. He explained blister beetles were toxic to horses and cattle. When accidentally ingested in hay, the beetle bodies caused blisters in their mouths and guts and can cause death. The only value the dying plants had at this point was to become chicken fodder.

"Won't they hurt the chickens too?"

"I've never seen a chicken eat one, even if they had a good chance to. Birds will eat them, though. I would just pull the plant and whup 'em off and throw what's left of the plants to the chickens."

"How do we prevent them from attacking other plants?"

"Oh, you can sprinkle the base of the plant with diatomaceous earth and that may keep 'em at bay. They's a fifty-pound bag in the garden shed. Help y'erself."

"What's that?"

"Its ground up fossilized plankton. Its death by a thousand cuts for the little critters. Yet it's safe for humans. We put it in the grains we grind for bread. Keeps the boll weevils outta 'em."

Intrigued, Zoe found the bag and sprinkled it at the base and around the plants to see if it would keep the bugs at bay.

An hour later, she was weeding around the pumpkin vines. She noticed swarms of beetles in and under the vines and pumpkins—feasting on some leaves yet not others and on shriveled pumpkins but not the healthy ones. She recognized them as stink bugs.

"Why isn't this plant dying?" Zoe said aloud. But this time Abe wasn't there to hear her. Nobody was.

She pulled the leaves back to see how bad of an infestation there was. The little stinkers had munched through the original vine where the plant had come up, yet it hadn't killed the plant. She kept looking. The bugs seemed to only be eating the dead or wilted parts of the plant.

What is going on? She wondered.

She sat and thought about her time out in the garden that morning. She had cried a good portion of it. Releasing all she had on her mind: fears over her future and the danger posed by Rayden's ex-husband.

Jael had been even more overbearing than usual. She protected Rayden in a weird alpha male way. It was like she considered Rayden her own, wanting no one to talk to her. Ironically acting like Rayden's husband once did. She wondered if their relationship was more than friendship. So strange.

Then there was Wyatt. Uncharacteristically absent, leaving a void in her she pined to have filled. He had said his former boss had a huge job they could use him on well into the fall. She wondered if it was a handy excuse to stay away.

She looked back at the pumpkin vine again and shook her head. *Why?* She stared at a bug half expecting an answer.

Then it came, almost a voice but mainly a thought. *There is life and death here. It is good.*

Zoe thought about the finality of death, as she knew it. It had never been good.

Another thought came with a light breeze: *Decomposition of the dead—feeds the living.*

Compost *does* feed, she thought. But how can it survive if the main vine has been severed?

Poor vines left to whither—new roots set to feed fruit.

The voice or whatever it was, was poetic, whispering thought provoking prose.

The poor parts of her life had withered. A chill ran up her spine and the hair on her neck stood on end. She looked around seemingly alone, but she wasn't alone. Someone was there. Someone was watching. She looked around more carefully. Nothing was out of place. Maybe she had been in the sun enough for one day. The wheelbarrow, full of dying plants, weighed on her like her thoughts. She dumped them in the chicken run, put the wheelbarrow in the garden shed and ran to the house.

The two glasses of water she chugged made her feel dizzy. Not in the mood to eat, she went upstairs to her room and closed the door. The coolness of her room felt good.

The faint sound of music and conversation were coming from the studio. At least she knew Rayden and Jael were okay. Her shoes hit the floor with a thud as she stared at her Bible and stretched out on her bed. She was reading through the Bible in a year and hadn't read her assigned passages yet that day. That might take her mind off the feeling that someone was there watching her. She thumbed the pages. John fifteen was today's reading.

"I am the true vine, and my Father is the gardener. He cuts off every branch in me that bears no fruit, while every branch that does bear fruit he prunes so that it will be even more fruitful. You are already clean because of the word I have spoken to you. Remain in me, as I also remain in you. No branch can bear fruit by itself; it must remain in the vine. Neither can you bear fruit unless you remain in me ... "

Her heart was beating out of her chest. She shut the book letting it fall to the floor. Maybe she was living in the twilight zone. Things like that don't just happen.

At that moment, everything in her wanted to see Wyatt. She had never called him to just chat. Without a cell phone and only the community landline in the house, the thought of it sounded strange. She reasoned if everyone knew they talked on the phone, just because, they would assume they were dating. Regardless of what it looked like, she needed to talk to him.

She peeled herself from her bed and quietly made her way downstairs to the phone in the parlor, hoping she would be out of earshot. She picked up the phone and dialed his number without a thought to what she might say.

It rang a few times before going to voicemail. "Hey Wyatt here—leave a message and I'll call you back. Have a blessed day."

148

"Uh yeah, Wyatt, this is Zoe. Ummm I'd like to uh talk to you sometime when you're not busy. If you could give me a call back, I'd appreciate it."

Zoe could hear the girls coming downstairs, so she walked quickly toward the kitchen.

"Hey girl. What are you doing?" Jael looked past her into the parlor.

"Nothin'!" Zoe smiled sheepishly. "Thinking about getting something to eat. Do you guys want to join me?"

"Sure, we're starving," Jael said, not looking at Rayden for confirmation.

"Yes, we skipped breakfast to go dumpster diving early." Rayden paused, tilted her head and through narrow eyes she asked, "Are you feeling okay?"

"Yeah, fine. Why?"

"You look peaked."

"I know what will make you feel better. You can come help us at the store. We came across a bunch of wooden crates you can help us move and you can also help us clean the upstairs." Jael ribbed.

Zoe smiled at the thought of "accidentally" running into Wyatt at his home.

"Sure. I'm not doing anything the rest of the day. Let's get some lunch first. I'm famished."

Abe and Evelyn joined them. Lunch was simple: beef salad sandwiches, pickles and watermelon. Dessert was a light and refreshing strawberry Jello cake.

~~~~~~~~~~~~~~~~

The transformation of the hardware store amazed Zoe. The girls had been working day and night trying to organize the space to make it work for their vision. They begged Wyatt for the artistic leeway to remake the space into a store on one side and a meeting place on the other. They planned to use the charmed area with the original bins and sliding ladder to house and display Miss Evelyn's pottery among other treasures.

149

Wyatt relented to all their wishes, giving them free rein. His only request was they leave a place for tables and chairs in front of the rustic stage, so people could sit and drink coffee, read the paper, play games or simply hang out.

The garage in the back was to remain a shop where guys could meet to fix cars. Once repaired, the cars were given away to needy families or individuals who needed a hand up. Pastor Wyatt's main vision for his church was to relate to people where they are, in a comfortable setting. A lot of the guys that came to the church were more comfortable in a man cave or bar. Wyatt wasn't willing to give up that part of his ministry.

The redesign included using large wooden spools, leftovers from utility companies, for display pods on the floor. Rayden had stacked the spools, small on top of large to use more vertical space. Rustic industrial with a touch of organic homestead was Rayden's vision.

Goods to sell would include: hand thrown pottery, canned goods and home-dried teas from Kit's kitchen, crocheted hats and scarves, fiddles and repurposed items that the girls had found or bought for very little. It was an eclectic mix of all things Homestead. The beautiful space and the experience itself were enough to bring in people searching for treasures.

Rayden's business plan was unique. Because the church and Homestead were both nonprofits the board decided the store would be a nonprofit as well, at least for the time being. Rayden and Jael would be paid executive compensation for their time and contributions.

Whatever misgivings were assigned to Rayden's ideas subsided as her vision came to life. Plans pitched to the board with a timeline of years were being fast tracked by her undying focus and energy. Her contagious vision spread to whoever came in contact with it.

Rayden had big plans for the future of the store. She envisioned a kitchen with cooking classes from area chefs, murder mystery dinners at the Halfway Homestead mansion (with some help from the community theater), marketing of grass-fed beef and eggs from the farm and Razed to

Redeemed classes on how to repurpose items. The message here was clear—everything and everyone has value.

Razed to Redeemed is what Jael called the future store most of the time. A fitting title. Most of the items sold would have to be razed, or torn down, and redeemed—to show their real value, similar to the girls from the Halfway Homestead. The name would be finalized closer to the grand opening.

Rayden didn't take a breath while painting word pictures of what was to come. She explained there was even more room upstairs in front of Wyatt's apartment to expand. Zoe giggled at the idea.

Moving their studio downtown into a bigger work space needed to happen soon. The double granary at the Homestead was full and didn't make a good place for the pieces that were ready to sell. If all Rayden's plans took hold, Pastor Wyatt and his church may get edged out of the building.

The heat of the upstairs didn't seem to affect Rayden's energy.

"So, what you do think?" Her eyes were bright. "Can you see it?"

Zoe looked around at the mess the upstairs. "I see it. I just can't believe it. You say we are focusing on cleaning this part out today?"

"How do you plan on moving this?" Zoe asked, pointing at a large scale.

The scale had two columns held together by an iron molded crown that had FAIRBANKS embossed across the top in gold and another iron connecting bar half way down the columns.

"The gentlemen from church said they would move it. I plan to sell all the scrap iron except for the beautiful columned part with the counterweights."

"What are you going to do with that part?" Zoe asked.

"We will put it along the rear side wall of the sanctuary. Isn't it fantastic? It will be our new coffee and tea bar at church. I have the perfect table to go with it."

Zoe always marveled at Rayden's vision.

"It is a neat piece," she said, envisioning it in place.

Jael had been unloading the crates downstairs while Rayden gave Zoe the tour.

"Okay you slackers, it's time to clear some of this out. I left the doors open and we can haul all the stuff we plan to throw away down to the dumpster. We can make a pile of scrap metal and other things that we will need a pickup to haul away. At least it will be down in the alley and not up here. Remember, we have to leave a spot for Wyatt to park when he gets home."

The girls got right to work moving the stuff downstairs. The work was grueling. A nice change of pace for Zoe.

It was almost seven in the evening. Everything the girls could do was complete. They were ready to go back to the Homestead for supper when Wyatt pulled in.

His genuine smile made Zoe's heart jump. He got out of his work truck dirty from the long day working outside and gave each of the girls a hug. He turned and cocked his head to one side, raised an eyebrow while looking at the piles of stuff the girls had brought down to be removed and said, "Looks like you all have been busy."

"We have," Jael said. "You won't recognize the upstairs. Come check it out."

"Alright," he agreed. "I hope you at least left me a bed."

The girls laughed as they led him upstairs.

"Wow! We could have a dance up here now," he said, walking around the room stopping to do a little dance and continue on his inspection. "Impressive."

"Do you girls want to stay for supper?"

"No." Jael and Rayden said together.

Zoe was disappointed they had answered for her.

"We've got to get home. It's our night to go curb robbing in the city. Besides you can't cook." Jael slugged him in the arm.

"I can too! I put a pork loin and a can of sauerkraut in the crockpot this morning. All I have to do is boil potatoes and make a salad.

"Are you sure? I would love to have company for dinner." He looked at Zoe.

"Are you going dumpster diving tonight too?" he asked. "I can take you home later," he added, with a boyish grin.

Zoe looked at the girls. Rayden nodded, encouraging her to stay. Jael rolled her eyes and walked to the van.

"Well, I'm leaving," she said, slamming the van door. "Who's coming with me?" She started the van.

Rayden turned to Wyatt.

"Pastor, do you think you and the guys could move the scales down to where I showed you, before church on Sunday?"

"Probably so. They will be over Thursday for Bible study and to put a starter in a car we are giving away. If I had some homemade cookies that night, it might persuade them."

"I can arrange that," Rayden beamed. She gave Zoe a hug and squeezed Wyatt's arm. "Thank you, Pastor," she said, before turning back to Zoe.

Jael honked the van horn.

It didn't decrease the intense look Rayden's eyes held for Zoe when she turned. "Stay. Enjoy your time. Thank you for helping us today." She hugged her neck.

Rayden's intuition was very perceptive. Zoe smiled back at her and bid them good night. Jael drove off in a huff.

Wyatt waved, turned to the door and held out his hand to guide Zoe into his apartment.

"After you," he said.

His studio apartment was small but inviting. Two walls were white painted drywall and the other exposed brick. White metal kitchen cabinets hung on the brick, salvaged from a 1950s kitchen renovation project. A white enamel stove and refrigerator were given to him by the same clients who wanted new kitchen appliances. The 1950s chrome dinette set with gray top and white chairs were an unexpected find on trash night. A denim loveseat divided the kitchen from the living area. A coffee table sat in front of a small television holding a few magazines, a remote control and an aloe vera plant. Over an iron bed, a giant clock made from a wooden spool end commanded attention. His loosely made bed was dressed in a simple gray comforter and white sheets.

Zoe stared at the clock.

"Rayden made that for me for sharing my space with her. Isn't it cool?"

"It's beautiful, so bold, like her."

"Yes. She is my brazen little sister." His words were full of love for Rayden. He shook his head as he walked to the sink to clean up. "She really seems to be coming into herself lately."

Zoe continued to study the flat. A large window and a glass door gave the room a lot of light, even late in the evening. The door lead to the roof of the garage where a small table and two chairs sat waiting to be filled.

"I was thinking we could eat out there tonight. It's a little warm in here, but it's cooling off nicely outside. Does that sound okay?"

"Sounds great."

He scrubbed the potatoes and cut them into a pot.

"Skins okay?"

Zoe looked at him funny.

"On the potatoes." He smiled, his blue eyes sparkling.

"Fine," she said, blushing. May I use your bathroom to clean up?"

Wyatt nodded.

The bathroom held a tub with shower, toilet, a small sink and a washer and dryer. Next to the room was a closet with hanging clothes, a dresser and storage space.

Zoe washed her hands and face. She wasn't dressed or made up for a date, but she didn't care. Wyatt was so laid back and real she felt like it didn't matter. She dried her hands thinking about what the night might hold. She hoped at least for some answers and maybe more.

The mood had changed when Zoe came out of the bathroom. Dimmed lights and music relaxed the tone to match Wyatt's easy demeanor. The door leading to the garage roof was open. Wyatt was seated at the small table, on which a candle burned and two glasses of tea with lemon sat. His eyes met hers with a smile. She sat down.

"Thanks for staying for supper," he said, reaching for her arm. "It's not much, but it's nice to have someone to eat and hang out with this evening." His touch was warm and deliberate.

"Thanks for asking," she said.

They sat in silence for a while watching a black and white cat make his way across the roof.

"Who is that?" Zoe asked.

"That would be Ned. He comes to visit me every evening about this time. Excuse me."

Wyatt got up to check the potatoes and returned with a small saucer of milk while Zoe introduced herself to Ned.

Ned enjoyed the attention until the milk arrived, then turned his focus to dinner and a bath. Wyatt returned to the kitchen and was back soon enough with two plates of food.

The simple fare was similar to what she could have had at home, comfort food.

Wyatt took her hands and bowed his head. "Jesus, thank you for the company You brought me tonight. Will You bless our evening together? Amen."

He held her hands a little longer, took his napkin, smiled at Zoe and placed it in his lap.

Zoe took a bite of food.

"Yum! You're right, you can cook. This is delicious!"

Wyatt talked about his day and listened while Zoe talked about her day with the girls. He got up for another plate of food and glass of tea for himself and settled in for more conversation.

"So, I got this message from you today. I tried calling you back, but Abe said you were here. Was there something you needed?" His face was concerned.

Zoe looked down at her empty plate, a little embarrassed. What seemed pressing at the time didn't seem as much so now. She looked at Wyatt who lifted an eyebrow as if to encourage her to speak.

"It was nothing, really," she said.

"Nothing? Really?" he said, with a smirk. "I would love to be the judge of that."

Zoe shrugged, anxious that Wyatt might think her crazy if she shared her incident in the garden. Wyatt continued to eat.

"Remember the day we picked strawberries together?"

He nodded.

"Remember our conversation about listening to the still small voice? And other times you've talked to me about praying to God and listening for His answer."

Wyatt laid down his fork and nodded, his eyes wide and inviting.

Zoe watched Ned bathe before telling Wyatt the story.

"Well, I've been trying to talk to God. I don't know if I would call it praying. It's more like a one-sided conversation, or at least I thought so until today. I'm usually in the garden when I do it, because I'm alone with my thoughts and weeds. My mind wanders to, you know, life stuff—where I'm at, where I'm going. You know, just stuff." She felt like she was babbling.

Wyatt had his chin resting on his fist listening intently. She couldn't tell if he thought she had lost it or not. She plowed forward.

" … And I don't know if you know this about me, but I talk to myself—like a lot. Anyway, I also interrupt myself quite often too with questions about what's happening in the present. Like today, blister beetles had destroyed a squash plant, yet when I saw stink bugs attacking the pumpkin plant the whole plant wasn't dying. I didn't understand why. So I said out loud to myself, 'Why? What's going on?' And … " she took a drink of her tea.

"And it was like the answer came to me. I didn't hear it verbally but felt it. Like God Himself answered. Is that even possible?"

"What did He say?" Wyatt was uncharacteristically serious.

"*There is life and death here. It is good,*" she said. "Then I thought how death is never a good thing. Then He said, *'Decomposition of the dead—feeds the living'.* And I know that's true, because I use compost—dead and decaying parts to feed living plants every day. Then I thought, but the main vine had been severed—so how is the plant even alive? And He answered again, *'Poor vines left to whither—new roots set to feed fruit'.*"

She took another sip of tea and looked at Wyatt. He was deep in thought and offered no insight. She figured there was no turning back now from crazy, so she rattled on.

"I felt light headed and went to lie down on my bed. While I was there, I read my daily passage in John … " Her mind went blank. "John … "

"Fifteen?" Wyatt offered. "About the vines?"

"Yes!" she blurted, and pressed on but stopped and looked at Wyatt. "How did you know that?"

He shrugged.

"It's about vines and how unproductive vines are cut off. It made me think of my life and how parts of my life have died and been cut off. My past is breaking down, starting to compost and is literally feeding my future."

Zoe took a breath and let it out. Her hand was shaking when she took another sip of tea. Tears welled up in her eyes. She was embarrassed she had even brought it up. As her tears spilled down her checks Wyatt got up from the table and pulled her into a bear hug.

"Do you think I'm crazy?" she said, laying her head on his chest. She wondered by doing so if she was crossing an unseen pastor—parishioner boundary. If she was, she didn't care. It felt good to be held again.

Wyatt waited a while before answering, causing Zoe's heart to jump.

"No. You're not crazy. You had a face to face with the Almighty." Wyatt continued to hold her.

"I did?" she pulled away to look at his face.

His face was peaceful yet beaming. He nodded.

"Then why do I feel like this?"

"Like what?"

"Like I'm nuts?"

"You mean like you're not alone? Like your universe just got a lot bigger and you feel small and there's a whole lot you don't understand right now?"

"Yeah. I guess that's what I mean. I feel insignificant."

"I would argue you are feeling very significant."

"Why did He answer my dumb questions and not my important ones?"

157

"Zoe … "

She loved the way he said her name.

"I don't pretend to know or even understand the mind of God. But I do know He is all about relationship. Think about this. The Creator of the universe took time today to seek you out in your garden and answer one of your so-called dumb questions. He enabled you to hear His answer, and in the process, revealed His character to you through something that happens every day in His creation."

He let his words simmer in silence for a while as he held her. "Maybe the small everyday questions are the most important to Him because they hold the most promise to any personalized relationship."

Zoe thought about his words. It was true. Deep relationships are built on the intimate knowledge of seemingly small details of another's life.

"But I have so many questions." Zoe looked like a child. It made Wyatt laugh out loud.

"Like what?"

"Like, is He always so poetic? Will He talk to me again tomorrow? Why me? Why today?"

"Well, He has all the answers. And in time He will answer every one of them." He pulled her close again.

When he pulled away, his eyes sparkled. "You know what you need?"

Zoe's mind raced. "No," she said.

"Ice cream," he said, helping her down in her seat and picking up the dinner plates.

"I hope you like cookie dough. It's all I have."

He returned with two small bowls of ice cream which sat on his Bible as if it were a tray. He settled back into his seat and held his Bible up to the last light coming from the setting sun and read the first half of John fifteen aloud while taking bites of his ice cream and pondering the words in the book.

When he finished reading, he laid his Bible down, finished his ice cream and put the bowl down for Ned to lick clean. Ned purred between licks.

"I think most of your answers are right there. The Word *is* poetic. Why you? Because He loves you and He chose you.

Why today? I don't know—maybe because you're ready? Will He talk to you again tomorrow? I hope you don't wait until tomorrow to talk to Him again.

They soaked in the stillness of the evening, waiting to see if His whisper might return with more answers.

When He didn't, Wyatt said, "I better get you home. I've got a long day ahead of me tomorrow."

"Can I help with dishes?"

"No. I'll get them later. Come on, let's go."

The night was ending sooner than Zoe had hoped, but she knew it was probably for the best. They both had lots of work to do that week and Wyatt was careful to keep most dating boundaries intact. Their conversation was lighter on the way home. Wyatt drove slowly with the windows down soaking up the summer night. At the Homestead, he stopped where Zoe had been dropped off her first day.

She had come so far since then. The house was dark. Abe's fiddle could be heard under the canopy of trees.

Wyatt got out to walk Zoe to the door. He was old fashioned in a lot of ways. Zoe loved that part of him.

"Hey, thanks for staying for supper. I loved having you there with me."

"You're actually a good cook. I really enjoyed being there."

"Thanks," he said, and was quiet.

He finally broke the silence by taking her face in his hands, "I want you to know I do think you are crazy."

Zoe's shoulders slumped.

"You're crazy blessed—beyond words—'one appointed to bear fruit'. Not everyone can say that. Not every life on this earth is lived out in His purpose."

"What's my purpose?" Zoe asked.

Wyatt rested his forehead against hers. "You're asking the wrong guy—that's above my pay grade. Maybe you can ask the right guy later tonight."

Zoe could tell he was smiling but couldn't see his face.

"I have another question," she half whispered.

"No way!" Wyatt whispered back. "What is it?"

"Are you my pastor? Or something more?"

Wyatt put his hand on her neck, stroked her face with his thumb and said with a raspy voice, "Yes." He kissed her on the forehead and held her there for a while without words.

"Is that okay?" He spoke the words into her hair.

Zoe nodded. "I like that."

"Me too. I'll call you tomorrow. Good night," he said, as he opened the front door to let her in.

"Nite," she whispered.

She floated upstairs to shower and get ready for bed. She had been involved in her share of romances in her young life, but this was different. In the past they had focused on the physical. This one was all about relationship and spiritual depth—two things lacking in her other forays in love or lust or whatever they were. She missed the physical, but somehow the longing and mystery added to her deepening desire to really know Wyatt before connecting physically. She was in a free fall. For the first time in her life, intimacy felt honest—without expectation or worry.

~~~~~~~~~~~~~~~~

Most things on a homestead revolve around the weather. After weeks of scorching July heat, the rains came bringing rest and growth.

The girls had been hounding Evelyn to teach them how to throw pottery. The respite from the heat seemed as good a time as any for a day free of regular duties to play in the mud and learn a new skill.

Evelyn had been teaching pottery classes for years at the recreation center and had donated many of the supplies needed to teach the craft. Because of her clout and investment, she commandeered the pottery room on a Saturday for the Homestead's personal use. That gave the four girls and Wyatt their own pottery wheel on which to throw. They were already set up with the tools needed all the tools to make art.

Always relentlessly joyful, Evelyn wore homemade white cotton pants held up by elastic. Her short sleeved, light blue buttoned shirt was untucked and free flowing, like her breasts

160

and her spirit. Aged Birkenstocks stretched out by her bunions nestled her weary feet. She looked at home in her wrinkled skin, mostly toothless smile and her classroom with Frank Sinatra playing in the background. Despite the strangeness of the setting, the students enjoyed the relaxed atmosphere and felt compelled to make art.

Evelyn's laid-back teaching style matched her personality.

"Pastor, you will give everyone ten pounds of clay to start, yah." She pointed toward the clay wrapped in plastic, while donning a well-soiled apron over her head.

In a sing-songy voice she danced toward a short table covered in fabric. "And we will gather at the wedging table to wedge our clay."

She picked up a wire attached to two small dowels and slid the wire through the clay cutting it into five equal pieces.

"Cut, cut, cut and weigh, weigh, weigh, yah." She hummed and smiled as she weighed each piece at precisely two pounds.

The group watched as she wedged without explanation.

"Cut, cut, cut and weigh, weigh, weigh," she said again.

Evelyn was a monkey-see, monkey-do type teacher, like a mother teaching her children.

The group cut and weighed their pieces on old kitchen scales while Evelyn continued.

"Now we wedge!" she exclaimed.

She hummed while she pressed the clay with heels of her palms into the table at an angle, then up on end, repeating the motion continuously. She nudged Kit with her elbow and smiled pointing to the clay. The wedged clay had a spiral on each end with a ram-shaped nose between the horns.

"Like a ram's head, yah," she said, pointing to clay. "But not like bread, no."

To demonstrate, she pushed the clay into the table folding it over like she *was* kneading bread shaking her head no the whole time.

"Adds air, and is no goot."

She adjusted her technique again and soon had it shaped right and set it down on the table and said, "ram's horn". She patted the clay into a sphere and picked up another piece to wedge.

Her students wedged their clay.

While waiting on her students, she poured coffee into a stemless clay wine glass and walked around the table looking over their shoulders, commenting or correcting.

Frank was done singing. Evelyn changed the CD to lively Celtic music that filled the room with fiddles and flutes. She clogged the best she could until one of her Birkenstocks went flying. This caused her to snort and flop down on her rolling office chair by her throwing wheel.

Bored with waiting, she used her feet to pull herself over to her fallen shoe. After putting the shoe on, she spun in circles with her head tipped back and eyes closed, humming to the music.

The students watched the silly scene with interest.

"I wish I could live so freely," Zoe said, watching the old woman.

The others agreed.

"What's keeping you from doing it?" Wyatt questioned.

"I don't know." Zoe's eyes fixed on Evelyn who had quit spinning and had gone back to dancing, this time with an imaginary partner.

"I'm not at home in my own skin," she said, to anyone who would listen. "Or maybe I care too much about what other people think of me."

Wyatt winked at her. Without hesitation he stepped into his place in Evelyn's arms. Evelyn's eyes popped open, she smiled at him and the dance was on.

Jael claimed a wheel and looked back at the girls.

"I don't think he shares the same fears as you," she said dryly.

The song changed to a faster jig. Their dancing followed suit. When the song was over, Evelyn bowed to her audience and took her place at her wheel after kicking off her shoes. It was time to create.

Without introduction, she picked up a round plate looking object and after placing it on the wheel, dampened it with a sponge.

"This is a bat, artists," she said, with a pat.

"First, we center." She placed a piece of clay in the middle of the wheel.

The foot control made the wheel spin quickly while she wet her hands in a bucket of water.

"I like to cone the clay, to center." She demonstrated by cupping her hands, putting pressure at the bottom of the clay and coming up.

"Others hammer," she said. Wetting her hands again, her right fist hammer pressed down while her left hand cupped slightly, pressed into the side of the clay.

"I cone, yah." She demonstrated the coning technique again after rewetting her hands.

"Begin with the end in mind." Her eyes twinkled as she slowed the wheel with her foot control.

"Zig Zigler!" Wyatt exclaimed.

She giggled. "Ziggy, yes!" she exclaimed, clapping her hands together, not minding the spattering of mud on her face and clothes.

Her eyes widened with her next words, "This piece wants to hold flowers from a garten."

Rayden nodded, taking it all in.

"How do you know?" Jael asked sarcastically.

Evelyn leaned forward staring deep into Jael's soul, "Because I listen," she said.

Jael's tough persona usually kept her from breaking eye contact, but not today. Truth has a way of stripping away anything false. Today she broke eye contact quickly. Her body language told the others she wasn't buying voices from clay or whoever else had done the speaking.

Unphased, Evelyn continued like there had been no clash between good and evil.

"We open," she said, placing her thumbs at the center and pressing down.

The clay opened. She stopped the wheel and picked up a large needle with a wooden handle, similar to what a biologist might use to hold skin back while dissecting.

"Pig poker," she said, squealing like a pig stuck in a gate.

Everyone laughed.

"Yes," she said, pointing the poker at them. "Laugh, artists. Laugh when you create. This is goot, yah!" She smiled and stuck the poker in the center of the clay, slid her finger down until her finger rested on the clay and pulled it out, measuring its thickness.

"Perrrrfect!" She tried rolling her r's like someone from Italy, but failed.

"You don't want it too shallow or too tick," she said, tossing the poker aside.

Ironically the music changed from robust and rowdy Celtic fiddles to melancholy Celtic flutes, fiddles and harps. Evelyn bowed her head and breathed deeply, swaying to the music. In the softest voice, she said, "It's time to pull, yah." Moved by the music and maybe a memory, a tear broke from her eye.

She held up her hands to demonstrate position, then dropped them into place, not touching the clay. Then up again pointing to where the pressure would be and back down as she made the wheel spin. Her eyes closed as she pulled the clay up and opened as she came off the rim straight up. She looked so young and full of life, comfortable in her purpose.

She picked up a sponge and cupped it lightly on the rim. "Compress. Pull and compress. Pull and compress, yah."

Her eyes closed again, hands pulling. Opening to compress and closing to pull.

She used a sponge to remove the water inside the vase.

"We will make a rounded place for water to live," she said, pushing from the inside out near the bottom.

She used a flat, flexible metal bean-shaped tool. "A rib to smooth and shape sides," she said.

"The inside should match the outside."

Wyatt shifted his weight from one foot to the other thinking about that statement. There was much more to the day than just learning a craft. Everything Evelyn said was deep and thoughtful. She was a woman of few words. The few that escaped her lips were worthy of consideration.

"Collaring in to hug the flowers." Her hands were in the air in an L shape with three fingers tucked away. She touched

164

the three contact points on each hand, demonstrating near the top of the vase. The clay came in somewhat.

"Or," she said, "collaring in." Her fingers encircled the clay gradually shortening the diameter.

A wooden tool was utilized next to shape where the clay contacted the bat. She removed the flare at the bottom along with the clay that stuck to the bat.

The wheel stopped turning.

She picked up a wire with round clay pieces tied to each end and slid it under the vase cutting the base from the bat.

"Done," she said smiling.

The fledgling artists gasped. It had only taken her a few minutes to make a vase.

"Clay in the hands of a master," Wyatt said, staring at the vase.

"Dah. His hands through mine," Evelyn hummed quietly nodding.

"Beautiful," Rayden whispered.

Everyone nodded. It wasn't just the vase that was beautiful. The whole experience was beautiful. A grotesque human twisted and wrinkled with time transformed into radiant beauty while fulfilling her purpose. It was spiritual.

"Okay, artists, your turn. Make what you wish," she said, with a wave of her hand. Evelyn got up with much effort. The moment of youthful endurance was gone. Caffeine and home remedies would have to do in its place for now. She shuffled off to fill her mug with coffee while the hum of wheels turning on filled the room.

Classical Mozart encouraged the budding potters.

Conversation was limited, in its place, concentration.

Evelyn rolled around on her chair placing hands on hands to instruct further. Jael's clay was the first to fall.

"Set your mistakes aside, yah." Evelyn said, with a shrug and a wave of her hand, dismissing any gaffe that might hinder progress. "It's just clay. We will pug it later," she said, pointing at a large clay mixer and compressor. "Try again."

Jael's heart wasn't in it. She huffed and slammed another piece down on a bat to try again. Jael was all about force.

Kit had been through several classes with other girls who had passed through the Homestead. She was working on bowls for Christmas gifts with varied success.

Zoe was doing okay, but felt like she had two left hands. So far, her favorite part of the class was the interaction between student and teacher and teacher and Creator. What she wouldn't give for a camera to record the moment in time. She tried to make a vase similar to Evelyn's. But when she tried to pull the clay up, she pulled out instead. A short wide bowl with an uneven top was left. She started to destroy it when Evelyn came rolling over.

"Roll away," Evelyn said, pushing Zoe's arm.

"Away," she said, again pushing the air around the piece still spinning—like the piece needed to breathe.

Zoe rolled her chair back and tipped her head, staring at her bowl.

Evelyn slapped her leg and pointed to the bowl.

"Undulating," she said smiling.

"What?" Zoe said.

"Undulating," she said again.

"What's that?"

Evelyn got out of her chair. Starting at her ankles to the tip of her raised hands waves made their way through her body.

"Undulating! Undulating! Undulating!" she said, in succession as her old body billowed.

Evelyn looked like a dancing blowup attention-getter at a car wash.

"It means, wave-like," Kit said, laughing.

Jael couldn't help but get up and mimic Evelyn. "Undulating. Undulating. Undulating." She mimicked with her body.

They all laughed.

"Is that good?" Zoe asked perplexed.

"Dah!" Evelyn said. "That piece is done, yah!"

Satisfied, Zoe stopped the wheel, cut the bowl off the bat and set it all on a shelf to dry when she heard Wyatt exclaim, "Ohhh man!"

His large bowl had collapsed. He stopped the wheel to cut the clay off the bat.

"Nah!" she hollered, hobbling over to his wheel.

She carefully hung the bat upside down between two shelves. The collapsed sides of the bowl came unstuck and hung in a wavy circle.

"Let that dry, yah, and you can be undulating too," she said, bending at the waist. Her upper body hung limply upside down.

Wyatt studied his bowl half expecting the bowl to come off the bat and land with a splat. When that didn't happen, he turned his attention back to making something else.

After centering the second piece of clay, he leaned back in his chair and studied Evelyn.

"What's the secret?" he said, to Evelyn's side.

She was back in her own little world. Her eye's closed, oblivious to the class going on without its instructor.

She didn't answer right away.

"Get out of the way," she said finally.

The students exchanged looks.

"Get out of whose way?" Wyatt asked.

"The Lort's," she said. Her eyes still closed.

"I didn't know I was in His way," Wyatt teased.

She opened her eyes. Her spirit was back in the studio. Her face bewildered, she continued her thought. "Are we not a vessel of clay ourselves? From dust to dust, yah? A vessel for His purpose?"

She closed her eyes again. "Get out of the way," she said again, hugging herself and humming a tune.

"So, it's spiritual?" he asked.

Her eye's slammed open.

"Broken pots." she pointed at Jael. "Undulating pots." she patted Zoe and Wyatt's faces with her mud dried hands. "Pots waiting to be filled." she looked at Kit's bowl on her wheel. "Pots waiting to be made." her eyes locked on Rayden. "All different and useful to the Potter."

"Get out of the way. Be moldable. Be hardened and refined with color by the heat. Be ready to hold something." she looked around.

167

"Or nothing." Her eyes and body froze. "Just be."

10

Washed in the Blood

I prefer dangerous freedom over peaceful slavery.
Thomas Jefferson

August

The back door slammed hard and opened as Abe made his way through it coming quickly toe to toe with Jael. The heat from the kitchen matched the scorching sun outside and the heated conversation inside. August seared hot on the Homestead.

"Now don't go making this what it ain't," Abe said, his voice measured.

Jael's eyes flared, darting back and forth holding Abe's gaze.

"I'm not," she snarled.

"Child, you don't know it yet, but you defeated and have been 'to who laid the chunk'. You so convinced you know what is, but ain't. And when you try to build on what ain't, theys no way to get to what is." Abe's voice was soft yet firm with truth, his eyes sad.

"No I haven't," she spat.

"We gotta get you to where you'll at least entertain what is, 'fore you ever gonna grow."

He poured himself a jar of iced tea and took a long drink while watching Jael hold her defiant pose, unwavering in her seemingly poor stance. He finished the jar and poured another while staring at her.

"I guess *we* don't have to do, nothin'. All this is on *you*. Y'er choice, in y'er time," he said, and took another long drink.

Jael wasn't about to give in but couldn't come up with a comeback. So she slipped through the kitchen with a huff and stomped upstairs.

Zoe set a plate of cookies on the table.

"Anything we can do?" she asked, laying her head on the old man's shoulder.

Abe shook his head.

"She enslaved by her old ways so long, she can't get free of 'em. If a person don't think they a slave—can't set 'em free."

Abe sat down with the paper and his tea. "Glory be," he said, shaking his head while he noshed on a cookie.

Abe had been outside most of the morning with Rayden and Jael for more shooting practice. Teachability wasn't one of Jael's strongest suits, hardheadedness was, however.

Zoe returned to the stove where water was boiling in two pots.

Rayden came in the back door with a smile. Despite the fear of her husband, she was becoming more confident and outgoing by the day.

She got a drink from the tap.

"What are you doing?" she asked, looking over Zoe and Kit's shoulders. Both were manning a pot of boiling water filled with tomatoes.

"We are talking these tomatoes out of their clothes," Kit said, with a wink. "Hot water makes their skins crack, allowing them to slip right off. After they are naked, we will make them into salsa, spaghetti sauce or just can them whole."

Rayden looked around the kitchen at the buckets of tomatoes that littered the floor.

"You will be canning for days. If you want, I can sell some of these at the farmer's market for you."

"That would be great," Zoe said. "With all this heat, we'll have even more to contend with, and we already have more than we need. We can go pick more anytime we want, but are trying to get as much done as we can before this weekend."

"What's this weekend?" Rayden asked.

"The bluegrass festival," Kit answered. "Abe insists everyone goes to at least one a year. We will leave Thursday night and come back Sunday afternoon. We will sleep on the ground in our tent, so enjoy your beds this week," she said, teasing.

"And it's mandatory?" Zoe asked.

"Ummm hummm," Abe affirmed, without looking up.

"What about the farm?" Zoe asked.

"I've got automatic waterers for everything including the chickens. Some guys from the church will be looking in on Miss Ev'lyn. It's all set." Abe said, looking out the top of his eyes as if he had glasses on.

Zoe laughed. "My idea of camping is room service."

"You'll come 'round to it," Abe said, from behind the paper.

"Well, I'm off to the recycling center to drop off and maybe pick up," Rayden said, smiling as she left.

~~~~~~~~~~~~~~~~

Rayden didn't like driving the huge van, but was getting used to the larger turning radius and cumbersome size. She constantly checked her mirrors. She noticed a black Mercedes a few yards behind her. Though hidden behind the glass, she knew he had come for her.

Her heart pounded in her chest and her breathing accelerated, making her lightheaded. She tried to focus on the road. Should she call the police? She looked in the empty passenger seat next to her. She didn't have her new cell phone with her.

Should she drive to the police station across town? There wasn't time.

Pastor Wyatt wasn't at the church, so she couldn't go there.

The black car window soaked up her stare. She racked her brain. A random thought came.

Turn left.

She turned left without signaling.

The car followed at more of a distance.

Her heart raced as she drove into the residential area. What should she do now?

The thought returned.

Turn left.

Without signaling, she turned left again. Wondering where her random thoughts would take her.

The car followed but at an even greater distance. Rayden strained her eyes to see who was in the car. The darkness couldn't be penetrated.

Her eyes looked for a house with people in it, but the streets and homes in the quaint neighborhood were empty, at least for the day. Dying wasn't on her "to do" list today. She checked her mirror again.

The Mercedes pulled into a home that looked vacant.

Thank God, she thought. *I'm crazy, but alive.*

She drove on checking her mirrors again.

The car, barely visible, backed out of the driveway in a distant pursuit.

The thought came again.

Turn left.

The car followed.

"I wish I were crazy," she said to herself. "But I'm not imagining this."

She drove back to the road she had originally turned off of.

Left.

The thought continued.

She knew for sure if the car turned left, they were following her. Why else would someone drive in a circle?

The car followed.

Driving across town to the Sheriff's Office didn't seem like a bad idea any more.

The Mercedes continued to follow her to the Sheriff's Office. When she parked and went inside, it rolled by like nothing funny was going on.

She requested to speak to the sheriff since he had taken the report of the mysterious items left at the Homestead. While she was waiting for the sheriff, she called Abe to tell him about her close encounter. Abe assured her she was doing the right thing and told her to be sure to get an incident report before leaving.

The sheriff asked numerous questions about the color, make and model of the car, license plate number, etc. She only knew it was a two door, black Mercedes with Illinois plates, probably a rental.

The sheriff tried not to come across as belittling, but his attempts failed. Rayden already felt her fears were irrational, but deserved attention in case her husband tried to kill her again. The sheriff thought the "evidence" was circumstantial at best.

They would contact her if they found the car. She drove straight home. When she stepped from the van, Abe put a protective arm around her and walked her to the house.

"Miss Rayden, if you have things you could do around here this week, maybe you should. That way, I can keep an eye on ya," he said, as cheerfully as he could with a comforting wink. His glance over his shoulder before coming into the house, told her he was taking her odd premonitions seriously.

"I might could bring a couple shotguns in for you girls, too. We can't be too careful," he said, as he squeezed her arm and went to do just that.

~~~~~~~~~~~~~~~

The feeling of dread is hard to shake. The residents of the Homestead were on edge and weary. Between the heat and the impending doom everyone was tired and grouchy, except for Evelyn. She was never one to succumb to tales of Armageddon. Life should be lived to the fullest, not feared. Pottery class continued. This week they would learn about trimming and how to fire the molded clay using the kiln.

"Goot morning! Goot morning!" she sang. Evelyn came alive in her purpose. Her skin was radiant though wrinkled. Her energy contagious, but body begrudging. The ailments in her old body were put on temporary hold leaving the appearance of youth and stamina in their place. Basking in grace and maximum freedom, Evelyn's spirit relished the reprieve and her pottery studio leaked creative juices.

"Today we trim and fire, yah," she said, putting in a jazz CD of John Coltrane.

"I've found, yah, in many years of teaching, students are afraid of creating and making mistakes. So I made for you bowls, many bowls to trim, no worries." She pointed to a shelf filled with smallish bowls, leather dry, still damp but not tacky.

"Take one each to your wheels and find a loop trimmer, yah," she said, holding up a tool. "Now, yah, go!" she encouraged.

Everyone moved as she sat at her wheel.

"This is a pottery trimming chuck ... " She pointed to the circular vise—looking tool mounted to her wheel. She didn't wait for the classes' full attention before continuing. " ... to hold your pots in place upside down."

She demonstrated how the sliders moved into place to hold the project in the center while trimming with little explanation.

"And trim the foot." Her pot spun slowly as she pressed the tool lightly towards the middle of the flat bottom cutting away the clay making a shallow bowl in the bottom. The clay cut away in long ribbons.

"Ribbons are goot, yah. Remember the inside should match the outside. We don't want any bowls that are hypocrites, nahh." The old woman laughed to herself.

With Evelyn there was always a deeper meaning to her art. Her teaching tips doubled as life lessons.

"You may trim some of the sides if you wish," she said, continuing her demonstration.

She stopped the wheel and picked up an ink pen that had long since stopped working and signed the clay piece with one large E centered in the middle of the foot.

"Done! Ready to dry and fire," she said. "Your turn. Trim my bowls first, yah and then yours. If there's time left, throw."

The students returned to their places and got right to work.

174

Trimming Miss Evelyn's bowls went pretty well for most of them. The undulating pots presented the most problems. Wyatt was the first to speak.

"Miss Evelyn, how do you trim an uneven pot?"

Evelyn, who always doted on Wyatt, was standing behind him twirling one of his dreadlocks around her finger.

"You must level, yah." She turned the pot over and shimmed up the low parts with pliable clay until the base was level and ready to be trimmed.

"You may trim or not. It's up to you. You're the artist." With a flit of her wrist she walked off as if she didn't care about his answer.

"Where are you going?" Wyatt asked.

"To fill Melvin." her smile filled her face as she turned and her body shimmied in a flirtatious dance.

"Melvin, huh?" Wyatt held his head sideways checking out his progress. "Who's that?"

"Kelvin filled Melvin," she said, dancing with a Mexican flare. "He is so hot, hot, hot."

Evelyn continued being light and silly while her students over-focused on new tasks. Her antics usually left images that were hard to erase from one's mind, but made happy memories.

Wyatt left the bottom flat but beveled the edge so it wouldn't chip off easily.

"I think I'll end on that note," Wyatt said, lifting his pot and taking it over to the shelf to finish drying and watch Evelyn fill the kiln.

~~~~~~~~~~~~~~~~~

The girls were giddy about the idea of their first field trip as they called it. Kit was the only resident who had been to a bluegrass festival before. With the van loaded down with tents, bedding, coolers, instruments and people they set off. Wyatt and Abe in the front seats and the girls in the back.

"Where is this place exactly?" Jael asked.

"Galax, Virginia," Abe said.

"Why are we doing this?" Jael asked rhetorically.

"Simply because you girls need some culture," Abe sighed.

In his best preacher voice Wyatt shouted, "Can I get an amen?"

Everyone but Jael responded enthusiastically. Her amen was dry and tired which made everyone laugh even more.

"How far is it?" Jael whined.

"Just down the road, south a piece," Wyatt mocked.

~~~~~~~~~~~~~~~~

Galax, Virginia sits on the edge of the Blue Ridge Mountain Parkway. A scenic drive through old Virginia. The van quieted as they got closer. The scenery demanded attention and reverence. Meadows and farms, creeks and ponds reflected the natural beauty of creation. It was picturesque. The town had unique shops, selling everything from fiddles to ice cream.

The landscape and old bridges made Zoe realize why they say Virginia is for lovers. Wyatt held her gaze more than once in the rearview mirror, impressing this idea further. She wondered what the weekend might bring with him. Just the thought of being in such a magical place made her stomach flip with anticipation.

The festival park buzzed with people.

Rayden gasped, "I had no idea there would be so many people."

The girls sat taking it all in while Abe and Wyatt bought tickets and camping spaces.

Halfway Homestead covered the cost.

Soon they were unloading and setting up camp. They had four tents to erect: a large ten-man tent for the girls, a smaller five-man tent for Abe and Wyatt and a couple of large pop-up tents to shade the kitchen and instrument picking area complete with carpet and solar lighting. This obviously wasn't the first time Abe and Wyatt had done festival life together.

Wyatt stretched his hammock between two trees where he would sleep unless there was rain. According to Abe, rain was a given at some point.

Kit busied herself in the kitchen area setting up the metal table where she would cook their meals in Dutch ovens using only charcoal. Everyone was hungry and thirsty from the increase in activity and the road trip down the Virginia roads. She had packed roast beef sandwiches, chips and homemade cookies for the crew which were devoured quickly.

She announced that after today they would be on a two-meals-a-day plan until they returned home: brunch and supper. Otherwise they were on their own to pilfer through the snacks and beverages she had brought or pursue food elsewhere if the mood struck them. At festivals, there was always plenty of food to share or be shared depending on where the music took you.

Abe and Rayden seldom missed an opportunity to sell their wares. They busied themselves arranging the goods in the van. The store would open or close at the whim of the owners or the weather. They were on festival time, as Abe called it—not beholden to set hours. The cowboy coffee was always hot, the instruments in tune and ready for company.

Abe was well known at the festivals for his luthiering skills and kind humanity. Soon old friends came around to play a song with him.

The girls explored the park, people and activities. Zoe took her camera to catch the essence of the festival.

Smells of festival food and people engulfed the area. There were pockets of musicians playing old time music, mountain music, bluegrass, new grass, folk, roots and old rock and roll on acoustic instruments. Age differences didn't matter here. Children played with other children as well as people ten times their age.

Zoe had never seen so many instruments in all her life, much less people who knew how to play them. She didn't know the names of all the instruments, but enjoyed their beauty and the artistry behind them. She took detailed shots of instruments and humans.

The cloggers fascinated her too. They carried boards around, stopping here and there at the different jams to dance a jig or two before moving on.

177

The thought of sharing music and movement with total strangers was foreign to her. She didn't have the moxie to ever do something that would expose her to so many. But she enjoyed recording the unique relationship in photo images.

The stage held paid entertainers belting out their offerings to a sea of people seated in lawn chairs. Music competitions were held here and there on the grounds: from fiddling to flat foot dancing. Abe was right. This place oozed with culture.

Vendor booths sold everything from handmade treasures to junk. Zoe was relieved that they didn't have a booth to man. This was a much, needed vacation.

As the sun fell the first evening, Zoe made her way back to camp. Kit came back early to start the coals to heat the ham and beans and bake the cornbread for their supper. Kit had preplanned all the meals. Most of them were precooked or cooked in part and frozen at home to cut down on prep time and dishes. Paper plates and bowls were used to keep the focus on rest and relaxation.

"So how do you bake without an oven?" Jael looked quizzingly at Kit. It was out of character for Jael to ask for cooking lessons.

"There are some loose rules. Take the pan size times two." She pointed at the twelve on the Dutch oven lid with her extra, long tongs. "So, twenty-four, right?" She poured the briquettes out of the briquette starter onto the metal table. "Put a third on the bottom and two-thirds on the top and you're ready to bake at approximately 350 degrees. Every fifteen minutes I turn the top a quarter to a half turn and the bottom a quarter to a half turn to keep the heat even. Halfway through baking I remove the pot from the coals on the bottom and let the top brown—nothing to it," she said, with a smile to the crowd gathered around to listen in on the free lesson.

"There's twenty-nine briquettes," Jael said matter-of-factly.

Kit just smiled and shrugged, "That's okay, my focus is about freedom and the community of cooking—the journey. Wind, weather and elevation affect the outcome. Things change and you adjust. Cooking is more art than science for me."

"How do you know when it is done?" A lady in a sun hat asked from behind the wall of people.

Kit smiled and said, "Of course, you don't want to peek at it all the time. I can usually smell when it is getting close. After twenty-five minutes or so, if I can smell it, I'll check to see if it is done in the middle."

"Why the tin foil lining?" another person asked.

"For easy clean up." She shrugged. "I'm on vacation here." She smiled again reaching for her tea. Cooking class was over.

Some of the people moved on. Others shifted their focus to the music being played.

Predictably, there were a fair amount of extras around at supper time. Abe called them strays. People longing to share in relationships. Halfway Homestead's policy was the same on the road, under the stars or on the grassy, oak covered knoll of the Homestead. Everyone was welcome to partake after returning thanks.

Zoe was tired. At midnight, she decided she could sleep, even if it meant on the ground, and bid everyone good night. Wyatt smiled at her. The low light made him look younger than he was, boyish and beautiful. She longed to have him to herself, but knew tonight wasn't the night for conversation.

In the tent she could clearly hear the music and conversation and made a mental note. The next time she came to a bluegrass festival, she would bring ear plugs. Much to her delight, a harp and a penny whistle showed up to the jam and played a song that seemed like it was from another time or at least another dimension.

~~~~~~~~~~~~~~~

"Ma-ma." The little girl's voice was distant but clear like it was carried by a breeze or a spirit being.

Zoe opened her eyes, but there was nothing to see except light. The light wasn't bright and shocking, but bright and soothing with no shadows, just light and the smell of rain.

"Ma-ma," the voice came again. "Come find me, Mama."

Zoe's heart quickened as the words she had longed to hear from a child's mouth sat easy on her ears. She tried to speak, but words wouldn't come.

Peering into fog she couldn't find a body to match the sweet voice, only light.

Maybe she was in the middle of the game of hide and seek. She ached to find the one who belonged to the voice but couldn't move. She grew anxious as the girl's giggles grew faint.

"Be still," another voice spoke.

She calmed. An overwhelming peace surrounded her.

"It's not time."

There was finality in the voice.

The light faded.

~~~~~~~~~~~~~~~~

Zoe smelled Abe's cowboy coffee and could hear voices talking low in the picking area. The sun had been up for a while and the tent was warm. She closed her eyes, trying to get back to where she had been only moments ago. But the land was swallowed up in the chasm of time and place or wherever dreams go to rest.

She sat up and looked around. Everyone was up except Jael and her. By the looks of the wet clothes that lay by her bed roll, Jael may have gone swimming, maybe even skinny dipping, in the wee hours of the morning. Zoe hoped Jael hadn't overstep her bounds last night. Jael had an edgy side that didn't want to stay squashed in memories. It was a reoccurring point in conversation between her and Abe. Zoe wondered how much longer Jael might be with them on the Homestead.

She struggled out of bed and found her toothbrush and a bottle of water. Brushing her teeth outside and spitting into a bush wasn't her first pick, but she was getting used to adapting to the new and uncomfortable.

Evelyn was always saying, "If you want to change, you must do someting you have never done, yah." Change was

180

part of her mantra and goals ... *beauty for ashes*, she thought as she slipped back into the tent.

~~~~~~~~~~~~~~~~

The girls spent most of the afternoon watching the shows at the big stage. Jael and Rayden went to learn how to clog. Wyatt found Zoe checking out pottery that was for sale.

"Hey there," he said, in her ear. "It looks different when you understand the process, doesn't it?"

"It does," Zoe turned and smiled, setting the mug down she had been holding.

"Want some ice cream?" He tipped his head and lifted one eyebrow. "Of course, you do. I'm buying." He grabbed her hand and led her to a large, wooden belt-driven ice cream freezer that made forty quarts at a time and sat in the shade of a covered wagon.

Wyatt paid for two large dishes of homemade vanilla. They strolled off toward the outer boundaries of the festival.

Her eyes got big when she took her first bite, "Mmm. It's not Kit's but it's pretty good."

"I've never met an ice cream I didn't like," he said, savoring his first bite.

They exited the festival.

"Where are you taking me?" she asked.

"Away," he said, with a wink.

Away sounded delightful to Zoe.

They soon came to a small creek flanked by hardwoods that reflected the once brilliant sunset making the banks of the creek and their faces glow in the warm light. There were two large stones next to each other. He helped her down on one.

"You look beautiful today," he said, before taking his place next to her on a vacant rock.

Zoe looked down at her long skirt and tank top, not typical for her. She thought about her face with no makeup. "Thank you," she said, returning his smile. She hoped her ice cream would cool her burning cheeks." Kit explained that

181

sometimes skirts were cooler at festivals. Today, cooler would be good."

"It looks like you have taken to festival life pretty easily." He stared at the water. "What do you think so far?"

She slipped out of her flip flops. "I love it. It is so relaxing and beautiful. There is no expectation of time. I love that."

She continued, "The people are so nice too. They're all so different. Some I would never hang out with, but they are beautiful people none the less. I'm challenged by this." She smiled to herself.

"And that's a good thing?" Wyatt was teasing but genuine.

Zoe studied his face for a long time, realizing he wasn't someone she would hang out with either. But she had grown very fond of him, his tattoos and dreadlocks.

"Yes," she said. "I'm being changed from the inside out." Unexpected tears fell in her lap. She glanced at Wyatt. "At least I hope I am. Some days, like today, my past seems so far away. Yet the shame of what I've done is always just under the surface, ready to spring out and remind me of who I really am." She wiped away a tear.

Wyatt threw a small stone in the water. "Wanna elaborate on that?" His voice was concerned.

This wasn't the light romantic conversation she had imagined. Since when did her expectations mirror reality? She let out a sigh.

~~~~~~~~~~~~~~~~

Darkness had stolen the last bit of sunset as her story ended. There was no moon. It was dark and quiet like nature was the courtroom and they were awaiting the verdict and the finality of the fall of the gavel. Judgment is never comfortable.

Wyatt was stretched out on the ground with his head resting on the rock where he had sat. "Not remind you, accuse you."

Zoe was confused by his statement.

"That's not who you are, it's choices you made once," he said, sitting up. His hand found hers in the darkness.

182

"If our poor choices become our identity, we may never change," his voice ached. "Is that what you really believe?"

"Not most days." Her bottom lip quivered.

Wyatt sighed. "A picture of the human condition: We will choose the loneliness of shame, over a victory when one is as close at hand as the other."

She felt a little better knowing she wasn't alone.

He stood and pulled her to her feet. His hands held her face. She could barely make out his face but knew he was looking into her eyes. "You know what you need?"

"More ice cream?" she asked, with a sniff and a giggle.

"Always." He looked away and then back at her. "You need to forgive yourself. You. Need. To. Forgive. Yourself." he said, again but slower. "And you need to stop the voice, that constant recording in your head, that accuses and tells you who you aren't. It's not speaking the truth."

"I know." Her voice was weak.

He hugged her close, trying to squeeze out the conflict he felt in his own soul. His feelings were strong for Zoe. He wanted so many things for her. He wanted to fix it for her but knew she wasn't his to fix. He wanted her in other ways too, but he knew he couldn't go there either. Sometimes it was hard to pastor when you need to be led as well. He prayed silently that God might make a way.

"How do you do that?" she asked slowly.

"It's hard at first, weird even," he said, pulling away some to let the moment pass and breathe. "The Bible calls it taking your thoughts captive." He let out the breath he had been holding. "I guess I can't say it any better than that." He chuckled.

She laid her head on his shoulder. Her breath felt good on his neck.

He continued. "When a thought comes into your head, like 'I'm worthless', you mentally pick it up and turn it over and ask yourself. 'Self? Is that the truth?' And if it isn't, throw it down and say, 'Nope! I'm not going to believe that.' Does that make sense?"

She looked up at him and nodded. They were still in the moment.

"Wyatt?"

"Yeah," he said.

"Will you baptize me?"

He picked her up and started toward the water. She let out a little scream when he kicked off his flip flops and waded into the water until he was waist deep.

"Right now?" he said, his smile wide.

As much as Zoe wanted to say yes, she thought of Abe and her sisters back at camp. She wanted to share this part of her journey with them too.

"Tomorrow," she sighed.

When Wyatt dropped her legs into the water, she screamed again, clinging to him.

"Yes," he said, his voice hoarse with emotion. "I would be honored to."

"I want Abe and the girls here with me."

Wyatt hugged her to himself as a tear fell silently onto his shirt. He sniffed. "It's hard not to show emotion when someone you love asks you to join them in announcing their rebirth."

"Someone you love?" Zoe's question was barely a breath.

"Yes. Someone I love and someone *He* loves. Remember? I trusted Him with you, and He showed Himself trustworthy." His kiss was soft and gentle.

Zoe didn't want it to stop when it did. She opened her eyes and let out her breath that had been caught in the moment and whispered, "I love you, too."

They hugged again.

"Precious words," Wyatt said, and fell into the water, taking Zoe with him.

Zoe squealed when they came up.

"Sorry. I needed to cool off," he said unapologetically. "We best make our way back to camp for supper, before ... " His voice trailed off. He didn't need to finish his thought. He squeezed her hand.

They both laughed knowing that was one statement which didn't need to be held up to the light of truth.

~~~~~~~~~~~~~~~~

Abe saw them coming at a distance, "What have y'all been into?"

Wyatt couldn't contain the news. "I have an announcement to make. Tomorrow at sunset, I will baptize Zoe in Chestnut Creek."

"Is that why you're wet?" Kit asked.

"Yes," Zoe answered. "We were practicing." She smiled and winked at Wyatt while hugging Kit.

The news was met with hugs all around. The air promised a musical celebration through the night. They changed and ate the leftover chicken ranch roll-ups.

Wyatt's eyes followed Zoe all evening, a fact not missed by Abe. To celebrate the moment, Abe played "Kentucky Waltz". Zoe yearned to dance with Wyatt like she had at the branding, but settled for a silent prayer of thanksgiving.

This trust stuff was getting easier.

~~~~~~~~~~~~~~~~

True to the predictions, Saturday showed itself cool and rainy. The deluge started about eight in the morning, complete with thunder and lightning.

The girls watched the water pool on the roof of the tent.

"This is why I prefer room service to camping," Zoe said, with a half-hearted laugh.

Jael sprang from her bed and lifted the sags in the tent where the pools had been, encouraging the water to move on. The tent started leaking in the places she had touched. Her fingers had somehow broken through the invisible seal that kept the water from coming in. At that point there was no stopping it. The dam had broken. The water pooled on the tent floor where Zoe and Kit's bedrolls were.

The girls scrambled to keep bedding and clothing dry. There was no hiding from the storm. Aggravated with Jael and the lack of dry clothes to slip into, the girls soon found themselves outside their tent.

Abe chuckled to himself at their discomfort and didn't bother looking up at the emerging mess until they were all out of the tent in various forms of disarray. "Well good morning, Glories," he said, while looking out the top of his eyes. "Coffee?"

The girls started toward the coffee pot, sloshing through the river of water that now ran through camp.

"I hate camping," Jael said.

"I can tell," Abe said. "Y'er not very good at it. You made a rookie mistake by touchin' the tent."

Jael glared at him. "You made a rookie mistake by not water proofing. Why doesn't our tent have a rain fly anyway?"

Abe shrugged, amused.

"How are we going to dry all this out anyway?" Jael asked.

"Whelp," Abe started. "We'll wait until the rain stops and send a few of you to the laundromat to dry out the clothin'. Since laundry duty is usually Rayden's responsibility, we'll send you and Miss Zoe." Abe's words always carried finality with them.

"I've got to cook breakfast," Kit said.

Abe stood up from his chair and handed her a dry blanket. "I'll cook my famous breakfast casserole. You just sit tight. We will eat, let this rain play out some and the rest of us will take care of drainin' the water outta the tent while they dry out the contents."

There was a bright flash and a loud clap of thunder as if to emphasize his point. The conversation was over before breakfast was started.

Abe lived fully in any moment. Cooking breakfast in the rain was no exception. He sang another silly song as he checked the coals: "The Biscuit Song".

Wyatt appeared from their tent, unphased by the rain, singing the high tenor part of the song. When the song was over the two exchanged a quick brotherly hug and morning pleasantries.

"Ole' Pee-Duub," Abe drawled. "You gonna get in on cookin' breakfast this mornin'?"

"It looks like I better," he said, kidding his friend, "if you want it to be good." Wyatt smiled over his shoulder while pouring coffee.

There was more thunder, further away.

"Storms 'bout played itself out," Abe said, looking into the sea of campers.

"Yep. Perfect day for a baptism," Wyatt said. "So, what are we doing here?" He turned his attention to the mess Abe was making.

"We gonna make my famous breakfast casserole. Hashbrowns on the bottom, then sausage, then gravy, eggs and cheese, topped with biscuits. Ummm-mmm mighty fine. Yes, sir."

They exchanged a smile.

"So, you the egg man. Crack about a dozen or so, and add a cuppa milk to make 'em fluffy. I'll get to work on heatin' the ovens and gettin' the biscuits ready to go in."

The guys worked while the girls scrounged dry blankets to cover up with. They hugged their coffee mugs, to keep the warmth from escaping.

"Are you going to stack the ovens?" Wyatt asked.

"Yeah, we'll stack 'em to save on coals. Abe explained.

Wyatt watched while beating the eggs with a fork.

"I'm gonna use liners to make clean up easier." Abe shrugged. "When there's music to play, don't need to be scrubbin' pots." He chuckled to himself.

"Miss Kit made up the sausage and gravy ahead of time. Takes all the mess out of it that way."

"Are you gonna stir up some biscuits, my friend?" Wyatt asked.

"No, we gonna use these whomp 'em biscuits." Abe held up two tubes of biscuits.

"Whomp 'em, biscuits, huh?" Wyatt shook his head smiling.

"Yeah, 'cause you whomp 'em on the counter to open 'em." Abe demonstrated and everyone laughed. "We'll have casserole with biscuits on top in one and just biscuits in the other."

"Why so many biscuits?" Rayden asked, from inside her quilt tent.

"'Cause biscuits make the world go 'round," Abe answered. "I gotta have at least one soaked up in the

187

casserole and some more to sop up butter 'n honey. Never have too many biscuits. No, sir."

Abe was busy layering his concoction when the sun baked away the clouds. The girls found a few pieces of clothing that weren't wet from the rain and decided a shower would go a long way in making them feel better. They gathered up their stuff and headed off to a neighboring camp to ask to borrow their outdoor shower.

"When will breakfast be ready, Abe?" Zoe asked.

"'Bout an hour, child. You gonna wash away that swampy smell you sportin' this mornin'?"

Zoe smelled herself, a little embarrassed by her findings. "Yeah, swimming in the creek last night left me a little musty this morning."

Wyatt smiled to himself.

"You gonna be back in that creek come this evenin'. No sense in showerin' twice. You have enough money to pay 'em folks for showerin' twice?" Abe loved to tease.

Zoe had kept walking with the girls and said over her shoulder, "Nope. I'll just invite them to breakfast."

Abe smiled while stacking the ovens, now full. His daughter was coming into herself. "Ummm hummm. She's learnin'. We best put on another pot of coffee, sound like we gonna have some more cump-ny." He winked at his cooking partner.

"There now." Abe stepped back surveying the stove. We'll rotate the lids and ovens ever so often, to keep them from getting hotspots.

"It's time to drain the bathtub."

"What bathtub?" Wyatt inquired.

"That one they call a tent." He pointed to the girls' tent. "Have you looked in there? It's a foot deep on that low end. It may leak from the top but the bottom is pretty well water tight." Abe chuckled.

"How do you plan to do that?" Wyatt asked.

Abe's eyes twinkled, "You gotta knife?"

Wyatt nodded pulling a knife from his pocket, he opened it with one hand and handed it to Abe.

Abe sloshed over the myriad of clothes and bedding to the deep end of the pool where the water had collected along with a healthy amount of leaves and grass clippings. "No need goin' to the creek to baptize Miss Zoe, P-Dub. They's plenty of water in here to do the job. Yes, sir," he said, shaking his head. He stabbed the knife into the floor of the tent four times and watched it literally drain like a bathtub, leaves swirling in the drain and all.

"Sometimes the biggest calamites in life makes the best memories." Abe smiled at his young friend and handed his knife back. "How 'bout some 'Whiskey 'Fore Breakfast'?"

Wyatt said, "I'll drink to that," and went to get his guitar and Abe's fiddle.

~~~~~~~~~~~~~~~~~

He watched through the window of Evelyn's studio as she placed the clay onto the wheel and wet her hands in the bucket before her. Sinatra was wailing in the background.

He knew the guys from the church wouldn't return until evening.

She turned the wheel on full speed to wedge the clay on the wheel.

He hated Rayden and hated those who protected her and everything they stood for.

Evelyn closed her eyes. Her left hand was stone still, unwavering, while her right hand pressed down. "Hard pressed on every side," her spirit sang. The clay came into perfect center.

Because you love me ... a voice whispered to her spirit.

She answered finishing the quote in an airy voice inaudible to human ears, "You will rescue me ... "

She opened her eyes and slowed the wheel.

He was no longer afraid of the light. All unbelievers must die. She must die. He grasped the knife firmly and slowly turned the knob on the door.

"Open now," she whispered, to her creation as her thumbs opened the clay as she pressed down.

The door opened behind her. A rough looking man from the church entered. Evelyn knew him as Brother John.

"Miss Evelyn, I forgot to tell you this morning I got a message from Pastor Wyatt. He plans to baptize Miss Zoe tonight at the festival down in the creek, there. I'd be happy to take you down if you would like to go."

The man let the knob rest back at center.

"Yah. When?"

The deacon said, "Well, Miss Evelyn, I was thinking now. It will take us a few hours to drive down there."

The conversation was hard to hear from the other side of the door, but the man listened intently. It sounded like the reckoning would have to wait another day. Perhaps the all-knowing, all compassionate would deliver more to kill. He must be patient.

Evelyn smiled like a child. "Almost ready," she said, focusing on her pot.

The kind man smiled. With Evelyn that could mean five minutes or five hours. He settled into a chair not wanting to interrupt the master.

~~~~~~~~~~~~~~~

The day passed quickly with the hullabaloo of trying to dry out everything. Creation itself seemed an anomaly, mirroring the humans that inhabited it. Jael was in a foul mood, hell-bent on ruining Zoe's baptism day. The sun beat back the clouds just in time for breakfast, making the hot air heavy. Then a cool wind came up suddenly, making the sky roll dark and angry.

Jael's words at the laundromat earlier kept ringing in Zoe's ears.

You think getting dunked in the creek will make your boyfriend more into you? Not! Water can't change who you are. It will just make you wet ... like your dreams.

The words were cutting enough. But it was the high pitch of her evil laugh that turned her warming feelings for Jael cold like the stone that covers sleeping souls. Zoe hated everything Jael stood for. She knew her reaction wasn't the right one, but she couldn't focus on anything but her anger.

~~~~~~~~~~~~~~~~

The time had almost come. The sun had surely begun its descent but they couldn't tell because of the light rain that had settled in. Miss Evelyn hadn't made her appearance yet, so they waited at the camp. Jael, not surprisingly, was M.I.A. as well. They would walk down to the creek together when Evelyn got there.

Zoe was conflicted as she waited. Wyatt was the first to break the silence.

"Everything okay, Zoe?" his voice concerned.

She wanted to be alone with him to discuss her feelings. But everyone here was family and knew her secrets. "I'm just so torn. Jael said some hateful things today. Maybe I should wait to do this."

"Were they true?" Wyatt asked.

Zoe remembered their conversation the night before. "I don't think so," she whispered. "It's just, I don't understand the hate Jael insists on spreading—not just today, but every day. It's like she wants everyone to accompany her in her hopeless hell."

Wyatt picked up where Zoe left off staring into the coals that were keeping the coffee hot. "Reality is, she is an addict like the rest of us, only active. She is actively addicted to the chaos of her past. She chooses daily to live in the torment of her past abandonment and abuse, like she deserves nothing better. The familiar chains of self-loathing are her high. Her drug of choice is the brokenness she sees on other's faces. These embittered endorphins course through her in dark orgasmic waves. No need to put gates on hell, when it's her choice to live in a crypt of self-pity martyrdom."

The words hung heavy in the thick air. The rained stopped as if to hear the next thought.

He continued, "Yes, sister, you are right. The words she speaks aren't steeped in truth, even if they seem true to her."

191

Abe studied Zoe. Kit and Rayden sat with their eyes downturned, their hearts heavy.

A breeze moved the stagnant air.

"Miss Zoe, if I may." Abe looked to Wyatt as if to ask permission to interrupt.

Wyatt nodded.

"You may wait, if you want. They's no pressure or expectation on this day—just a possible announcement about one's belief. That is all—nothing more. The day doesn't seem perfect to you because it's been filled with chaos: chaos in the weather, chaos in your emotions and chaos in relationships. A sad comedy of errors, indeed. Yes, sir." His face was old and tired.

The breeze picked up.

"Child, you hear me when I say they's no better day than today to stand. And say to the darkness in the clouds, 'y'er storm cannot dissolve my hope'. And to the accuser, 'y'er lies will not change the truth'. And to y'er past, 'y'er failures will not infringe on my freedom'. The war was won over two-thousand years ago, Miss Zoe. You just announcin' y'er claim on y'er inherent victory through Christ. Tell me. Who waits to claim victory?"

"Not me," Zoe said finally, through tears. "Not today."

An old car rumbled to a stop outside their camp bringing with it a peek of sunshine and Miss Evelyn who was perpetually late.

She opened the door, amused as if holding a joke for the right moment. "Let's all go down to the river … " she sang, holding her hands up in praise, or for some help out of the car that lacked air conditioning—but not personality. Wyatt and Abe obliged.

Zoe let out a sigh. Miss Evelyn was a breeze that carried the secret intercession of life, giggles, spontaneity and praise. It seemed she only accepted the "goot" things and dismissed the bad. How she longed to live her life in a fearless freedom like that.

The procession began in the warm air. The sun made the earth glow and the colors on the trees were vivid greens, not common in this world. Its beams pierced the dark clouds; in not a warning but a statement that light never runs from darkness.

Strangers joined the parade with their offerings of music, well wishes, voices in song or a dance from giggly girls who couldn't help themselves. Young boys nervously followed the girls.

Abe was right, Zoe thought, as always. This was the perfect day—perfectly imperfect.

Pastor Wyatt waded into the creek. He looked at the patchwork of people who had gathered and smiled an easy smile. "Wow! Isn't this a beautiful setting?"

The crowd answered in various ways.

"We are here simply to announce in a traditional way that today we have people who choose life over death. They will bury the ways of their old life in the waters of baptism and rise a new creation in Christ. Zoe ... " He held out his hand to summon her.

She came into the water, arm in arm with Abe. He was her mentor and father figure when she needed one so desperately.

Abe turned her so Wyatt was on one side and he was on the other.

Wyatt continued, "State your name."

"Zoelander Renee Dempsey," she said, voice wavering.

"Zoelander Renee Dempsey, do you believe Jesus is the Son of God?"

"Yes."

"Do you believe He died to pay for our sins and rose to life on the third day?"

"Yes."

"Do you accept Him as your Lord and Savior?"

"I do."

Wyatt smiled at the choice of words. "Is there anything you would like to say?"

Zoe's eyes were wide and wild-looking as she looked to Abe. He nodded. She wished she could remember what Abe had said earlier. It was exactly how she felt, but his words escaped her.

"I just want to say," her voice somewhat weak. "I've lived in fear much too long." Her bottom lip quivered. "And the only way to overcome that, as I see it, is to give that to Jesus and … " she sniffed, "and live in His fearless freedom."

"Amen, Yah!" Evelyn hollered in support.

Zoe couldn't help but laugh. "That's all," she whispered, while blinking back tears.

Wyatt whispered back, "That's enough." He gave her hand a squeeze.

"Yes, sir," Abe echoed.

"We baptize you in the name of the Father, Son and the Holy Ghost."

Abe and Wyatt lowered her into the water and brought her back up. Wyatt hugged her first and then Abe.

Abe hugged her closer than usual, "Where demons dance and angels sing. Yes, sir." He whispered in her ear and kissed her on top of her head.

Rayden met her in the water to give her a hug.

Evelyn met her at the water's edge patting her face with one hand and holding her hand with the other. "My goot girl. I am well pleased." Tears of joy filled the old woman's eyes and creases.

Evelyn turned at the commotion in the water.

Rayden was now standing between Abe and Wyatt. She wanted to be baptized too.

"State your name," Wyatt began again.

"Rayden Alima Alexander," she said.

He went through the questions one by one with her as he had with Zoe.

"Do you have anything else to say?" Wyatt asked.

Her voice was strong and unshakable, "Today, I will no longer be held captive by the lies of an ideology, but live free in truth and love." She nodded as if to emphasize her point.

Evelyn again burst into praise at the water's edge. "This is my girl! Praise the Lort!" Clapping again.

Wyatt and Abe lowered her into the water and again Wyatt hugged her first.

"Welcome to the family, my brazen sister," he said.

Abe took his turn at hugging as well, "Another daughter comes home. Welcome, child," the old man said.

Evelyn waded into the water, "Goot, goot girl. May the Lort bless you," she squeaked.

"Anyone else?" Wyatt asked.

There were a few others that took the opportunity to be baptized that evening until the sky subdued its color. Afterwards they stood on the banks of that small creek in various forms of dryness with their heads bowed in prayer.

Abe's booming voice put an exclamation in the evening.

"Father, we thank You for the additions to Y'er family. Another few sittin' at Y'er table. Y'er gracious, Lord and we honor you today with the tradition of baptism and the redemptive story of Y'er Son's sacrifice. We ask for Y'er blessings on these lives in Jesus name! Amen."

The crowd echoed his amen.

"Ya'll are welcome to join us at our camp for dinner and music."

Kit made her way to Abe's side. "I hope we have enough," she said, hugging Abe's side as they walked back to camp.

"I bet they'll be just enough," he said, looking ahead.

~~~~~~~~~~~~~~~~

Zoe felt like she had come full circle. She was graduating today, not away from the Homestead but into her purpose—whatever that might look like. Ironically, the menu was the same as it was Zoe's first night at the Homestead: beef stew. homemade bread, oatmeal cake and cowboy coffee; only with one addition … wine.

Evelyn insisted on having communion before dinner. She literally broke the bread and passed it around so everyone could retrieve a piece for themselves. The wine followed. Drinking straight out of the bottle after Evelyn could be a little unnerving but tonight people didn't seem to mind.

Wyatt was amused by this. He turned to John who had driven Evelyn to the festivities. "You bring the wine with you?" he asked, before tipping the bottle up and passing it to his friend.

John smiled widely. "Yeah. She insisted."

"So, you're a bootlegger now," Wyatt said, tossing a piece of bread in his mouth.

John took a sip of wine and followed it with bread while he formulated his answer. "I 'spose so," he drawled. "Just add it to the list of things I've been forgiven for … "

"Amen!" Wyatt said.

From the shadows she watched like a banished child driven from her tribe. A voice told her she didn't belong—would never belong.

She believed it.

Flames from fire cast unique shadows. There was no shadow as unique as the one that fell across her face from her place in the dark. A perfect cross from forehead to throat and temple to temple. It was to that darkness the voice of the Spirit spoke of freedom, but her heart was deaf to its call.

Abe was sure his wandering child was watching from the night. He stared into the chasm where he thought she might be and whispered, "Where demons dance … " He turned his sad eyes to his fiddle and played the most sorrowful tune.

The crowd hushed while the old man poured himself into the strings allowing his own offering to waft up into the stars and beyond to their Maker—the Maker of all lonely pilgrims.

Zoe stood near Wyatt. Their eyes locked for a moment and then focused on Abe. His hand found hers and pulled her into his side.

"What's he doing?" she asked, into his dreadlocks.

"Interceding," he barely spoke. "Sweet Hour of Prayer."

11

Fishin' for Whales

Your time as a caterpillar has expired. Your wings are ready.
Unknown

September

The leaves weren't the only thing turning in the Shenandoah Valley. The cooler weather awakened the earth and its inhabitants to the possibility of revision. In the cellar, some of the cider had turned hard or to vinegar. Not the original plan, but still usable. Out in the pasture, monarch caterpillars hung their chrysalises from milkweeds in anticipation of morphing and the first flight that would take them to worlds unknown. By design, lives at Halfway Homestead were in the state of perpetual alteration, echoing the changes found in nature.

Abe pondered these things as he sat on the back of his horse watching a monarch unfold its wings for the first time, expanding them to dry in the sunlight. He enjoyed nature's show every year in early fall and made it a point to take the time to watch the creature lower and raise its wings before taking flight. His spirit told him by this time next year things at the Homestead may be radically different.

As he rode back toward the barn, a butterfly landed on the mane of his horse, hitching a ride. He thought of the journey that lay ahead for the fragile beast. It had purpose prewired in its genes. For as natural as it is for a butterfly to migrate, fulfilling its purpose sure seemed beyond most humans. Only a human blessed or cursed with free will would go against the Creator. He wondered which girls would denounce their pride and ride the winds of humility to go the way of the butterfly.

Abe stopped before riding out from the cover of the trees, something he did instinctively since his Army days. He surveyed the land. Everything seemed in order, almost too much order, if that's possible. The hitchhiking Monarch grew impatient with the over watch and lifted to eye level, as if to say "thanks for the lift". Then it was off to find its like kind and a strong tailwind to push south on to its destiny. Abe smiled at this. For years he had witnessed orphaned purposes, long ignored, become adopted and nurtured, maturing into merciful miracles. Where an old soul was laid to rest over time, a healed spirit replaced it. He believed in the process even if it wasn't perfect.

He watched the butterfly until it was gone, wondering if it would make it. Only God knew. "Vaya con Dios," he said, a salute to its vapor trail. He leaned forward in his saddle, a clue to his horse it was time to move on and embrace whatever changes were coming.

~~~~~~~~~~~~~~~~

Miss Evelyn was in some kind of a mood. Reggae music was the choice of the day. She was sporting a tiered, ruffled skirt in a red plaid with a matching shirt and head scarf. Her outfit was obviously something she had picked up on a mission trip to the Caribbean years prior.

The years had taken away the knowledge of how to correctly tie the head scarf in a traditional sense, but that didn't matter to Evelyn. She tied it like her mother had tied a babushka, a bohemian head scarf from the old country—under her chin. The result was a comical and whimsical marrying of two vastly different cultures.

She had the windows of her studio thrown wide open. The music and wind were free to sweep people and papers to and fro as it wished. Jael and Pastor Wyatt were dancing in a line, grooving forward and back to the music.

Rayden, Kit and Zoe looked on amused.

"I can't wait to get old and wear costumes without having to explain myself," Kit said.

"Well, lucky for you, you'll probably inherit her most extravagant collection when she dies," Rayden said, ribbing her with her elbow.

The song ended with a group hug and face pats from Evelyn. "Okay artists, gather' round, gather 'round, gather 'round." Her arms were outstretched with her hands twisting inward in repetitive circular motions, making the loose skin on her arms wave back and forth. The scene may have seemed grotesque to some. To those who knew her, it was the carefree, childlike exuberance in her own skin (as ill-fitting as it was) that they loved and admired about Evelyn.

"The kilns are firing, that is why it is hot, yah. Your creations before you on the table have been bisque fired and are now ready to be waxed and glazed.

"You will learn how to pour or dip your pieces in glaze. I will fire them again before you return next time. But first, we wax." Her attention turned to a recycled container with a liquid wax in it. She picked up a small worn paint brush and painted the bottom of a bowl with the wax.

"We put wax where we want no glaze. No glaze on the bottom or it will stick in the kiln and ruin your piece. No glaze up a ways on bottom to stop the movement of glaze, yah. Remember my lines?" Her eyes shot open and looked around to get everyone's attention and she repeated herself to make her point.

"Remember my lines? Lines are goot, yah. They give the eye and the glaze a place to stop."

She went higher on the piece and painted a band an inch wide around the bowl just above the midline.

Rayden was perplexed by this, "Miss Evelyn, why would you put wax there? Isn't that where you want your glaze?"

"Nah," Evelyn said, with a slight shrug. "That's where *you* want glaze." Evelyn pointed to Rayden. "Evelyn doesn't want glaze there."

Everyone giggled at her response.

"Evelyn wants to feel da clay. Eart!" She hit the table with her fist, causing some of the wax to drip on the table.

"Eart'!" She said again. "All that wax will melt away leaving me with eart'. Evelyn is an artist and it's important for

199

her to feel the eart'. Evelyn is from dust, works with dust, is going back to dust—wants to feel dust. If Rayten wants to feel glaze, then glaze. Evelyn wants to feel life and texture. This piece, wants to breathe. You," she pointed at the group with an open hand, "You create and let dry."

She turned, waved her hand as if tossing a tissue over her shoulder and walked away from the demonstration table to find her hot tea and a chair. Her students got busy on their projects. She rocked and slurped and let the fall breeze blow past her.

Jael watched her old friend, her dancing partner, as she called her. Out of all the people at Halfway Homestead Evelyn meant the most to her. Rayden meant a lot to her too, but her feelings for her were conceived from a different place. Jael admired Evelyn's unabashed freedom. It was like she was baptized in it, fully submersed. No physical, mental or spiritual limitations on this earth could hold her in their prison. She was truly free. Jael was drawn to that. She longed for it more than anything in the world but it eluded her around every bend. To her credit though, she tried to stay close to what or who she thought of as the source, hoping to at least acquire some by osmosis.

"Miss Evelyn?" She approached the old woman like a child. "What are you drinking today?"

"Mullein tea," she answered, rocking.

"Mullein tea, I've never heard of that before. Is it something we grow in the garden?"

"Got's garden, yah. It's wile't. You gather in the summer and dry. Steep in winter when you can't cough up gunk." She tapped her chest and made the motion of something coming up from her stomach.

She leaned forward and put her forehead on Jael's. "But strain it first, through an old t-shirt or someting. It has the prickles in it. You don't want the prickles, nah." She shook her head and looked back out the window.

Jael had noticed her nagging, dry cough as of late. "Is it helping?"

The old woman shrugged. The conversation was over.

Jael went back to the table and Evelyn followed.

Evelyn rolled two five-gallon buckets on rollers over to the group and handed a whisk to Kit and Zoe and pointed to the buckets. "We will glaze now," she announced. "But first we mix." She nodded at the girls.

Wyatt helped the girls remove the lids while Evelyn lectured and they mixed.

"The color needs to be suspended to glaze." She stood on one foot, her other suspended in the air. Her arms outstretched like a scarecrow. Her best impersonation of the word suspended. "This is a chemical reaction, yah. The color you see, isn't what you'll end up with. So pay attention to the samples, yah. Or you could end up with an ugly color. We fire to cone eight. Cone eight is what we fire to."

"What's that mean, Miss Evelyn, cone eight?" Rayden was taking notes.

"Very hot. Dishwasher, microwave and oven safe, yah. Stoneware—stoneware pot'try," she said.

"Will it be hot when I take it out of the microwave?" Rayden asked.

"Nah, shouldn't be. This is durable, useable eart'. Form to follow function, yah. Foundation first and then beauty." She thought for a moment and continued, "From ashes to beauty, yah." She smiled showing her few teeth and winked at her students.

"First we pour." She picked up a spouted measuring cup and dipped it into the glaze. She then poured the glaze into the bowl to the rim and turned the bowl as she poured out the glaze turning it to coat the rim, to keep it from running down the side.

"And now we wait until that dries. Not long," she sang, "not long." She had time to dance with Wyatt while they waited for the glaze to set.

"And now we dip," she said, showing the group her two index fingers that went into the bowl and pressed against the sides so she could pick it up and dip it into the second bucket of glaze.

"Blot off any extra that has stayed on the bottom with a wet sponge and set on this shelf. It is ready for Melvin."

"Okay." She clapped her hands together. "It's time for color."

After class, Wyatt pulled Zoe aside.

"Hey you! Are you busy Saturday?"

"Depends." She smiled, teasing.

"It's supposed to be nice this weekend. John said I could borrow his motorcycle and take you on a picnic."

"Question: Is his motorcycle in better shape than his car?"

Wyatt laughed, "Yes, much nicer. It's his baby."

"Then yes." Zoe smiled. "Where are you taking me?"

"It's a surprise. Wear leather!" He winked, kissed her briefly on the cheek and got into his pickup to go.

~~~~~~~~~~~~~~~

Saturday was nice indeed, warmer than it had been but still had a bite to the air that whispered autumn was there to stay. Rayden had come to Zoe's rescue more than once while living on the Homestead. By some miracle or special knack, she produced a simple black biker's jacket complete with zippers and buckles in her size. Rayden also came up with a newer pair of designer jeans, a simple white t-shirt, some cowboy boots and a navy bandana for her hair. Rayden had reasoned Zoe would want to braid her hair and wear a bandana skull cap to keep her hair from being blown by the wind or messed up by a helmet. She was thoughtful that way.

Zoe got up early to get the chores done and get ready for her day with Wyatt. She felt a little like Evelyn donning a costume, that on a normal day would be ridiculous. The masquerade added to the mystique of where they were going and what they might be doing. He arrived at nine dressed in similar fashion.

He laughed out loud when he saw what she was wearing. "You're dressed perfectly," he said, looking her up and down before kissing her on cheek. "Are you ready?"

Zoe nodded. "Where are you taking me?"

"Away," he said, handing her a helmet. "Here, put this on. It has a headset in it so we can talk to each other."

He put his helmet on and checked hers before mounting the bike and helping her on. "This is Painted Reverend to Cowgirl. Do you copy?"

Zoe laughed at their biker names, "Awww, I was hoping to be Pepper," she said, into the microphone.

His shoulders slumped, the face of his helmet pointing into the heavens. He started the bike and said, "Okay, this is Painted Rev to Pepper, copy?" He said with joking frustration.

"Roger, Rev. You've got Pepper," she answered with a giggle. "Why is it when people use a CB or headsets they suddenly talk like a trucker?"

"Roger that, Pepper! Five-five-two-two c'mon," he said, as he pulled out of the drive and headed to the main highway.

"Five-five-two-two. What's that even mean?" she asked.

"Ten-four," he said, dryly with a laugh and picked up substantial speed.

"I should've guessed that," she said. "Where did you say we were going?"

"I didn't. Just sit back and enjoy the ride. We should be there in a couple of hours, give 'er take."

"A couple hours? Can I at least have a hint?" she asked.

"Fishin' for whales," he said finally.

"Are we going to the ocean?" she asked.

No answer.

"Is this thing on?" she asked.

Still no answer.

"Fishin' for whales. Roger that," she said, with a dramatic sigh and settled in for the long ride. She loved how Wyatt could make an everyday thing a mystery and wondered what in the world a hint like that could mean.

Wyatt smiled to himself.

~~~~~~~~~~~~~~~~

They pulled off the highway and parked near an old covered bridge. It felt good to get off the motorcycle and stretch their legs.

"Wow this is beautiful," she said, handing Wyatt her helmet.

"Humpback Bridge," he said, with a shrug holding his palms out. "Get it? It's the oldest covered bridge in Virginia. Have you ever been here?"

Zoe was taking in the whole scene. "It's been a long time," she said. "Like when I was a kid. It's so ... I don't know, enchanted here. Wow!"

Wyatt scooped her hand up in his and led her toward the bridge. "Enchanted, huh? Let's walk a while and find a nice place to picnic."

They explored the bridge and its rich history for the better part of an hour until their stomachs were ready for lunch.

Wyatt unwrapped the cheeses and meats he brought and laid them out with the crackers and gourmet olives. He smiled as she removed her boots and socks and lay back on the blanket. Her sexy feet were just a small fraction of what he loved about her.

A forked stick was stuck in the earth near their blanket.

Wyatt broke a small limb from the tree and tied a cord to it. Digging in his pocket he found a bobber he attached to it. Pilfering through his pockets he produced a washer looking weight, which he ran the cord through and tied it to the end.

Zoe leaned up on her arm and watched as he finished. "What are you doing?" she asked, with a big smile.

"Fishin' for whales." He smiled at her and checked his knots at both ends.

"What are you using for bait?" she teased.

"It's a secret." He flashed another smile.

"A secret? It looks like a piece of clay from Miss Evelyn's class," she said, lying down.

"Something like that," he said, as he carefully flipped the bait into the water and set the fishing pole on the forked stick stuck into the bank.

The water was clear allowing them to see the rocks on the bottom that made the water ripple in places.

Wyatt settled down opposite of Zoe on the blanket. He said a simple blessing over the food and opened his water to take a long drink. They talked about everything and nothing while they ate, each enjoying the other's company.

Wyatt took out his pocket knife and cut up an apple.

"Is that clean?" Zoe asked, taking a piece he offered.

"Of course not. I don't remember what I cut with it last, probably catfish bait or something." He smiled and blew into the knife and a piece of blue lint flew out and landed on the blanket. "I hear lint is a great disinfectant. Kills ninety-nine percent of the germs." He cut another piece and handed it to Zoe.

They finished the apple and Wyatt sat up quickly. "Did you see that?"

Zoe sat up quickly too.

"I think you have a bite!" he said seriously.

Zoe giggled at his antics. She got up and picked up the makeshift pole and acted like it had a big fish on it and then like the big one got away. Wyatt leaned against his hands. His blue eyes sparkled in a teasing way, "After a fight like that, you better check your bait."

She gave in to his request pulling the line from the water and looked strangely at the end of the line. Swinging it towards herself, she caught the weighted end. The "weight" was an antique silver ring with simple yet ornate carved holes that held a small diamond.

As she held the ring in her hands Wyatt eased up behind her wrapping his arms around her body and drew her back into himself. Zoe's heart was beating fast and her breathing was shallow. He held her there for a moment before he whispered in her ear.

"I love you, Zoe … "

Hearing him say her name made her feel weak.

He turned her around and got down on one knee. And continued, "I loved you when you were broken, scared and dying to your old life. I love you now, stronger and more vibrant, beginning your new life. I'll love you when our lives here on earth are dimmed and give way to eternity.

"I want you to serve with me in ministry, be my other half, and fill the spaces in my life I can't. Zoe, will you fish for whales with me, sit beside me in the boat through the storms of life, help me bait the hook and wait with me through the monotony of everyday to see what we'll catch?

"It's the ultimate fishing adventure. Fishing for whales on a cane pole and hollering' for Jesus to bring the net when you hook into a big one. I just need someone to share it with."

He looked up at her, their hands intertwined and asked, "Is that someone you?"

Zoe looked down at the ring still tied onto the pole and up at Wyatt. *Sometimes you have to humble yourself, trade fear for trust and say yes to the unknown,* she thought.

"Yes," she said, with fresh tears streaming from her eyes nodding. "I believe it is."

"Thought so," he said. He stood and cradled her head in his hands and kissed her passionately on the lips.

Wyatt dug his pocket knife out of his pocket. He cut the ring from the cord and placed it on her finger.

~~~~~~~~~~~~~~~~

They walked back toward the beginning of a new adventure, hand in hand carrying the remains of their picnic.

An old man in ragged clothes sat near the entrance of the bridge on a stone retaining wall. All of his worldly possessions slumped in an old sea bag behind him.

Wyatt nodded at the old man while he looked them up and down settling on the makeshift pole.

"Catch anythin'?" the old man slurred.

"You wouldn't believe it if I told you, man." Wyatt smiled easily.

"Yeah … " the transient said. "Try me."

"A keeper," Wyatt teased. "On my first cast, even."

"Well, I'll be." The bent guy looked at the water on its journey, spit into his warbled reflection and glanced back at the pole.

"You wanna have a go?" Wyatt said, propping the pole beside the old man along with the remains of their picnic.

"Why, shore!" His dark eyes lit up as he promptly dropped the naked line into the water. "What do I do if I hook into one?"

206

"That's the best part, brother," Wyatt said, over his shoulder. "Holler for the net."

"Yap!" the homeless man said, to the couple around a mouth full of food.

~~~~~~~~~~~~~~~~~

"How do you do that?" Zoe whispered.

"Do what?" Wyatt said.

Zoe nodded toward the lonely old man. "That."

Wyatt shrugged and came close for a kiss. "I'll show ya."

"I'm looking forward to that!" She kissed him back lingering for much longer than usual.

He started the bike. "Pepper this here is the Painted Rev. Do you copy?"

"Ten-four, Rev" she said, as they turned toward the highway. She pressed her body into his with her hands in his jacket pockets, thinking about what had just happened. The proposal was so … Wyatt. She couldn't put it into words.

"Wyatt?" she said softly.

"Yeah."

"Whatever gave you the idea to fish for whales?"

He waited a while before responding.

"Willie Nelson," he said.

"Willie Nelson?"

"Yeah. You know that song—'Hands on the Wheel?' "

"No. I guess I don't."

"I'll sing it for you sometime."

"Willie Nelson, huh?"

"Yeah," he said, with a snicker.

They drove on.

~~~~~~~~~~~~~~~~~

They were getting closer to home and she was looking down at the ring.

"Wyatt?"

"Yeah."

"It's beautiful!"

"You're beautiful!"

"Is it an antique?"

"Yeah."

"A family heirloom?"

"You could say that." He was being aloof.

"Where did you get it?"

"Evelyn gave it to me," he said softly.

"Really? Evelyn?" She was perplexed.

"It was her grandmother's. She wanted it to stay in the family. Said it was 'from the old country, yah.'" His impression was a dead ringer for the old woman they had grown to love.

"But you're not related."

"To be a part of Evelyn's family, you don't have to be blood kin, just adopted."

"Does that mean we will inherit her millions." Zoe chuckled.

"Oh, I'm sure," Wyatt said sarcastically. "'Course with wealth untold, prolly comes the Homestead, too. Are you up for running a halfway house?"

Zoe smiled at the thought and at the strange, but lovely turn of events in her life. She let out a long breath. Marriage 2.0, a former addict and con, a cowgirl and soon a pastor's wife.

"Am I up for the challenge?" she said aloud. "Probably not!

"I'm going to have to call for the net."

"Amen," Wyatt said, and drove on in silence.

~~~~~~~~~~~~~~~~

The cellar was dank and cold but he couldn't feel it. He was numb to anything that this world offered. He looked ahead to paradise and what awaited him there. "Grant me the patience to carry out your will," he whispered to the dark, as he peered through the crack that the warped cellar door had left.

~~~~~~~~~~~~~~~~

Evelyn sat at the wheel, chewing her cud like old people do, deep in thought or prayer—which for Evelyn was basically the same thing. Since hearing of the possibility of a store, she had been busy throwing bowls, cups, vases, tea pots and whatever else she could sell. Her offering to the venture.

Shep lay in front of the studio door. He was restless today, lifting his head and growling more than once, unable to settle into the deep sleeps he usually did. Evelyn ignored him.

~~~~~~~~~~~~~~~~~

The window in Abe's luthier shop brought in smells of fall. On any other day it would have mixed with the essence from Abe's pipe and the smell of wood and made a delicious combination, but not today. Instead the air coagulated and refused to mix as if nature was proclaiming a warning to whomever would listen. Abe stared out his window, his brow furrowed, his pipe in hand, humming an ancient tune.

~~~~~~~~~~~~~~~~~

Abe walked down to the barn. The cattle on the hillside weren't grazing. Their heads were high, looking toward the house. Before disappearing into the barn, Abe stopped to survey the farmstead, searching for the danger the cattle perceived but couldn't see. He studied the setting sun just below some angry looking thunder heads that had built up in the last couple hours. He surveyed the iron gate that was always open and strained his ears hoping to hear a motorcycle, but there was nothing. A calmness had settled over the valley. Against his better judgment he turned to see about the evening chores and walked into the barn.

~~~~~~~~~~~~~~~~~

The old woman straightened herself and stood and bent her body back. The dog jumped up eager to go outside.

209

He barked and took off out the of the studio. The old woman shook her head, said a few words in Bohemian and shuffled back to her work at the wheel.

Abe heard the dog barking from the barn. He stopped to listen about the time Shep quit.

~~~~~~~~~~~~~~~~

Blood dripped from his blade. The man watched as his victim's eyes went from wild fear to blank. His throat gargling blood as his body fell limp. He disappeared back into the cellar dragging the dog in with him, like a deadly trap door spider. Shep's blood moaned out a final warning to his Homestead, staining the grass and smearing the opening of the cellar. The man hoped the impending darkness would cover the evidence and give him enough time to carry out his plans.

~~~~~~~~~~~~~~~~

Abe's trip to the big house was diverted by Rayden and Jael getting home. The mood in the van was solemn. "Ooh, here we go," Abe said to himself, scanning the property.

Things could change quickly on the Homestead, especially living with a bunch of women. "Lord, help me."

Rayden was the first one out of the van. She could tell things weren't what they should be. "What's wrong, Abe?" she asked concerned.

Jael wouldn't make eye contact with Abe. Instead, she walked straight toward the house.

Abe, ignoring Rayden's question hollered at Jael. "Before goin' to the house would you ladies join me in my cabin, fer a second?"

"Why?" Jael spat.

"Oh, come on now. I generally don't ask fer much … " he said, as easily as he could, making another quick scan all around.

She huffed but turned and fell in behind Rayden and Abe.

"What's going on, Abe?" Rayden asked again, her eyes big.

Abe glanced into the windows of his cabin, before opening the door. "Right in here now," he said. Looking over Jael's shoulder, he whistled for Shep.

The girls had only been in his cabin once in the year they had been there. They looked questioningly at each other.

Abe whistled again, but Shep didn't show himself.

He rested his hands on the counter for a few seconds before turning toward the girls. "I'm afraid something ain't quite right," he said, with grave concern in his voice. He went to the corner where a shotgun was leaning. He picked it up and racked a shell into the chamber.

~~~~~~~~~~~~~~~~

"Miss Ev'lyn?" he said, knocking on her studio door. "You still in here?" He tried the door. It was locked.

"Miss Ev'lyn," he said, knocking again. No answer.

"You gals don't happen to have one them cell phones on ya, do ya?"

Jael produced hers, "Who do you want me to call?" She said, at the ready.

"The sheriff," Abe said.

Her eyes were big. "And tell him what?" Jael asked.

"To come a runnin'. I ain't sure, but I think someone's around here."

He handed Rayden the shotgun and he picked up his handgun. "I'm gonna check on Miss Ev'lyn. Ya'll stay here. Don't be shootin' me when I come back, now … "

~~~~~~~~~~~~~~~~

He slinked across the yard without being detected while the man and the girls disappeared into the small house. A sign he was indeed in god's will. He prayed a silent prayer of thanksgiving as he searched for the best place to lay in wait.

~~~~~~~~~~~~~~~~

The sun was down and the clouds cast an ominous glow over the Homestead. Colors were getting harder to distinguish. Abe eased around the corners outside.

Dim light spilled from the crack in the studio door. Abe edged closer to get a better look. The room was empty. A bowl half thrown sat on the wheel, still spinning. Abe heard a door slam outside his cabin.

He turned off the lights and eased toward the door leading outside. Someone was approaching.

He raised his pistol to cover the door. His finger resting on the slide. A body filled the doorway.

~~~~~~~~~~~~~~~~

The law enforcement officers left their sirens mute. They parked in the residential neighborhood across the road hoping their stealth might prove beneficial. The four-man team divided into teams of two. They advanced in a leap frog pattern—one team providing cover for the other until they reached the mansion. One man was posted on opposite corners of the house to cover the exterior. The other two made entry to clear the house.

~~~~~~~~~~~~~~~~

"Miss Ev'lyn!" Abe breathed out what breath he had. "What 're you doin' out here in the dark messin' 'round?" Abe threw on the light.

"Using the facilities, yah." She nodded toward the outhouse.

"Abe, are you all okay?" Rayden asked through the door.

Abe laughed nervously, "Yeah, honey. We fine." He had forgotten how much Evelyn used the outhouse during the summer. He unlocked the door to allow passage into the main part of the cabin.

Jael was still on the phone. "They are supposed to be here right now," she said, over the receiver.

Abe nodded toward the house where he thought he saw the outline of an officer posted outside. "We'll hole up here then."

Evelyn looked a little puzzled, then sat back down at her wheel as if everything was fine.

~~~~~~~~~~~~~~~~~

The man breathed in deeply. Oh yes, this is where she lays her head at night. Her scent was still familiar to him. He swallowed his acidic spit. The taste just before the kill—he lived for it.

~~~~~~~~~~~~~~~~~

The officers cleared the first floor of the home. Finding nothing, they moved to the second floor.

~~~~~~~~~~~~~~~~~

It had been a glorious day. Zoe couldn't wait to tell her friends the news. She knew Rayden's help would be instrumental in planning her wedding.

~~~~~~~~~~~~~~~~~

Rayden's bedroom door flung open. The lights from the officers' guns cast eerie shadows in the room. The man lunged toward the lights yelling something in a foreign language. The knife flashed in the light just before the deputies' gun muzzles flashed consecutively, lighting the room like lightening during a thunderstorm.

~~~~~~~~~~~~~~~~~

Zoe's heart sunk as they rounded the curve to the Homestead. Squad cars, ambulances and fire trucks dotted the driveway. The combined lights made a sickening kaleidoscope of colors. Every light in the house was on. A gurney with a covered body slid into an ambulance.

"Oh my God," she said, more a plea than a statement.

Wyatt was quiet as he pulled into the driveway.

Zoe was off the bike just after it stopped.

Wyatt placed a protective arm around her shoulder to guide her or stop her as he saw fit.

Resistance met them.

"What happened? Where's Abe and the girls?" she said, to the first person who approached them.

"Ma'am, we are processing a crime scene here." A deputy explained. "I'm going to have to ask you to leave."

"But I live here." She pushed. "I need to know what happened—if everyone is okay."

Abe appeared from around the corner. "It's okay. They supposed to be here," he said to the deputy.

"Abe!" Zoe threw her arms around his neck. "Are you okay? Where's everybody else?" She saw Rayden wrapped up in a blanket over his shoulder.

"Everyone is fine, Miss Zoe. Just a little shook up is all."

"Oh my God," she said again. "I saw a body, whose ... "

"My husband's." Rayden said dryly.

~~~~~~~~~~~~~~~~

The following day they buried Shep on the hill with Abe's family.

12

Weaning

Forget what hurt you but never forget what it taught you.
Shannon L. Alder

October

Fall revealed itself overnight in a brilliant array of colors announcing change was indeed here and intense in color and temperature. There was so much to do to get ready for the grand opening of the store that Rayden and Jael had been working nonstop since coming home from the festival. The recent turn of events made the girls put the store opening on hold until October.

Since the death of her husband, Rayden was busy trying to re-establish contact with her children. She prayed that she might one day get them back. She didn't know how it would all work. Since going into hiding, she didn't know if her husband had a will to specify who would get the children or if her being their mother would trump any of his previous direction. If granted custody of her children, could she have them at the Homestead? What would they think of her? Had he brainwashed their babies into thinking their mom was dead or worse, some kind of monster? These were just a few of the questions she had for the attorney Miss Evelyn had graciously hired on her behalf. Regardless of the unknowns, she felt she needed to continue with the grand opening even though it had been postponed a couple of weeks.

The dam had broken in the garden and canning and freezing would continue until it froze hard. Kit and Zoe enjoyed cooler days in the kitchen with the windows open and the first of fresh apple pies. It had been a good fruit year and they had dried a considerable amount of fruit from the orchard along with the normal canning and freezing.

Abe was muttering about the need to bring the cattle in soon to wean and complained of the lack of help he was getting out of Zoe lately. Deep down Abe was delighted P-Dub had asked for Zoe's hand in marriage. He hated the thought of losing Zoe as a worker and a ranch mate, but understood that time marches on and the Good Lord's end game hadn't changed. He would continue to draw His children to Himself. How that would play out would stay a mystery until further notice.

But first things first, he and P-Dub were to install a wood-burning stove in the store side of the church so the girls could serve homemade hot apple cider from its top. Flanking the store on either side were tables with large woven checkerboards for men to pass the time while mama shopped or a place for children to try their hand at the old-fashioned game.

"It's a good thing we have these young bucks," Abe said, as he observed the young men from the church moving the stove with the help of dollies and rolling supports.

Everything else was in place at the store. The stove was the cherry on top. It sat on salvaged red bricks laid out in a single basket weave pattern. The old wood-burning cooking stove came out of the old mansion but had spent many years in the double granary waiting patiently for its next home. Rayden had discovered it, the original kitchen cabinets, farmhouse sink and the like while organizing the space to store her treasures that were awaiting repurposing. Abe admitted it went a long way in making the store look like an old general store.

Miss Evelyn's pottery or Chamber's Pots, as they were respectfully known now, were artfully displayed behind the long counter in the bank of cubbies. It seemed like Miss Evelyn had long since known a plethora of pottery would one day be needed. Her years of hoarding the earthy pieces wouldn't be in vain.

Sharing the cubbies were home canned goods and home-dried teas, with labels gracing the front and brown paper tied with twine on the top of the jars. Kit had spent her spare time getting the church's kitchen up to code and registered with the health department as a commercial kitchen.

A rustic ladder served as the quilt display, leaning against the wall. The walls held wooden spool end clocks, corrugated tin initials and an array of tin art.

Abe supplied fifteen revoiced instruments with cases. Cattle hides, homegrown on the Homestead littered the floor, donning their brand. It seemed every living thing at Homestead had contributed something precious to the store.

The repurposed furniture was the most stunning and unique attraction to the store. Rayden offered to customize pieces for patrons from their own collection or from the collection upstairs that hadn't been redeemed yet.

Orders for organic beef by the quarter were taken. Depending on the day, fresh fruits and vegetables may also be an option for purchase.

Eclectic offerings as unique as the hands that offered them could be found here. Shops like this had a hard time making it, especially parked in a dying main street store. Rayden knew it had multiple strikes against it, but with the help of the internet they could expand beyond the borders of the small town.

The grand opening was a huge success. The stove crackled happily, music from the church stage kept people there longer than expected. By the end of the day it was evident, if God's plans are carried out by man, they will not be thwarted.

Wyatt and Zoe spent the evening planning for their future in Wyatt's apartment. Abe took Miss Evelyn and Kit back home early so he could do chores, leaving Jael and Rayden to count the money and evaluate the day.

They sat by the fire, drinking the last of the hot cider and eating stale cinnamon rolls for supper. They were giddy with their success. Today was a blessed turn of events in their troubled lives. A chance to do what they loved and get paid for it.

Jael was especially happy. Abandonment had been her home for so long, the sense of a loving family appealed to her. She got up from her place near the stove and gave Rayden a shoulder massage.

The massage felt good to Rayden. Jael had proven to be a good friend, despite the fact they were polar opposites.

The feelings Jael had suppressed so long for Rayden were too much for her to contain any longer. She took Rayden's hair and twisted it gently laying it over her left shoulder while she bent and kissed her on her neck.

Rayden leaned forward quickly. "Jael! What are you doing?" she asked, with one hand on her neck where Jael had placed the kiss.

There was deep hurt in Jael's eyes. "I was … " she started, "I was just trying to show you how much you mean to me." Her voice cracked as she looked away. "We have shared so much for so long, I thought maybe you loved me … the way I love you."

Rayden felt for her friend. "I do love you, Jael," she said, placing a hand on her arm. "I do. But I don't love you *that* way." Her eyes were sad.

The thought of that kind of relationship with another woman was repulsive to Rayden. She wondered how she could say that without breaking her friend's heart.

Jael studied her friend's beautiful face. The feelings she was hoping to find weren't there. In their place was the truth. Jael had misread Rayden's vibe. Embarrassed by the turn of events she didn't want to be there any longer. She turned and ran out the back of the store.

Rayden heard the door slam and the van peel away into the night.

She focused on cleaning in order to get ready for business the next day and to sort out what had just happened. Life could change in a moment. She thought about the possibility of being able to raise her girls. Nothing would make her life more complete, except maybe to find love someday. Real love with a man though, not a woman. She shook her head, saddened by the dampening this incident had put on the day.

~~~~~~~~~~~~~~~~

They could hear footsteps coming up the stairs followed by the softest knock.

Wyatt opened the door to find Rayden standing alone. He smiled at his little sister and motioned her in. Zoe sat on the couch with the remains of their supper, grilled cheese and tomato soup, on the coffee table before her.

Rayden sat next to Zoe and sat with her head in her hands. Not waiting for her friends to ask, she began, "I'll be needing a ride home when you go. If you don't mind."

"Sure, of course. Where's Jael?" he asked.

"She left," Rayden said simply.

"Where did she go?" Zoe asked.

"I'm not sure," Rayden said softly. "But I don't think she'll be coming back."

"What happened?" Wyatt probed sitting beside Rayden on the couch.

"I'm afraid I have hurt her deeply," Rayden began. "She wants more than I am willing to give."

Rayden explained what had happened. She recounted other times she failed to see Jael's advancements for what they were.

"I'm afraid I broke her heart." Rayden eyes were downcast.

"*You* didn't break her heart," Wyatt interjected. "J has a habit of breaking her own heart."

Wyatt looked at Zoe. She nodded in agreement. He looked to Rayden, gave her arm a comforting pat and asked if there was anything they could do to help close up shop before taking her home.

~~~~~~~~~~~~~~~~

She parked just off the road and walked onto the train's bridge high above the river. It had been a long time since she had come here. She didn't know where else to go.

She lit a cigarette and walked, her hand feeling the bottle in her pocket. Love was the most elusive thing about life— the most elusive and the most longed for. She took a long pull on the bottle after settling down with her feet dangling over the edge of the trestle.

The wind was chilly. But the warmth from the liquid numbed her to the wind and the wild feelings of abandonment and rejection.

She had prayed to multiple gods, repeated prayers of penance and mantras, fasted and hoped. No answer. It didn't seem to matter.

She would have to move on from the Homestead as soon as the news hit, but she didn't have a place to go.

Thoughts of Abe's pistol ran through her mind, and what it might feel like to have a hole in the roof of her mouth. Her tongue went to the spot where it would be. She imagined feeling the hole surrounded by jagged bone and beyond to the displacement of soft tissue. A final void to match her life. Oh to be void of feeling. Perfect.

They say in nature there are no vacuums. For as empty as she felt, she doubted that law of physics. But then there was one thing that filled the void in her heart, the familiar pain of abandonment.

She took a drink and lit another cigarette.

~~~~~~~~~~~~~~~~

Wyatt shut the pickup lights off before traveling the last few hundred yards to the train trestle. He wasn't surprised to see the van parked ahead. Why people always came to this place to sort out their lives, he didn't know. Was it because they felt suspended, between one world and the next? Maybe. Perhaps it was the closest place to in between. Like a suspended chord in music, the hanging bridge that paused life for a moment. It was the unresolved semicolon of life.

He glanced in his truck hoping to see Jesus in the flesh. The passenger seat appeared empty. Wyatt shook his head at his own antics and let go of a nervous laugh as he closed the door.

He walked toward Jael in the dark. Picking his way to the middle of the bridge, he wondered what to say.

"Got room for one more?" Wyatt asked, into the darkness.

"That d'pends," she slurred. "Are you preachin'?"

"Not tonight," he said softly. "Just chillin'." He sat down next to his friend.

The bottle she held out for him to take barely reflected the faint moon. She tapped his thigh lightly in encouragement.

He was perplexed about what to do. Hesitantly he took the bottle resting it on his thigh. *Would he be enabling or encouraging her by taking a drink? Where is the line between meeting someone where they are and encouraging poor choices?* He wondered. *Why in a world full of color is there so much gray?*

"Are you gonna drink that 'er just h-h-hold it?" she stammered.

When Wyatt didn't perceive any divine guidance, he took the smallest sip and handed the bottle back to her. A burning cigarette was offered in exchange for the bottle. He rolled his eyes in the darkness and begrudgingly took it. She laughed when the first drag made him cough.

His last two moves probably weren't the most pastoral, he guessed. But it was too late now. Life was chess and not checkers. Right? Darkness encompassed him. He took a long drag from the cigarette.

"Come here often?" He finally spoke.

Jael couldn't help but laugh at his pick-up line. "Not fer about a year," she said. "Jus' before going to that effin' Halfway Househead 'er whatever they call it … "

They sat in silence until Wyatt flicked the smoke into the water below.

"I s'pose she told you everythin'?" she slobbered.

"Not sure about everything … " he said simply.

"E-enough, though. Right?"

"Probably, but there's always two sides ... "

"S' now you hate me tooo?" she drawled.

"Nobody hates you, J. In fact, we all love you." Wyatt looked down into the darkness for answers. Since no good answers ever came from darkness, he glanced toward heaven before continuing, "And we only want what's best for you."

"And wass bes' for me is to be straight 'er leave?"

Wyatt didn't know what to say to that.

"Cause, you know, y'all think being gay is a s-sin. Right?" She hissed, finished the bottle and threw it into the river below.

Wyatt sighed. "J, a sin is only a sin if you act on it in your heart or mind."

"Well, I damn sure acted on it," she said. "'Er tried to … "

"We all have our battles," he said. "What tempts you, may not tempt me. But we're all tempted by something—or lots of things," he said.

"S-so I need to leave," she said matter-of-factly.

"I don't know that you need to leave. I'm sure there is still a place for you here," he said. "From my experience running from problems whether real or perceived, doesn't solve them. It just makes 'em pile up 'til you get around to solving them."

"Well in th' mornin', I'm leavin' and nobody can s-stop me."

He should have known better than to argue with a drunk, "Okay, little sis. But how about sleeping at my place before you bug out?"

"Only if 'y'er drivin', cause I cain't," she said.

Wyatt smiled to himself at her drink-induced southern twang. He helped her to her feet, praying they wouldn't misstep on their way back to his truck.

After tucking her into bed on his couch, he decided the best thing to do was get Abe and get the van back to the Homestead. They could sort it all out in the morning. He was walking to the door when she spoke.

"P-Dub?"

"Yeah, sis. What's up?"

"Y'er a good friend. If I ever decide to settle on a god, I think I'll pick y'ers. K? Night!" she closed her eyes.

Wyatt smiled at the young woman. How many times had he been where she was, caught in the chasm between the desires of the flesh and eternity? Why were choices of blessing or curses seemingly impossible sometimes? He didn't know.

"I hope so, little sis," he turned to go. "I really hope so."

Closing the door, he stopped to watch her fade into a deep sleep. He thought about her last words. Truth had a way of appearing in the wee hours of the morning. Sometimes the fog of this world whether chemical or mystical tries to cloak it—leaving one to question the authenticity. But Truth will not be hidden in this life, even if it means staying up past midnight.

~~~~~~~~~~~~~~~~

Wyatt knocked on Abe's door hoping he was awake for the day. When he had to knock a second time, he figured the old man was still sleeping.

A light came on in the window.

"Who's there?" Abe said, from behind the door.

"It's Wyatt, Abe," he said. The door opened.

"P-Dub, what on earth are you doin' here at this hour?" he asked, wiping the sleep from his eyes.

"Sorry to bother you, brother. Can I come in?" He walked over the threshold before Abe answered.

"Everything okay?" Abe asked, while smelling the contents of the coffeepot.

While Abe made coffee and built up the fire, Wyatt explained the reason for the early visit.

"So ya said all that just to ask if you can camp here tonight?"

Wyatt chuckled. "Yeah, I guess so. And I may need a ride in the morning."

Abe poured them each a cup.

Wyatt looked at the cup of coffee and Abe's short couch.

"You not thinkin' a beddin' down are ya?"

Wyatt sighed. "Well I was … " his voice was tired.

"It's 'bout time to get up anyhow." The old man looked out the window into the darkness as he took the first sip of coffee.

Wyatt shambled to the old wooden rocking chair. He sat down, rested his head on the back and closed his eyes. "You don't seem surprised by any of this."

223

"Son, after watchin' girls come in and outta here for years, not much is a surprise anymo'. They's no normal or surprise in the human condition."

Abe continued to look out the window while Wyatt dozed in the chair.

"Abe?" Wyatt broke the silence. "Do you think I did the right thing?"

"You mean drinkin' and smokin' and what not?"

"Yeah." Wyatt's eyes remained closed.

"Well, P-Dub," Abe lifted the coffee cup from Wyatt's knee and set it on the table. "I don't understand all the ways of the Lord. But I do know He meets people where they at. Not where He want them to be, 'cause they ain't there yet.

"Would Jesus 've handled it differently? Prolly so. But we not Jesus. We humans. So, we do our bes' and let God do the res'." He went back to the window.

Wyatt opened his eyes and watched the old man. "What are you looking at?"

"The possibilities." The old man kept looking into the darkness like it was a television.

"It's too dark to see anything out there yet," Wyatt said, taking a sip of coffee, giving into the fact that sleep would elude him tonight.

"It's never too dark for that," Abe said.

Wyatt looked thoughtfully at the old man and wondered who was pastor to whom.

~~~~~~~~~~~~~~~~

Jael made goodbyes easy. She simply avoided them. Sometime in the night she left the protected world she had known for the past year without so much as a thank you, a goodbye or a trip to get her personal belongings.

Rayden mourned the loss of her friend. Zoe and Kit would miss Jael, but not like Rayden. Abe, Evelyn, Pastor Wyatt and the rest of the board met about what happened, but there was little they could do. Jael had come on her own accord and left much the same way. The group agreed that Zoe and Kit would have to help with the store in order for it to be open and to give Rayden time to focus on getting her children.

The only positive thing about Jael leaving was the space in the house it had opened. Which might allow Rayden's girl's a room of their own. Evelyn's place had always been a place of change and this fall was no different.

~~~~~~~~~~~~~~~~~

It had been a good year for keeping cattle on grass with plenty of rain to hold them until October, but it was now time to bring in the pairs and wean the calves. The calves would go to another ranch and the cows would stay with Abe. Like at branding time, it was all-hands-on-deck. Some of the old hands came to help gather and sort.

Gathering went smoothly. Soon the folks were back at the Homestead cutting the calves from their mothers. The calves would bawl and the mamas would hum, calling for each other. Abe described the scene, "Bawlin' weaners, the music of fall."

13

A Final Farewell

How lucky I am to have known someone who was hard to say
goodbye to.
Unknown

November

A hard freeze brought colder days to the Homestead. The garden had been laid to rest and the tradition of saving heirloom seeds was taught to Zoe. She put the last of the seeds in the pantry. They had saved enough seed to stock dozens or maybe hundreds of families over the years.

Next month would mark a full year for Zoe. She wondered where the time had gone. She thought about the broken person she had been then and marveled at the healing that had taken place. Most of the growing she had endured was organic and not from a book. The twelve steps she had expected to dictate her life wasn't at all what had happened.

Change had come through serving others whether plant, animal or human. The law of the harvest ruled. Plant, water and grow. Birth, feed and care. The living aged, reproduced and their death fueled the other lives on the Homestead. Nothing was wasted. Lives of any kind were respected, encouraged to grow to potential and the harvest brought a richness to be shared. As a whole, their cups ran over in abundance which they shared with others. The natural order of things was in place on the Homestead and when implemented in a life—lives and society were forever changed.

Zoe was thankful for the experience and her new skills. In the process she learned to live beyond herself and trust her Creator, but wondered where she would go from there. She was no more equipped to be a pastor's wife than the man on the moon. Nonetheless, Mrs. would be added to her name next month in a simple ceremony at the mansion.

Her new life would be a life of service to others, a continuation of homesteading. Planting seeds, watering words of prayer and waiting in anticipation to see what would grow from the seeds saved from a past life—she could hardly wait.

~~~~~~~~~~~~~~~

Abe came into the warm kitchen from doing the morning chores. He was earlier than usual. Zoe could tell it wasn't because the chores were done. He looked his age today. His wrinkles looked cavernous and his gray-black hair more white today, echoing the feeling of the approaching winter. The kitchen once alive with wedding plans fell quiet as the old man made his way slowly through the door.

Zoe got up and Wyatt followed suit. Wyatt was the first to break the silence.

"Mornin', brother," Wyatt stuck his hand out to meet Abe's. His body followed with his typical hug.

Abe held the hug longer than usual while whispering in his friend's ear.

Wyatt's shoulder's drooped with the weight of the news.

"What is it?" Zoe rushed to Wyatt's side.

Kit leaned into her mug of coffee, breathing heavy into the warm liquid before drinking as she listened to the man she had grown to love.

"Well now, it seems Miss Ev'lyn has made her way to the other side this mornin'." The old man's eyes filled with tears that spilled over and ran down his cheeks.

"Right there at her wheel, propped up in her usual tripod. Look like she just placin' her last piece of clay, just before bringin' it to center. Yes, sir," he said, wiping his face with his sleeve.

"She died with clay on 'er hands and a prayer on 'er lips I s'pose ... One minute she creatin' next minute she be talkin' to the Creator, face to face. Hard to fathom how quickly we can step from one place to another. I imagine she be dancin'

228

now, not talkin', though." His voice was a hoarse whisper. He tapped Wyatt on the stomach with the back of his hand and smiled through the blur of tears. "She always liked dancin' better than talkin'." Abe stared into the most mysterious of dimensions, beyond our 3-D world and into the unknown, imagining what he might see if he weren't temporarily blind to it. "Yes, sir."

They stood quietly as the clock ticked and the news settled on them.

"We best call the county so they can send the right folk out to care for 'er," he said. The old man shuffled across the room, looking every bit his age. He dialed the sheriff to request the coroner.

~~~~~~~~~~~~~~~~

The rest of the day was a blur. Law enforcement came and went. There was a trip to the mortuary to plan the funeral and one to the lumber yard. Abe insisted on building his friend a hand-crafted box for her well-worn body to rest in for however long it was needed. Phone calls were sent out. Friends, food and condolences brought in.

Rayden, devastated by the news, closed the shop and came home early. Miss Evelyn had been so much to her. Besides being the obvious grandmotherly figure, she had taught Rayden to be still and trust in the midst of the unknown. A lesson she hung onto now while trying to get her girls back. All that aside, she wanted to help plan a celebration for a life well lived.

~~~~~~~~~~~~~~~~

Evelyn's area of the house was a place that few entered. Abe had only been in it a handful of times over the years, Kit only once and the rest of the girls had never set foot in her place. It added to the mystery of what was behind and what was to come.

Evelyn left much history, pictures, quirky attire and plain old curiosity to be discovered in the space that held her for so

229

many years. The day after her passing, they descended on her lair in search of things to be shared and uncovered.

The smell hit them first. A person's scent is always the first thing that leaves, a fleeting footprint, their personalized signature. Words to describe it exactly were hard to come by. Maybe it was a cross between the great depression (the smell of an old house closed up for a long time), roses, powder and just Evelyn.

Her space was a small apartment her parents had added on after the war. It must have been evident to them that their Evelyn would probably never marry. So they made a space just for her, complete with a small kitchen, living room, bathroom and bedroom.

A simple mahogany bedroom set with double bed, dresser, dressing table and night stand sat waiting for their owner. Her closet held only a few of her favorite wardrobe pieces from around the world, an old pair of snow boots and a pair of simple leather shoes.

A period bath with a bath tub only, toilet and small vanity had few additions past the absolute necessities. Homemade lye soap, Pert shampoo, powder, budget toilet paper, a simple hair brush and bobby pins were the extent of Evelyn's toiletries. The girls commented on the missing necessities: deodorant, toothpaste and razor. Kit corrected them by pointing out a small hand-thrown dish of baking soda and salt. A mixture that Evelyn used instead of toothpaste. And a bottle of ethyl alcohol with rose petals in place of deodorant.

"Rose petals and ethyl." Abe handled the old bottle gingerly, carefully removing the lid and smelling it as a tear ran down his old cheek. He replaced the stopper on the bottle and set it back on the sink.

"Wouldn't surprise me if she'd use it as 'snake bite', for medicinal purposes as well. Pits and lips," he said softly, as he patted the sink before leaving the small space in search of other signatures of his old friend.

The kitchen area had simple plywood cabinets with Formica countertops with an apartment-sized stove and matching refrigerator.

There was nothing fancy in the space. It was surprisingly sparse for a wealthy, aging globetrotter. Pictures and knickknacks from afar were abundant, however.

Evelyn in front of the pyramids on a camel. Evelyn in India at the Taj Mahal. Evelyn fishing in the Amazon. Evelyn throwing a pot on a Japanese kick wheel. Evelyn dancing in praise in South Africa. Evelyn on the beach in Jamaica at a baptism. Evelyn peeking out of an igloo in the Arctic. Evelyn in Russia donning a fuzzy hat with the Kremlin in the background. Evelyn praying at the Wailing Wall. Evelyn floating in the Dead Sea. Countless pictures of babies delivered in thatch huts in the rain forests as well as a Bedouin tent in the desert. The group took these moments in time off the wall for her final earthly celebration. It was clear the world had lost a favorite citizen.

~~~~~~~~~~~~~~~~

The day was sunny and warm with the cool air that told you the illusion was fleeting. A melting pot of cars, trucks and motorcycles lined the streets and spoke to the cross-section of lives that Evelyn had touched. The church couldn't contain all the people who came to pay their final respects.

Her current ragtag family who remained at her homestead decided the best way to welcome her friends and salute her memory was to play bits and pieces of the CDs and records she had played while throwing her pottery. There was something for everyone: reggae, rap, bluegrass, country, hymns, Irish jigs, praise and worship and of course, Frank Sinatra.

Wyatt whispered a simple prayer, and squeezed Zoe's hand a final time before approaching the simple pine box where his friend lay. Against the back drop of old doors— connected to make the back of the stage, hung a garland of pennant-type mismatched fabric flags attached to brown cording each with a letter on it that formed six words that spoke briefly to the profound life the precious lady had lived. *She said yes to the Lord.* John 11:27

231

Around the garland hung pictures of the saint's worldly adventures that came from saying yes.

Wyatt looked hard at the photos, some black and white, yellowing with age and others dripping with color. What does one say on a day like this? Wyatt took a deep breath. He thought about the lives touched by this woman and looked up to address the throng of people that spilled out the doors—front and back. The welders and bikers were just inside the garage at the back. The smoke from their cigarettes wafted into the building. Normally offensive, it mixed with the other smells of the day: coffee, people, cinnamon rolls and settled as the comforting scent of a mixed bag of the common and uncommon who loved the eccentric old woman. The sounds of smokers' coughs, scraping of chairs being moved and babies babbling were welcome and familiar; comforting the people who came to pay their respects and mourn.

"When we were going through Evelyn's possessions this week, they were pretty well void of earthly things," Wyatt's voice wavered. He stopped to clear his throat and gather himself while the throng of people settled in to focus on his words.

"She lived in a world where possessions are everything. Yet she had given all of her possessions away, except a very few things that were most precious to her." Wyatt rested his hand on her well-worn Bible that sat on her coffin.

"The earth where she resided for so many years commands focus on technology, space, and expansion. She was grounded to the soil: living on it, eating from it and physically taking it in her hands and molding good things with it." He pointed to a hand thrown vase that sat near her Bible. It held a simple bouquet of rust colored mums picked with her private porch where Shep used to lay.

"The planet where she frolicked had boundaries that held other races and ways of life—yet she crossed the divisions seamlessly, like a breeze crosses a meadow." He glanced over his shoulder at the pictures on the makeshift wall behind him.

"This macrocosm, now absent one of its members, claims everyone needs a cellphone or internet to be connected, should be dumbfounded by the fact that Evelyn never owned a cellphone or surfed the world wide web, yet touched more people in more places than most people can with a megaphone, cellphone, computer or even an international telecast.

"How is that even possible? How can a strange introvert with hermit tendencies, change the world? And not just her part of the world, but a part of almost every continent." He paused for effect and to let the question settle on the mourners.

"She said yes to the Lord.

"When God said, 'Evelyn, be a good steward of the land I gave you.' Evelyn said, 'Yah, I'm on it.' When He said, 'Evelyn, share what you grow.' She said, 'Of course.' He said, 'Evelyn, go and deliver babies here and beyond.' She said, 'Absolutely.' 'Evelyn, visit my girls in jail and the lowliest of places.' She said, 'Yes, Lort. Let them live in my house, my mansion.' 'Evelyn, Life, (that's what her name means), worship me in song and dance.' And she did." His voice cracked and wavered and tears fell from his face.

"Loud and off key, she sang and clumsily, she danced. And we joined her. Didn't we? Why? Because we wanted what she had. That same spirit that was alive in her, came alive in us. When we said yes to her invitation, it was if we were saying yes to His invitation." The room was quiet.

Wyatt continued, "Finally, He said, 'Evelyn, be still and create with me from the dust.' And she did. Her body bent now with age, her hair gray, she created at a wheel, body bowed in submission, a prayer on her lips and 'plenny of time for tink'. Right? Isn't that what she would say? That is how she humbly left on her final journey."

He sniffed while looking down at the floor. When he finally looked up, he said again, "She said yes to the Lord."

"She focused on people. She built relationships. The rich, eccentric from Virginia doubled down, and was all in on relationships. She invested in the only thing she could take with her to the other side. She literally clothed herself in them. She didn't record her experience on a phone. She scribed it on her soul. She took pieces of the people she came in contact with and wove them into her being—her garment of praise.

"That, my friends, is why we are hurting today, because the part of us we shared with her is gone, and now resides in heaven."

Wyatt picked up his guitar, sat down on a bar stool and finger picked a song. Zoe didn't recognize it. It wasn't written on the paper that summarized the service and the events for the day. Others recognized it. Some hummed along, others danced. She thought it must be an old hymn.

When he had finished, he looked at the casket and said, "Well done, my sister. Well done."

Abe said, "Amen," in his booming voice and stood to address the crowd. Wyatt went back to Zoe's side.

"We would like to open it up now to y'all to share whatever you want about our friend, Miss Ev'lyn, here … " His strong voice trailed off.

For the next thirty minutes or so, people of all stripes recounted what the old woman had meant to them.

Abe ended the service with a simple prayer of thanksgiving and invited whoever wanted, to come to meet at Homestead for the burial and to share in communion and food.

~~~~~~~~~~~~~~~

It was late afternoon when a small crowd met on the hillside where Abe's wife, daughter and Shep lay in the ground. The sun bathed the small cemetery and barely took the bite out of the late fall day. The simple pine box sat on the logs that stretched over the hole. Three ropes were tied around the box, ready to help lay the old woman to rest among the other souls who had gone before her.

Evelyn's homemade wine was passed out in small cups, along with some homemade bread. Wyatt talked about the importance of remembering that freedom comes from sacrifice and Jesus came to set the captives free. We were all captive to at least one thing and Evelyn had joined Him in His mission. They gave thanks for the broken body and

234

spilled blood that precedes true freedom and drank and ate in agreement.

An old car without a muffler bumped its way across the pasture to the hill. The people watched to see what would come out of the ruckus. The crowd recognized the driver as Brother John, a welder, who had fondly toted his late friend wherever she wanted to go in his old beater.

His eyes were clear from the alcohol that once clouded them but were red from the tears he had wept for his friend. He got out of his car. A fresh cigarette hung from his lip. Nodding at the crowd while loosening the wire that held his trunk down, he lifted a heavy sheet metal piece out of the back and walked it to the front of the hole where he pounded it into place.

The beautifully crafted metal grave marker was shaped like an old wooden tombstone, rectangular with rounded corners at the top and at the bottom spikes to go into the ground. John had cut a cross out of the middle. Over the cross her name had been welded in a raised bead with the year of her coming and going beneath. Below that was Isaiah 61:1-3 followed by the six words that summed up her long life …
She said yes to the LORD.

Abe and Wyatt looked on in support of the rough-hewn man as he struggled to settle the marker into place. John grunted as he pressed and tears and sweat fell through the smoke from his cigarette. Finally, he stood, with one leg out, the rest of his body perched on the leg that remained, his head bowed, his dirty cap in his rust covered hands. He whispered something, made a patting motion with his cap and hand, wiped his tears on the sleeve of his flannel shirt and looked up at his friends, satisfied with his contribution.

Abe nodded at him and said, "Amen," as Wyatt comforted his friend with a side hug.

John nodded to the grave and said, "In lieu of flowers." And laughed a big nervous laugh.

Others joined the men to lower her well-used body into the dirt from which it had come. They dropped the ropes into the hole and buried their friend a handful of dirt at a time. It comforted them to feel the dirt that would hold their friend until one day her grave would burst open.

They shared soup and desserts in the house where Evelyn was born. The crowds dissipated, leaving Abe, Wyatt, Zoe, Rayden and Kit in the living room to decompress from the day. They sat staring at the fire in the fireplace sipping their coffee not saying much of anything.

Wyatt, drained from the day, was soon fast asleep on the couch. Zoe covered him with an afghan, placed a kiss on his forehead and excused herself to run a hot bath.

~~~~~~~~~~~~~~~~

The news of Evelyn's quiet exit into eternity caused people to murmur as it usually does in a small town. People love mysterious and unique figures and Evelyn was certainly that. With the news of her death came rumors and speculation on what would happen to Halfway Homestead. Who would get the millions she was rumored to have? Would the girls be on the street?

Thankfully, Evelyn had her affairs in order. The nontraditional nonprofit would receive everything. Abe would be president of the board and could continue to live on site until he couldn't or didn't want to anymore. The mission of the Homestead hadn't changed. Halfway Homestead was a place that would set captives free until there was no more time or no more captives, whichever came first.

14

A Bride for a Groom

*To fall in love with God is the greatest romance; to seek him, the
greatest adventure; to find him, the greatest human achievement.*
St. Augustine of Hippo

December

December came again, bringing a crisp world adorned
in fresh white. It was a new season for Zoe with
hardly an echo of her first winter at the Homestead.
This season didn't feel cold and dead like the first season
here. Like a tree, she had stored up the nutrients from the
fertile layers of the earth that would bring new life to her
branches in the next season. She slid her hand over her
stomach. A prayerful hope for the future. No more marking
the time of a sentence. Today she would ask time to stand
still so she could soak up every nuance of blessing and
promise.

She took one last long look in the mirror. One of Evelyn's
final gifts to her was a wedding dress never used. At one
point, Ida Red, Evelyn's mother, had a woolen suit made for
Evelyn's wedding day. A day that had never taken place.
Instead, Evelyn married adventure. She became a breeze
refreshing the earth, while the finely crafted hope lay in a
cedar chest. Discovered by whom it was originally meant for,
it was truly a work of art. Zoe felt so special that the Lord
had sanctified the woolen pieces just for her long before this
world knew her.

There was a soft knock at the door. Her father opened it
slowly. His nervous smile was calmed by seeing his daughter,
healthy and healed.

"Oh, sweetheart, you look beautiful," he said, his eyes turning misty.

"Listen," he began. "I know I've failed at so many things with you and your mom … " While he searched for the right words, Zoe interrupted.

"Dad, please, not now. Not today."

She looked just like her mother, beautiful and radiant. "Right," he said. He filled his cheeks full of the air from his lungs and held his arm out for her to take.

She gently took his arm. As she did, he placed his opposite hand on hers and turned slightly towards her. "Can I at least say, thank you?"

Zoe giggled at the strange comment. "For what?"

"For giving me a second chance when I didn't deserve one."

She softened a little toward the first man she had ever loved. "Of course, Daddy."

They put their foreheads together. "With God's help, I will get it right this time," he said, with a whisper and a wink.

She smiled at the words long overdue and placed the softest kiss on his cheek.

"Me too," she said. They started toward the door.

Rayden's girls had transitioned to the Homestead beautifully and were immediately conscripted into being the keepers of the rings. Zoe's throat tightened when she saw the girls for the first time. They were tiny like their mother and shared her fiery spirit. Spirits that hadn't burned long before being snuffed out by their father. Zoe prayed their fires would rekindle and burn again.

Rayden had dressed them in white A-line dresses with furry cuffs that she had sewn for them. Their black hair hung straight and shiny. A woven tierra of grape vine, cotton and baby's breath crowned their heads. They were beautiful creations.

A crown of beauty instead of ashes … she thought. How fitting. Isn't that just like God to put reminders of His goals for her life in her wedding day?

The girls held fishing poles made from small branches and twine like the one Wyatt made the day he proposed. The poles held the rings. Each girl had a basket of dried flowers from the gardens on the Homestead to sprinkle as they made way for the bride.

Rayden placed a quick kiss on her sister's cheek and slipped down the stairs to her seat.

The mansion was decked out for the season. Pine boughs on the staircase held burlap ribbon and white lights. In each window, a single candle glowed. White lights, pinecones, burlap and lace covered the tree. The top was crowned with a single white cross. Under the tree lay Jesus, swaddled and asleep. Zoe took in the image of a baby of meager beginnings, who was tasked with setting the captives free.

Only a few close friends and family were invited to the wedding. Zoe wanted the ceremony to be intimate and take place exactly where her new life began. The wedding supper would be much larger and at another location. Abe played a thoughtful tune on his fiddle as the bride and her father descended the stairs behind the keepers of the rings.

Wyatt was waiting in front of the fireplace where a fire crackled happily. He looked handsome in his brown slacks, white shirt, white vest and white tie. A loose ponytail held his signature dreadlocks. His blue eyes sparkled more than usual when he saw his wife to be. He exchanged a warm look with Abe.

After Zoe and her dad got to their place her father turned, kissed his daughter on the cheek one last time and took her hand and placed it in Wyatt's. He squeezed the union and turned to sit by her mother.

Abe placed the violin on the mantle nestled in the greenery of the season.

"Ya'll can sit," he said, nodding at the small crowd.

"We are here today to unite our friends, family and brother and sister in Christ in holy matrimony. It's a good day.

"I've had the pleasure of watchin' Wyatt and Miss Zoe grow through the dark despair of their trials into the presence of freedom. I've watched as they became friends, courted and now have the pleasure of escortin' them into their life together as one. For these things, I'm honored."

239

He spoke directly to the couple, "Y'er new individual lives started here and I find it fittin' y'er new life together will start here as well. A life built on service to others on a Homestead where we find ourselves halfway home. It is my prayer that y'er love will grow like the gardens here, y'er seed long stored will find fertile ground and this place will someday be filled with arrows from y'er quiver."

He turned to Rayden's girls and gathered the rings, handing a ring to each and nodded at Wyatt.

Wyatt took Zoe's hand and placed the old ring on her finger. "Zoelander Renee, I have loved you from the first time I saw you. I promise to keep you safe in my arms whether sick or healthy, love you like Christ loves the church and provide for you and for any family He chooses to bless us with until we are divided in death."

Zoe took his ring and placed it on his finger. "Wyatt, I never knew what real sacrificial love was until I came here. I gave myself to work on behalf of others and it healed me. I promise to stand with you as we continue to serve others, rich or poor, healthy or broken. I will respect your role as the head of our home until Jesus comes to take us to be with Him."

She smiled at Abe and he continued.

"Folks, with the blessin' in the name of the Father, Son and Holy Spirit, I present to you Mr. and Mrs. Stratton. You may kiss y'er beautiful bride. Yes, sir." Abe smiled broadly.

Wyatt cradled her face in his hands and kissed her easy and then hard, a promise of things to come.

~~~~~~~~~~~~~~~~

Outside a rusty rat rod held a banner which read "just hitched", compliments of Brother John, of course. The car would deliver the newlyweds to the church for a simple reception and a music jam.

After being pelted with birdseed, Wyatt and his bride crept slowly out of the driveway in the old car romping on the gas to the joy of the onlookers.

Zoe's exuberant exit from Halfway Homestead, differed from her arrival. She entered an orphan clothed in a blanket of despair. She departed a princess, donning a crown of beauty instead of ashes and a garment of praise. Another day this captive, finally free, would return to this place wielding the sword of redemption, to set free the captives. But first, a celebration and a cruise down main street ...

~~~~~~~~~~~~~~~~

The semitruck driver never saw the stop sign.

The sound of metal crushing metal was deafening.

15

The Wedding Supper

The Sprit of the Sovereign LORD is on me, because the LORD has anointed me to proclaim good news to the poor. He has sent me to bind up the brokenhearted, to proclaim freedom for the captives and release from darkness for the prisoners, to proclaim the year of the LORD'S favor and the day of vengeance of our God, to comfort all who mourn, and provide for those who grieve in Zion—to bestow on them a crown of beauty instead of ashes, the oil of joy instead of mourning and a garment of praise instead of a spirit of despair. They will be called oaks of righteousness, a planting of the LORD for the display of his splendor.
Isaiah 61:1-3

Eternity

I've been looking forward to this day for a while now. Seems like a great while some days and other days—like just a moment has passed. Regardless of the matter of time and the sacrifices that have brought us all here, it's a good day. A day of much anticipated celebration.

If I had to choose one word that would describe it, it would be color. There is brightness on the lawn, the light of goodness. It flows from not one place in particular, but more like everywhere in between, it just seeps out. No shadows here, not today. Light says, "Today is my day, Darkness, you have already had your day." And Darkness went and hid. True color was revealed, singing like a prism, the harmony of color that is just light.

Today the grass is standing straighter, each blade is announcing the presence of the King. The animals still adorned in their slick suits, trumpet the Bride's arrival.

That's what I've been waiting for, my Bride.

243

The tables are all set up in a circle today, never ending. My children, the Bride of Christ, are dressed in royal robes. Today, they will sit at my table and enjoy my riches freely.

Oh, how I love my children.

~~~~~~~~~~~~~~~

Zoe was finally at peace. A peace her flesh never fully understood. Gone were the questions, fears and doubts—like a wisp of smoke on a windy day. Hope and faith were gone too. Here, products of hope are revealed at last. Faith is finally sight. In their place was the peace that understanding love brings. Real love. True love.

It was perfect.

The day was bright and the place familiar. It reminded her of the place where her dark secrets were once revealed, but Light lived there now.

A little red-haired, green-eyed girl dressed in a simple white dress came dancing along a path of woodchips. Her knees were scuffed and dirty. When she spun, an assortment of white daisies and strawberries fell from her basket onto the path. Some of which she stepped on, leaving her dirty toes stained red in between. The little girl approached, gave one last spin, then a bow that turned in a somersault causing her to land softly on her back. Looking up at Zoe, she was giggling, her eyes dancing and her red hair spilling perfectly around her pale, freckled face. The rest of the strawberries and daisies spilled out all around with the basket laying empty by her side.

"A little help, here?" she giggled and held up her hand.

Zoe squatted down, and took her hand in hers and pulled up gently. The little girl sprang into her arms knocking Zoe to her back while the girl covered her in kisses and strawberry juice. After her kisses stopped, she laid her head just above Zoe's breast and reached out twirling the grass next to the path around and through her dainty fingers humming a song. That song. The familiar song with no name, that Abe once hummed and Evelyn would sing. What was the name of that song? It was a curious and delicious moment for Zoe.

244

The little girl rolled off of Zoe and offered her a hand. Zoe placed her hand in the girl's and pushed with her other until she was in a squatting position. She picked up the basket and picked up the daisy tops and strawberries and placing them back into the basket. The little girl helped, picking up one strawberry at a time putting one in the basket and eating two, putting one in the basket and eating two.

"Here, try one," she said forcing a handful into Zoe's mouth. "Aren't they delicious?"

Zoe bit down on the perfectly ripened berries and said, "They are the best I have ever eaten. Where in the world did you find something so yummy?"

The little girl shrugged, put her nose on Zoe's, set her forehead against Zoe's and said, "From your garden, silly. Come on. Let's go."

"My garden?" Zoe asked perplexed.

"Well yeah, they were ripe this morning. When I found out you were coming, I picked them along with your favorite … dai—sies," she said, with a sing-songy voice. "Evelyn told me she would make strawberry shortcake for us with fresh whipped cream if I picked them for her."

"Oh, she did, did she?" Zoe said, as she stood up.

"Yep. Have you ever had her strawberry shortcake?" the little girl asked, taking Zoe's hand. "It's the best!" She wandered down the path from where she had come, leading Zoe by the hand, stepping on a berry here and there and giggling when it squished up between her toes. She continued humming the song.

Zoe's spirit was alive with excitement, like the mysteries of her past would soon be illuminated or the last piece of the puzzle would finally be in place. It was as if she was looking at a picture painted in one lifetime and improved upon in another, becoming complete—washed in the colors of Truth. Anticipation filled her soul.

Around the first bend was a bunny nibbling on a strawberry with a river lying just beyond. Once a dry rocky bed, a river flowed, babbling over rocks. The little girl squealed when she saw the rabbit and ran to give it a pet. She spilled more strawberries out on the ground as she skipped to the river's edge.

Zoe stopped where the water started and watched as the little girl jumped from stone to stone to cross. With each stone daisies, but no berries, spilled from her basket, and floated downstream while Zoe watched them go.

"What are those?" Zoe asked, as the flowers passed from sight.

The little girl spun. "Those are choices from yesterday. We will let them go. Maybe they will take their seeds, plant themselves along the stream and become flowers for tomorrow."

Zoe picked her way across the river and looked up at the top of the bank where the little girl stood humming.

"What is the name of that song you are humming?" Zoe asked.

The little girl smiled and rolled her eyes as if to say, "Do I have to tell you everything?", let out a sigh, put her hand on her hip and said, "It's the song that a chicken sings." Then turned and ran.

Zoe laughed, giving chase. When she topped the bank she said, "I see. But what is it called?"

The girl stopped running when she got to a rope with a loop in it hanging in a tree. She set her basket down and leaped toward the rope catching the loop perfectly on the arch of her right foot. She was swinging into the air tipping her head back as she watched Zoe approach, seemingly up-side-down.

Zoe gave her a little push and asked, "Where are we going?"

The little girl's eyes sparkled in the light. She bailed from the swing landing on a fern, turned with the biggest grin, shrugged and said, "To the wedding supper, duh." She giggled. "I can hardly wait to show you! We have waited so long for this day."

Without hesitation she picked up her basket, took Zoe by the hand and walked purposely on in silence. The scenery was beautiful, like Eden restored.

"What is your name?" Zoe asked.

246

The girl stopped and turned to Zoe pulling her down until she was face to face with her giving her a light kiss on her nose. Then taking her dirty hands and holding Zoe's cheeks within them, she looked into her eyes, resting her forehead on Zoe's and said, "Grace. My name is Grace. But my mama calls me, Gracie. I went a while without a name. I was sitting on my Father's lap when she named me. It made me happy, very very happy. It made my Father happy too."

Gracie laid her head on Zoe's shoulder with her nose close to her mama's neck and held her close. The child breathed in and out. She closed her eyes as if asleep and drank in the moment. Zoe closed her eyes, too. *My child's breath against my neck.* The Light around them intensified. Zoe was blessed. A lifetime of tears fell to the ground.

As quickly as the tears started, they stopped. While the lasts tears stood on her cheeks, Gracie pulled away, reached down to take a hold of the skirt of her dress and gently wiped the tears away from her mama's cheeks.

Giving her a peck on the nose she said, "Those are the last tears you will ever cry, Mama. Beyond here, there are no more tears."

She picked up her basket and her mom's hand and walked. After a few steps, she glanced over her shoulder and nodded with her head behind them and said, "See, flowers for tomorrow."

Behind them a peaceful garden of daises covered the ground. A troubled past laid to rest.

They walked on now, quicker than before and more reverent. Grace was still quietly humming. Zoe leaned down sensing a change in mood and whispered her daughter's name for the first time, "Gracie?"

Grace kept walking but looked back, her eyes alive with anticipation, "Yes, Mama?"

"Gracie, tell your Mama the name of that song."

Gracie smiled and rolled her eyes as if tired of telling her mom the obvious, "It's Evelyn's song," she whispered. "Come on, Mama, we are close."

The final bend gave way to a valley. A garden paradise adorned with every precious thing but mostly one thing: Light.

Wyatt joined them there. Now in their robes of dazzling white, their heads topped with crowns, Grace lead them to their place at the table. His table.

The table was short, like in ancient days, covered with the richest of purple tapestries and set simply with clay dishes. On each plate was a piece of broken flat bread and beside it some wine. For what would a wedding supper be without wine?

Grace knelt down first, next to Evelyn, Adriel and Hannah. Her mama and Wyatt did the same. Grace fell prostrate, face down. Zoe and Wyatt echoed her movement.

And in a moment…in the twinkling of an eye … the trumpet sounded … the angel sang an announcement … and Love drew near.

The end … or actually, the beginning.

A note from the author

I didn't want the book to end when it did. It was hard for me to leave the final chapter. I wrote that chapter first. It sat on a crashed computer for ten years, while I wrote a story to prelude it. It grieved me to think how my story must end, to get to where we went. But after arriving, I didn't want to leave. Ever. But where was that exactly? That's a good question.

(Please understand there are spoilers to follow. If you haven't read the book you may want to first.)

The final scene opens at the Homestead, in a parallel space and progresses to the future. The manmade buildings are no longer. The land is perfectly healed, like Eden—with the river of life running through it (Revelation 22:1-2). Zoe is dying. She meets her aborted daughter, Gracie, who escorts her and Wyatt (Isaiah 11:6) to the Wedding Supper (Revelation 19:9). They are in a place of no time like we know it on earth. Contrary to what Bible says, Gracie wipes away her mama's tears (Revelation 21:4). I took the poetic license to pose the question. What IF God allows or delegates the job of wiping away our final tears to the person or persons we hurt the most on earth? What a time of complete forgiveness and healing that would be! But the Bible says He will do the wiping. I just took poetic license as an author to pose the question.

So why does it matter? Another good question. Like me, the characters of the novel are not perfect and struggle with how they fit into society. They are addicts, control freaks, worry warts, murderers, thieves, gossipers, slanderers, coveters, perverts and liars who are trying to navigate this broken, complicated world. We are all looking for the same things: peace, hope, love, grace and forgiveness. But when we seek it out in material things, drugs, alcohol, experiences or other people, we come up empty.

I believe that everyone is held captive by or addicted to something, or a lot of somethings. I know I have been. The characters in this book are all slaves in various stages of freedom. Jael's past hurts imprison her. Her self-focus poises her to hit rock bottom. On the other hand, Evelyn is selfless and at the pinnacle of freedom here on earth. The others are everywhere in between.

This book leaves some things unanswered ... Why didn't Wyatt and Zoe get to go on their honeymoon or have children? What happened to Jael? Was there healing for Rayden and her girls? Does Kit ever leave the Homestead? What about Abe? And the biggest question of all: **If God's so great ... WHY?** Why does He allow bad things to happen to good people?

We won't fully understand why, this side of heaven. That is frustrating and freeing; but shouldn't hinder us from asking. I seek answers in His word. While digging through the verses I've found some profound, life-changing answers. When I try to explain them to others, my postulates fall pathetically short. I encourage you to explore for yourself.

After losing a brother to a car wreck, I can assure you our eternity can start at any time. While it sounds final and sure feels like it in this world, the beginning in another realm that comes from an end in this one, is anything but tragic or final. NOTHING can separate us from the love of God, not even death (Romans 8:38).

As far as the story goes ... Wyatt and Zoe were healed of their addictions while on earth and their legacy will live on at the Homestead. That's worth celebrating. We live in a similar reality. Whether in an apartment in New York, a hut in the backwoods, a tent on a desert plain or (like me) a real-life homestead in the middle of nowhere—we are all halfway home.

With that in mind. God has more for you than you can ever hope or imagine. I challenge you to release the dark things that hold *you* captive and live the rest of this life in the light of God's freeing grace. After claiming your victory through Christ, tell your story to others or give them a copy of this book. Maybe you too can help set the captives free.

My deepest gratitude and love, *Angie*.

Acknowledgments

This book would have never seen completion if a few people hadn't said yes to my requests. The first, Kim Cooper, Leslie Baker, Shelly Wilson, Karen Groot and Kelsey Vine who coached, encouraged and prayed a weary manuscript into a book. Bless you sweet friends for saying yes to the Lord. I want to be more like you.

A special thanks to Phyll Kilma who led me on my first adventure in clay. She is an amazing artist and human. Over lunch one day she asked about my book. I shared that I may never publish it, because it didn't say everything I wanted to. With fire in her eyes, she banged on the table in that crowded restaurant and exclaimed, "Then write another book—but publish this one. Only selfish people don't share their art." Sometimes we just need a push, I suppose. I'm glad it was you.

Paul Gautchi, master arborist and gardener who divinely discovered the Back to Eden gardening method, granted me permission to directly quote some of his wisdom for Abe's character. I am so grateful for this. His gardening and spiritual wisdom has forever changed me, the way I garden and connect to my Creator. If you want to learn gardening from a master, watch his film for free at www.backtoedenfilm.com. Thank you, my humble brother, for finding the mysteries that God hid in nature and sharing these secrets with the world.

I'm so thankful for the support of my family. My parents taught me love isn't always easy, just worth it. David, my favorite half, who taught me love doesn't keep score. Our sons, Wayne and Mason, the music of our life, taught me love is dynamic and ever-changing. You all believed in this when I didn't. Thank you!

But mostly I give thanks to God, the caretaker of my homestead. He turned my weeds into the compost that nourishes the seeds that He planted in the garden of my heart. Your love and grace overwhelm me. I can't wait to see Eden, smell the dirt and walk with you there.

About the Author

Angie was raised poor (but not poorly) by an honest to God—no kidding, hell-raising, philosophic cowboy and a grace-filled, Bible-believing cowgirl. So, her story was bound to be wild and wooly yet interwoven with mercy and hope. Together they raised their children on poached deer meat, fresh ground whole-wheat bread and veggies from a garden. For flavor, they seasoned their lives with horses to be tamed, goats to be milked, bar fights, coon hunts and some Old Testament religion. Sex education was a discussion over a five-gallon bucket while cleaning calf nuts, backed by a fifth of whiskey. Her early years were filled with hard work and adventure the likes of which hadn't been seen in America for at least a half century, maybe longer. They taught her survival or self-preservation (some days self-destruction).

She left all that to be a nanny just outside of Washington D.C., where she met her husband, a Marine. After a six-month whirlwind romance, they married. He started a career in law enforcement. They added two boys, homeschooling, some bluegrass music, a little gun powder and Jesus to the mix. Twenty-four years later she's right back where she started. Still eating deer meat (not poached), garden veggies and whole-wheat bread. But she's better now than she was then.

Nowadays, she enjoys God's freeing grace while working their homestead and volunteering at places who specialize in healing broken women.

This book is simply a parable about the freedom she found in Christ. She hopes when people read it, they will go the way of the Homestead and choose to be set free through Jesus as well.

Pass it on

If this book affected you in a positive way and you think it would benefit others. Please share it with them without telling them how it ends. There are so many easy ways to do this: Blog about it, tweet about it, share your thoughts on Facebook, tell a friend about it over coffee or buy a few copies and give them to your church, a halfway house, rehab center or jail.

Find me online

Website
http://angierublewrites.com

Facebook

@angierublewrites

Instagram

angie.ruble.writes

This page is intentionally blank.

Made in the USA
Columbia, SC
01 September 2019